Praise for Becky Barker's *On Wings of Love*

5 Cups! "On Wings of Love was an amazing book. Ms. Barker has an ability that I found almost unbelievable to see into the hearts and souls of her characters, which she conveys to her readers...Jillian and Trey's sexual encounters are not particularly graphic but they are sensual and sensitive nonetheless. They are able to open up to each other, handle a terrifying situation and begin to trust. Ms. Barker, I am eagerly awaiting Cade's story!"
~ *Marcy, Coffee Time Romance*

On Wings of Love

Becky Barker

A SAMHAIN PUBLISHING, LTD. publication.

Samhain Publishing, Ltd.
2932 Ross Clark Circle, #384
Dothan, AL 36301
www.samhainpublishing.com

On Wings of Love
Copyright © 2006 by Becky Barker
Print ISBN: 1-59998-284-6
Digital ISBN: 1-59998-222-6

Editing by Jewell Mason
Cover by Vanessa Hawthorne

First Samhain Publishing, Ltd. electronic publication: August 2006
First Samhain Publishing, Ltd. print publication: November 2006

Dedication

"This one's for Thad, our youngest. May your life be filled with as much joy as you've brought to ours."

Prologue

Jillian Brandt heard Special Agent Bill Stroyer whispering to someone on the phone, and a chill ran down her spine. As she strained to hear his side of the conversation, the blood started pounding so loudly in her ears that she couldn't decipher his words, but his hushed, secretive tone set off a clamor of mental alarms. A highly developed sense of self-preservation warned her he was up to no good. She was on her own again. The government's safe house was no longer safe. Stroyer had never been very friendly, but now she suspected he was conspiring with her enemy.

Waves of fear and despair almost overwhelmed her, but she forced them aside as her survival instincts kicked into overdrive. She and Stroyer were alone in the house. The other guard had succumbed to a sudden illness and his replacement wouldn't be here for a while yet. It was just a little too convenient and beyond suspicious. She knew she had to escape before becoming just another grim statistic.

What few personal belongings she had were on the opposite side of the house, and she didn't want to risk trying to collect them. Stroyer's overcoat and hat were hanging on the back porch, so Jillian grabbed them. She'd need them later, but right now her main concern was putting as much distance as possible between her and her would-be assassin.

The safe house was located on the outskirts of Miami. Daylight had completely faded when she quietly let herself out the back door. She could see a collection of lights and hear the sounds of traffic in the distance. As soon as she'd picked her way across the rough yard to the alley, she began to race toward the more heavily populated area.

She hadn't gotten far when she heard Stroyer shouting her name in an alarmed, angry voice. Bundling the coat and hat into a tight wad, she tucked them under her arm and ran harder. He would be faster than her and in better physical shape, so she knew it wouldn't take him long to close the distance between them. He kept yelling at her to stop, but Jillian concentrated on running and breathing, running and breathing. By the time she reached a busy intersection, Stroyer's tone had grown harsh, and he was threatening to shoot her if she didn't stop.

She'd paused for traffic when she heard the first explosion of his gun. Panic surged through her. With the second shot, she felt the fiery impact of a bullet slicing her right side. The force of the blast knocked her sideways, but propelled her forward until she was darting recklessly through the traffic. Horns blared and brakes squealed as she stumbled her way to the opposite curb.

Stroyer followed her across the street. A renewal of angry honking alerted her to his continued pursuit. More brakes screeched, and then she heard the sickening, unmistakable thud of a human body being struck by a heavy vehicle. A frantic glance backward proved that Stroyer had been hit by a large commercial van. Jillian had no time for remorse or relief. He was just one of many who wanted her dead. She had to get as far away as possible before she could afford to rest or relax.

She ran for several blocks until the sight of a restaurant and truck stop offered the first real glimmer of hope. Her running had slowed to a labored, pathetic pace, so she wove her way between two big rigs to hide and catch her breath. Leaning heavily against the cold metal of one truck, she dragged air into her burning lungs. Chest heaving from exertion, she reached a hand to her injured side. Her blouse was already soaked with warm, sticky blood.

When she'd caught her breath enough to think straight again, she jerked the wide fabric belt free of Stroyer's coat and wrapped it around her midriff, tightening it over her wound to slow the bleeding. Then she slipped into the coat and tucked her hair under the felt hat. It was the best disguise she could manage under the circumstances.

Having been warned all her life that it was dangerous to accept rides from strangers, Jillian understood the risk she was about to take. She didn't have much choice, so she found a rig bearing license plates from several western states. The engine was running to keep the refrigeration system active. The cab door was unlocked, so she climbed inside and crawled into the sleeper section behind the front seat.

Inside the confines of the truck's cab, her ragged breathing echoed with frightening loudness, so she fought to regulate each breath. After covering herself from head to toe with a blanket she'd found, she managed to calm down just minutes before two men climbed into the front seat. Fortunately for her, their laughter and good-natured teasing made enough noise to block out any other sounds.

It didn't matter where the truck headed, so long as it was headed out of Miami. Jillian hoped they'd be a long way from Florida before making another stop. With two drivers, there was a chance of a long, nonstop night. She should be safely hidden until one of the drivers decided to use the sleeper. When discovered, she would handle the situation in whatever fashion necessary.

Her father had been a truck driver, so she instinctively trusted truckers. She knew there were good people and bad people in every sector of society, but she was desperate and had run out of alternatives. The price on her head was a cool million, dead or alive, but preferably dead. She had to trust her instincts.

It was a matter of life or death.

Chapter One

Jillian's fingers trembled as she dropped the necessary coins in the pay phone and punched the familiar numbers. A wave of dizziness assaulted her, but she fought to stay conscious. As one unanswered ring followed another, she whispered a fervent prayer. "Please, Trey. Please be home and give me one more chance," she chanted, knowing in her heart that he had little reason to respond to her call for help. She'd phoned him two months ago and begged him to meet her in Dallas for an attempt at reconciliation. Then all hell had broken loose in Miami.

She hadn't shown up for their rendezvous. The nightmare had begun, and she'd been desperate to protect him from all the horror. Now she was beyond desperation, and he was the only person left on earth she trusted with her life.

๛

Trey Langden stretched his long, jean-clad legs in front of him as he leaned his head against the back of his favorite chair. He'd eaten a solitary meal, taken a shower and pulled on a pair of jeans before settling himself in front of the living room fire. It had been another long, exhausting day. He hated March. It was a cold, windy month when spring tantalized but winter refused to relinquish its hold on the weather.

The lower elevations of New Mexico didn't usually suffer from extreme temperatures, but this winter they'd experienced record amounts of snow and more damaging winds than usual. It had been hard on the cattle, thus harder on him and his ranch staff. Now, every living beast—man and animal alike—was growing restless.

He watched the flames dancing in the hearth and sipped some whiskey before resting the glass on his stomach. It had become a habit, the whiskey—the need for something to dull his senses every night before he could sleep, despite his physical exhaustion.

The liquor was a crutch. He knew it and never risked the effects during daylight hours, but nighttime was different. He restricted the drinks to one or two glasses, depending on how restless he was and how persistently the memories fought to surface. He never allowed himself complete oblivion, even if he was tempted.

The night stretched before him, long, quiet and lonely. Damn! Sometimes the loneliness was unbearable. He could find entertainment and female companionship in the nearest town within an hour, but two years of trying to assuage his particular brand of loneliness had taught him it was a waste of time.

He wanted his woman, he thought grimly. A short bark of self-derisive laughter followed the silent admission. Despite knowing his wants would go unfulfilled, he still longed to see her sassy smile, to touch her soft, sexy body and to hear her infectious laughter. When he closed his eyes, he could easily conjure up the image of Jillian's slender, shapely body. The image was always gloriously warm, naked and needy.

His own body reacted with swift arousal at the thought. Trey cursed the too-vivid memories and his unholy need for one woman. He shifted his legs restlessly and emptied the contents of his glass in one long swallow.

The alcohol burned all the way down, making him feel more empty and lonesome. A loner by nature, he was more in tune with his land than with people, but lately he'd longed for the type of human contact his ranch hands couldn't supply.

Most of his life had been spent in a masculine domain, from the relative isolation of the ranch, to a tour in the army and then back to the ranch. He'd thrived on the challenges, but his was a solitary existence.

It was a life he'd chosen for himself and had been content with until he'd met Jillian. Since then, nothing seemed quite as satisfying. Something always seemed to be missing, some essential part of his being. She'd stolen his peace of mind, his dreams for the future and his heart. He deeply resented the loss of all three.

Trey shook his head to ward off the depressing memories. Then he stretched out in the recliner and closed his eyes. Some nights, his favorite chair was preferable to a big, lonely bed. This was one of those nights.

He'd just dozed off when the stillness of the evening was shattered by the ringing of the telephone. The sound ricocheted around the sprawling ranch house with annoying shrillness. He was tempted to ignore it, but the caller was persistent. After the fifth ring, he dragged himself from the chair to the hallway and the phone.

His tone wasn't cordial or welcoming. "Langden."

There was a slight pause on the other end of the line, and he felt a quiver of indefinable reaction.

"Trey?" The voice was softly feminine, huskily wary and achingly familiar. "Trey, it's Jillian."

He hadn't needed her name. The familiar sound of her voice made every muscle in his body knot with tension. The blood sang through his veins in a heated rush. Oh, hell! Not tonight.

"Trey?" This time her tone held a note of panic. The emotion was totally alien to his memories of her.

"What's wrong?"

Her soft, sad sigh hummed through the lines and over his body. "I'm in terrible trouble," she admitted. "I need a place to hide."

A rush of protectiveness bombarded Trey, but he quickly subdued it. He had good reason to be wary of involvement with the woman who'd caused him so much heartache. Jillian had never really needed anyone, especially not him. He'd learned that lesson the hard way.

"Who are you hiding from?"

"From everybody. From everything. From the whole world," she told him in a quivering voice.

The desolation and defeat in her tone slammed into Trey with unexpected force. The Jillian he knew was a die-hard optimist. She never, ever admitted defeat.

"Why call me?"

"There's nobody else I can trust. I was hoping you'd come and meet me."

Trey felt a hot rush of anger. "The last time you asked me to meet you, you didn't show," he reminded her grimly.

"I can explain," she promised.

"You could have explained two months ago, but you didn't. You didn't even bother to call. Why now?"

"I know you're furious with me, but I really need help, Trey."

Was there a sob in her voice, or did he imagine it? The tiny sound created an unwelcome clenching in his gut. Was she playing games with him? He hadn't believed her to be that type of woman, but that was before she'd coaxed him to Dallas and left him waiting.

Trey heard another "please" accompanied by a smothered sob, and he tensed. Jillian's attempt to stifle the sound affected him more than blatant crying would have done. She'd never used tears to manipulate him, so his curiosity was even more aroused.

There was no doubt he was furious with her, but despite his personal feelings, he wasn't the type of man who ignored someone in need of help. Jillian obviously needed help.

"Where are you?"

"I can't say much," she mumbled so softly that he had to strain to hear, "but I can hitch a ride as far as Albuquerque."

Hitch? What the hell was going on? He didn't like it. "Why can't you fly?"

"I don't have much money, and I stopped using credit cards because they can be traced."

Trey didn't waste any more time arguing. She had to be in deep trouble. "I can be in Albuquerque in a little over two hours," he told her.

Jillian's voice trembled with relief. "That's about how long it'll take me," she said, then cleared her throat. "There's a truck stop on the east side of town, just off the highway."

"I know where it is."

"I'll meet you there, but don't come looking for me. Just park, and I'll find you," she told him. "What will you be driving?"

"A dark blue Lincoln."

"I'm wearing a man's tan overcoat with my hair tucked under a hat," she said, then added, "I have to go now."

"I'll see you in a couple hours."

Trey broke the connection after hearing the click at the other end of the line. Then he wasted no time. Boots, shirt, hat, and he was out of the house. Wayne Reilly, his foreman, was making a nightly check of the property when Trey drove the car past the barns. He stopped to explain that he would be gone a few hours and headed for the main road.

Once on the highway, the powerful car ate up the miles. His impatience kept his foot heavy on the accelerator while he imagined every possible harm that could come to Jillian. He'd warned her that her fearless, headlong plunge into life would result in regrets. He'd always known that her eternal optimism would land her in trouble.

The trouble had to be damned serious for her to call him.

Two years ago, they'd had a passionate affair. They'd fallen in love and decided to marry, despite their incompatible lifestyles. They'd planned for Jillian to move to the ranch and accept freelance photography jobs if an assignment appealed to her. Before their wedding plans could be finalized, they'd encountered and failed their first real test.

A special assignment had been offered to Jillian by a man she'd dated in college. Trey had behaved like a jealous, possessive lover, demanding that she refuse the job. She'd accused him of not trusting her, of not having enough faith in their love.

He couldn't help his lack of faith. Their love had been too new, too precious. He'd never been in love before, never known he could love so deeply, and he couldn't control the feelings of possessiveness.

Instead of protecting that love, they'd destroyed it. They'd had a bitter argument, and the wounds had gone deep when they went their separate ways. Since then, she'd been traveling extensively. She'd called from time to time, from various parts of the world, but never when she was close enough for him to reach her.

When she'd called in January, he'd debated about the wisdom of seeing her again. He didn't need the grief their love had caused, but he'd gone to Dallas. The trip had reinforced his belief that Jillian would never be satisfied with long-term commitment. She'd stood him up without an explanation. She hadn't even called. Not until tonight.

She hadn't sounded excited or emotionally high, just damned scared. He found it hard to imagine her being scared. She'd been in a lot of situations that would scare the average person, but she was far from average. She was addicted to the adrenaline and excitement of world travel.

What could have happened to quell her fearlessness? How long did she plan to hide? Would he be able to help her without destroying his own peace of mind? It had been two long, lonely years. How much longer would it take him to get her out of his system if they spent time together again? Could he survive another separation? On the other hand, maybe he'd get lucky and seeing her again would finally break the hold she had on him.

It was well after midnight when Trey drove into the parking lot of the Albuquerque truck stop. He pulled in front of the gas pumps, had the car filled and paid the attendant in full view of the restaurant. There were several big rigs parked to the side of the building, so he circled the property. On his second time around, a lone figure stepped toward the car. The trench coat hung nearly to her ankles and most of her head was hidden by the hat, but Trey knew it was Jillian.

He stopped the car and hit the button to automatically lower the passenger window. She hesitated until he spoke her name. Then she dashed to the car and climbed inside. Trey rolled the window up and set the door locks. "Do you need to stop anywhere before we head to the ranch?" he asked.

"No," said Jillian. She fumbled with the fastener on her seatbelt, but finally managed to lock it in place. Then she stayed stiff and watchful until the lights of the city were far behind them. Eventually she pulled the cap off her head, shook out her heavy hair and heaved a deep, tired sigh.

"Thank you," she said quietly, turning wide eyes on Trey and studying him with searing intensity. "I don't know what I would have done if you'd refused to help me."

Trey felt her gaze on him and locked his jaw in frustration. He tried to get a better look at her but only had the dash lights for illumination. He had to give most of his attention to the road, but he sensed her desperation and could smell her fear.

Tension made his tone gruff. "Want to tell me what the hell's going on?"

A bone-weary sigh rattled from Jillian's chest. "All your dire predictions finally came to pass."

Trey didn't think that was possible. He'd imagined too many ways harm could come to her. He'd tortured himself with images of her being mutilated or killed while she traveled the world. "Tell me about it."

"I was helping a friend cover a story about a drug cartel," she started.

He made a rough sound of disapproval.

"I know, I know," she said. "I normally avoid stories that involve vicious criminals, but this friend begged me to do some photography for him. We'd worked together in the past, I knew he could be trusted, and I owed him a favor. He wanted pictures of a secret meeting, in the dark, that required special equipment."

Trey's stomach muscles knotted and he tightened his grip on the steering wheel. A long silence followed until he thought Jillian might not give him the details. When she spoke again, he had to strain to hear her hoarse words.

"We hid in an old warehouse, expecting to witness and photograph a big drug transaction. But it was a whole lot worse. I took pictures of the drug lord, Juan Gardova, orchestrating the torture and murder of an undercover agent named Rico Valdez."

A groan rumbled from Trey's chest. Was she totally insane? Did she have a death wish? What kind of lunatic had involved her in such a suicidal scheme? "It sounds like your taste in friends has disintegrated over the past couple years. Who the hell dragged you into such a dangerous situation? Where is he now?"

Jillian's response was slow in coming. Finally, her voice quivering with emotion, she replied, "He's dead."

So far, he didn't like anything about the picture she was painting. "Who was he?" Trey asked grimly.

"Jack Carnell."

His guts twisted tighter at the identity of her friend. The international reporter had been a well-known crusader against drug dealers. His brutal murder had made national headlines. How and when had Jillian's work taken such a violent path?

"I take it the two of you made it out of the warehouse alive, so what happened after that? What about the pictures?"

"Jack gave them and his testimony to the grand jury in Miami. Indictments were handed down, and then Jack was murdered. The photos were destroyed by a mysterious fire in the federal court's evidence room."

"So you knew there was a threat within the system."

"Probably just one of many," she said.

"But you had the negatives?"

"Yes," Jillian dragged in another breath.

"So what did you do?"

"I could have played it safe. God knows I wanted to!" she exclaimed roughly. "Jack made me promise not to put myself at risk as long as he could testify. After he was killed, I was scared out of my mind, but I just couldn't let them get away with it."

She shifted restlessly. "I had to tell the authorities that I was an eyewitness, too. I gave the FBI another set of prints and they said I'd have to testify against him."

Trey admired her courage and integrity, but he also realized the extent of the danger she'd put herself in. If the drug lord hadn't hesitated to kill a high-profile reporter, then Jillian's life would mean nothing to him.

"Weren't you offered protection?"

"I was surrounded by armed guards when I made an appearance in court for the preliminary hearing. Then I was taken to a safe house and kept under 'round the clock protection. That's where I've spent the past three weeks."

"Why the hell didn't you stay put?"

Jillian was sounding more and more weary, her voice fading to a near whisper. "One of the agents assigned to protect me must have been on the take from the cartel. I overheard him on the phone and realized he was planning another mysterious accident."

Her declaration fueled Trey's frustration. The thought of someone plotting to kill Jillian made him grit his teeth, and he battled a surge of impotent fury. It was several minutes later before he could continue the discussion.

"You can't trust anyone?" he asked tersely, shooting a glance at her.

"Only you," she murmured softly. Then her tone grew urgent. "I'm truly sorry for involving you in this mess, but I didn't have anybody else to turn to, and I knew there was no way they could trace me through you. I've been really careful. I hitched a ride with some truckers, and I don't think anybody could have followed us from Miami. Only a handful of people know about our relationship."

Trey heard the quiet desperation in her voice and felt the intensity of her fear when she reached out and grabbed his arm. Her touch sent a jolt of electricity scorching through his body. All hope that time had dulled his physical reaction to her was swiftly dashed.

"Get some rest," he suggested tersely. "It'll take us a couple hours to get to the ranch, and nobody will find you there."

Jillian grasped one of his hands and lifted it to her lips for a kiss. The light caress sent waves of heat through Trey. Despite the anger he'd been nursing for two years and the gravity of the situation, his body responded violently to the feel of her hot mouth on his flesh. He grumbled in annoyance, and then realized just how hot she felt.

"Are you all right?" he asked, trying to study her in the darkness. "Are you sick? Do you need to see a doctor?"

"No!" Jillian's tone was panicked. "Please, don't worry. I'm fine, just tired. I don't need a doctor."

Trey hoped she was telling the truth. There were no doctors or hospitals close to the ranch. "Would you like to stretch out on the back seat?"

"Michael Trey Langden," she whispered weakly. "That sounds like an immoral suggestion."

The unexpected teasing was a disturbing reminder of the woman he'd loved obsessively. It made his pulse accelerate, but it didn't distract him enough to drop the subject.

"How long have you been on the road?"

After taking a slow, deep breath, she straightened in the seat and asked, "What day is it?" Her long hesitation hinted at the depth of her confusion and exhaustion.

Trey swore under his breath. "It's early Wednesday."

"I left Miami on Sunday evening."

"You came the whole way by truck?"

"Yes."

"Then you made good time."

"We drove straight through."

"Who's we? Did you know the trucker you hitched a ride with?"

"Not at first."

Trey got the feeling she didn't want to go into details about her trip. "What do you mean, not at first?"

"I stowed away in the sleeper of his truck, but he and his driving partner were very kind. They were only going to Fort Worth, so they found someone they trusted to bring me the rest of the way."

His tone grew grimmer. "Have you eaten or slept at all?"

"Some."

Trey wanted a lot more details, but this wasn't the time or place to badger her. She needed to rest, so he controlled his impatience.

"Why don't you relax and take a nap," he suggested after another glance at her stiff posture.

Jillian sighed wearily and rested her head against the back of the seat. It didn't take long before her breathing became slow and even.

The car was equipped with a citizens band radio. Trey didn't use the equipment often, but he listened to news, weather and police reports when driving long distances. He flipped the scanner on and adjusted the volume.

There was a frequency that regularly gave police reports and reviewed the FBI's list of most-wanted criminals over the radio. He scanned the bands until he located that particular station.

His thoughts drifted as the miles passed, his mind replaying the details of Jillian's predicament. She'd landed herself in deep trouble this time. It was so like her to jump into a situation without considering the risks.

Once involved, her loyalty to a friend, her personal integrity and innate sense of justice would have made it impossible for her to turn her back on what she would consider her civic duty. Jillian was passionate about civic responsibilities.

They couldn't trust the authorities right now, so he'd have to find some other way to help her. It wasn't a problem that would disappear with time. They'd have to find a solution. In the meantime, she'd be safe at the ranch.

More than an hour after Jillian fell asleep, an FBI report began with a nationwide plea for assistance. The mention of an all-points bulletin interrupted Trey's thoughts and snapped him to attention.

"The Federal Bureau of Investigation has asked law enforcement across the nation to be on the lookout for freelance photographer Jillian Brandt. Ms. Brandt is the primary witness in the upcoming murder trial of drug lord, Juan Gardova. She disappeared from a government safe house in Miami, Florida, and officials fear foul play.

"Ms. Brandt is five-feet-six inches tall with a slender build, has shoulder-length blond hair, green eyes and was last seen wearing blue jeans and a white shirt. Photos are being faxed or emailed nationwide. Any information regarding Brandt's whereabouts should be immediately reported to FBI headquarters in Miami."

"They took their good ole time asking for help," murmured Jillian drowsily.

Trey glanced her way. She hadn't lifted her head from its resting place against the seat, and she looked very frail. "They probably concentrated their search locally before expanding nationwide."

"Probably," she agreed, but she didn't sound convinced.

"Do you think the FBI has something to hide?"

"The fact that one of their agents was trying to kill me when I disappeared."

Trey tensed. "You're absolutely sure of that?"

Jillian gave a rough laugh, then gasped and reached a hand to her right side. "I'm absolutely certain."

"Do they know their agent was responsible for you running from the safe house?"

Jillian shrugged. "I have no idea. Stroyer could be seriously injured or dead. He was hit by a car while chasing me across a busy street."

Trey's hands tightened on the wheel again. There seemed no end to the horrors, but she sounded calm enough. Was she numb from shock or hardened against all emotion?

"You don't know if he was killed or not?"

"I didn't take time to find out," she explained. "Since he'd just shot me, I wasn't overly concerned for his welfare."

Trey felt poleaxed. He controlled the urge to slam on the brakes as shock slammed through him. He managed to slow the car as quickly and safely as possible, then pull to the side of the road while he battled for patience and control.

Jillian sat up in alarm. "What's wrong?"

His hands were locked on the steering wheel in a death grip. He continued to stare straight ahead for another long moment.

"Trey? What's wrong?" she insisted, panicky.

When he turned his head, he looked directly into her wide, concerned eyes. He studied her face intently. "Jillian, you just told me you were shot."

She blinked in surprise. "Oh."

Trey could tell that she was confused. He reached out and touched her forehead. She was definitely feverish. "Where were you shot, Jillian?" he asked in a low, rumbling tone.

"In Miami," she muttered.

He sighed heavily and tried to quiet the pounding of his heart. He briefly closed his eyes, then reopened them and looked steadily into hers. "What part of your body, Jill?"

"Oh." Understanding dawned. "My side. My right side," she told him, reaching a hand to the injured area. "It's not too serious. The bullet just grazed me. I cleaned and bandaged it."

Someone had actually shot her. She'd been shot, and she'd been bouncing across the country in a trucker's rig. Trey ran a hand through his hair in agitation. "I've got to get you to a hospital."

"No!" Jillian cried. "Please, Trey, no hospitals!" she pleaded, grunting softly in pain as she turned toward him. "They'd have to report a gunshot wound. It's too risky, and I've come too far to let them find me now. Please, just take me to your ranch."

Trey thought about ignoring her plea and taking her to the nearest hospital. He knew that was the smart thing to do, but he couldn't do it. She'd come to him for protection. She trusted him, and despite his conflicting emotions, he couldn't let her down.

He'd dealt with plenty of medical emergencies on the ranch, but this was Jillian. He wouldn't risk a hair on her head, let alone her health or safety. Reluctantly, he put the car in gear and pulled back out on the highway.

"I'll take you home and have a look at your wound, but if it needs treatment, you're going straight back to town and a doctor," he insisted tersely.

His decision had her relaxing against the seat again. He understood that her fears were very real, and he knew she could be obstinate, but he wasn't going to listen to any argument if she needed immediate medical attention.

Her fever meant that the bullet wound was more serious that she realized. "How long have you had a fever?"

"I've kinda lost track of time," she confessed in a slurred tone.

Trey felt another stab of anger. "Just rest. I'll wake you when we get home."

Chapter Two

Everything was quiet at the ranch when Trey drove through the wrought iron gates. It was dark and there was nobody in sight as he pulled to a stop near the front porch. He got out of the car and circled to the passenger side, startling Jillian when he unfastened her seat belt. He calmed her sudden panic with soothing reassurances and carefully helped her from the car.

She leaned heavily on him as they walked to the porch and climbed the steps. Once Trey had the front door open, he helped her inside and switched on a light. She blinked sleepily, and, with his help, shrugged out of the oversize coat. He hung it on a coatrack and carefully lifted her in his arms so her left side rested against him.

Her delicate features creased into a grimace as she lifted her arms to his neck. She was shivering, yet hot with fever, and his concern increased. He carried her down the long hallway to his bedroom in the west wing, and then gently deposited her on the bed.

After flipping the light switch, he got his first really good look at his weary guest. The smile she gave him made his heart race. She was pale and fragile, yet still the most beautiful woman he'd ever known. Her thick, golden-blond hair was tousled and her emerald eyes a little too bright, but she looked gorgeous to his hungry eyes.

"Thank you for coming to my rescue," she mumbled.

"I didn't do any rescuing, just driving," he insisted.

"You were there for me when I needed you. You'll never know how much that means."

When tears welled in her eyes, Trey experienced a flash of panic. The Jillian he knew only cried over sad movies and beautiful music. He didn't like seeing her so vulnerable, so he swiftly changed the subject.

"Is that shirt a loan from one of your new trucker friends?" She was wearing a very large, neon green T-shirt with giant wheels on the front and the words "Keep On Truckin'".

She managed a small grin. "It was a gift. My blouse was ruined."

Trey stiffened in renewed anger. Someone had actually tried to murder her. She could have been maimed, left for dead or disappeared and never been heard from again. The thought generated a savage reaction in him, but he knew he had to rein his temper long enough to help her.

"I'd better take a look at your side. Can you get out of your clothes?"

She nodded, but didn't move. At first he thought she might be shy about undressing in front of him, and then he realized she was just too exhausted to begin the process.

He reached for her feet and slipped off her loafers. She wasn't wearing socks, so he went next to the snap and zipper of her jeans. Jillian lifted her hips slightly so he could slide them off her legs. He could see that the slightest effort was a strain for her. He was beginning to experience a considerable amount of strain, too. Just having her close after all these months was a shock he hadn't had time to prepare for.

Anger was swiftly replaced by more complex emotions. He silently cursed at the sight of her athletically slim, bare legs and skimpy French underwear. It had been a long time since they'd made love, since he'd had the pleasure of losing himself in her softness, but the memories were vivid and arousing. Her frailty at the moment didn't make him want her any less, it just reinforced his need for control.

"The shirt next," he insisted in a graveled tone.

She raised her arms over her head while he carefully pulled off her T-shirt. Her full, rounded breasts strained against the lacy confines of her bra, and Trey's pulse accelerated. He forced himself to breathe deeply and shift his gaze elsewhere.

A rough bandage covered Jillian's right side between her bra and her waistline. It was stained with dark, dried blood and a spot that looked like fresh seepage. He slowly removed the two strips of tape holding the gauze in place.

"Butch and Joe let me use their first-aid kit," she explained. "I was able to clean the gash and keep fresh bandages on it."

Trey tried to pull the gauze from her skin, but it was glued to her flesh by her own blood. "It's stuck to you. I don't want to pull on it and reopen the wound, but I need to see how bad it is and get a clean bandage on it."

"I could soak it off in the bathtub."

"I don't know if you should sit in water for very long."

"I already took a shower," she told him without expression. "At one of those truck-stop rent-a-shower places. I had to get clean."

Trey shot a glance at Jillian's face. Her eyes were closed. He knew she needed rest, but he didn't want her to pass out on him until he'd tended her side. If the wound was too deep, infected or needed stitches, he'd find a doctor.

"I'll draw a bath," he decided. "You can soak in some clean water for a few minutes. That should loosen the bandage enough to get it off without doing any damage." He hoped it would bring down her temperature, but he didn't mention that.

Jillian nodded in agreement, but didn't reopen her eyes. She was totally limp on the bed.

Trey went into his bathroom and started the water running, then searched the medicine chest for gauze and tape. He took a deep, calming breath before returning to Jillian.

"I'm going to take off your underwear now," he explained in a tight voice.

She seemed incapable of a response, and he hoped she was resting instead of unconscious. So far, she'd seemed fairly coherent, but she was getting more feverish.

He clenched his teeth and forced himself to slowly remove her panties. He wanted to accomplish his objective as quickly as possible, without hurting her. Being careful not to jar her whole body, he slid the scraps of silk off her hips and down her legs. Then he unfastened the front clip of her bra and removed the silken fabric from her equally silky breasts.

When Trey lifted her soft, naked body into his arms, he had to stop and fight for breath. His heart was thudding against his chest in such a riotous rhythm that it made breathing difficult. The feel of her in his arms was an exquisite torture. Tremors shook him, and he pressed her closer to his chest in a purely possessive manner.

Jillian clung to him until he lowered her into the bathtub. The water was cool and sent a chill over her heated flesh. She gasped softly and her nipples puckered. He couldn't help noticing her body's involuntary reaction, nor could he control his own body's response.

"It's cold," Jillian complained, teeth chattering.

"It's warm enough. It'll help with your fever." He grabbed a washcloth and began to sponge water over her face and shoulders, being careful not to get her hair wet. He bathed her quickly, and then gently tugged at her bandage. It slowly came loose, and he growled low in his chest at the sight of the raw, angry gash in her side.

Trey felt a black rage welling inside him again. His body quaked with fury. What kind of greedy bastard would shoot a woman in the back? What kind of a society created people with no conscience or morals? People who preyed on those who were weaker or vulnerable? He wasn't even appeased by the knowledge that the corrupt agent might be dead. He silently condemned the man to rot in hell.

Jillian was fortunate the bullet hadn't lodged in her side. The gash was deep and badly bruised, but looked like it was healing without the help of stitches. He tried to smother his anger while gently wiping away dried blood to clean the wound.

She moaned again when he lifted her from the tub and wrapped a thick towel around her. He held her in his arms until she stopped shivering, then urged her to stand still while he patted her completely dry. The process strung his nerves tighter than a bowstring.

He didn't own a pair of pajamas or a robe, so he found a long-sleeved cotton shirt for her to wear. She cooperated as much as possible while he slid his shirt over her arms, but Trey knew she was ready to collapse. As soon as he had the shirt around her, he drew back the covers on his bed, laid her down and tended her wound.

A tiny gasp slipped from her lips as he spread antibiotic cream over the angry welt. He was trying to be careful, but the wound was tender. It was healing nicely, yet he needed to stop any spread of infection. He tried not to press too hard when he taped fresh gauze against her skin.

His hands trembled slightly when it came time to button the shirt over her soft, feminine curves. His anger over Jillian's injury had briefly dampened his desire, but it was rekindled with a vengeance at the sight of her tempting softness.

His body was one big ache. He wanted to pull her into his arms and feel her naked flesh locked against his own. It had been so long. Instead, he finished buttoning the shirt and went to the bathroom to get a glass of water and some aspirin.

Jillian roused enough to take the tablets, and then dropped off to sleep. Trey stripped to his briefs, turned off the light and slid into bed beside her. She was flat on her back, so he turned on his side to get as close as possible without causing her any discomfort.

It was nearly 5:00 a.m. and he was beat, but he couldn't get to sleep. Having Jillian so close brought back a rush of memories, both good and bad.

They'd met two years ago when he'd been in Dallas for his brother Cade's college graduation. Their attraction had been instant and intense. While Cade went on an extended vacation, Trey and Jillian had turned his apartment into their private love nest. They'd kept the world at bay while their love blossomed and their passion raged out of control.

He'd never known another time so filled with love and laughter. Just the thought of those days made his chest tighten with emotion. They'd spent a month vowing eternal love. He hadn't known he could love so deeply and possessively. The feelings had been new, untried and difficult to trust. He could never be completely sure that Jillian shared them.

They were total opposites. She was vivacious, extroverted and eternally optimistic. He'd been thirty when they met, had already faced some serious hardships and had become cynical about a lot of things. She'd viewed the world as an enchanted kingdom, awaiting her enthusiastic explorations. She'd wanted to capture all of life with her camera lens.

This ranch was his life. The land had belonged to his family for generations, and it was as much a part of him as his arms and legs. He'd dreamed of marrying and teaching his wife to appreciate the beauty of his corner of the world. He wanted to help raise another generation of Langdens.

Jillian had teased him about being old-fashioned and as tied to the land as the most honorable of old-West cowboys. Maybe he was a throwback to an earlier generation, but he'd been prepared to alter his dreams and compromise with her.

Even though he'd loved her independent spirit, he'd resented her desire to leave him and travel the world. They'd agreed on an arrangement that included marriage and living at the ranch. Jillian had planned to use it as a home base while pursuing a career for several years before starting a family.

For a few weeks they'd lived a fantasy life. Then their plans had gone awry. She'd expected unconditional trust, and he hadn't been able to give it. If she'd loved him as much as he'd loved her, he was convinced she'd have understood his stubborn demand that she refuse a job offer from an old boyfriend. Instead, she'd flown away with him.

He harbored a lot of resentment. Their brief affair and the taste of real love had destroyed all desire for other women, a normal marriage and family. For the past two years, he'd lived without hopes or dreams for the future.

Trey curved one arm above Jillian's head and brushed stray strands of hair off her face. Just looking at her brought an unwelcome wave of bitterness tempered by possessive need. He had to bury those feelings until she was fully recovered. It was like trying to hide during a tornado. It wasn't going to be easy.

She still felt warm, but she seemed to be sleeping peacefully, so he gradually relaxed and fell asleep.

Several times during the next couple hours, Jillian stirred restlessly, mumbling and fretting until Trey calmed her in a low, soothing tone. Each time she grew alarmed, he pulled her closer against the protection of his body, and she seemed pacified. By the time daylight began to seep into the room, she was cradled tightly against his side.

A little after seven, the steady beeping of the ranch intercom woke Trey. He carefully stretched an arm to the bedside stand and punched the receiver button.

"What?" was the best he could manage.

Wayne Reilly responded. "Sorry to bother you, boss, but I thought you might want to be roused. The men are waitin' for orders."

For the past couple years, Trey's every waking minute had been spent working or worrying about the ranch. Today he had different concerns. "Just keep everybody busy rounding up strays and checking fences. I've got company and might stay inside all day."

There was a surprised pause on the other end of the line. Trey rarely had company except for his brother, and he never let a day go by without riding the ranch.

"I'll take care of things," Wayne promised, his tone a little puzzled.

"Thanks." Trey knew his foreman would be curious, but he could explain later—if and when he understood the whole situation himself.

He turned his attention to Jillian. Her eyes were open and drowsy from sleep, but they'd lost their fevered brightness. She was studying him with an intensity that made his nerves sizzle and destroyed any lingering sleepiness.

"How are you feeling?" he asked.

The smile she gave him was slow and intimately warm. It took him back in time and turned his insides to mush.

"I'm fine," she insisted, reaching a hand up to brush a lock of hair off his forehead. The action must have pulled at her wound because she sucked in a breath.

"Forgot that for a minute, did you?" he asked.

Jillian closed her eyes on a sigh. "I guess I did."

Trey slid his hands around her hips and rolled her closer, but not close enough for her to feel the strength of his erection. When Jillian rested her hands against his chest, a surge of hot desire pulsed over him. She'd always made him crazy with just the lightest touch. Apparently that hadn't changed.

"Are you hungry?" he asked.

She shook her head, closing her eyes and resting her head on his shoulder. Her hair tickled his chin, and he buried his face in the sweet-smelling softness until her breathing became even again. Soon she was sleeping, and he eased her to her back on the bed. He wasn't ready to leave her side yet. His body throbbed with an unappeasable ache, but Jillian wasn't in any condition to be seduced.

He closed his eyes and smothered a groan. What had he ever done to deserve this? He'd offered her everything he had to give, and it hadn't been enough. He didn't plan to make the same mistake twice. He'd never risk that kind of emotional involvement again, but he couldn't deny that the attraction was still strong. Vowing to keep their relationship impersonal or strictly physical, he drifted to sleep.

When Trey next awoke it was noon, and he was surprised to have slept so soundly. Jillian was still asleep, so he eased himself from bed. After pulling on jeans, he collected her dirty clothes and headed for the laundry room at the back of the house. He threw the clothes in the washer before starting a pot of coffee and checking the contents of the refrigerator. He needed some groceries, and Jillian would need something to wear besides one pair of jeans and her truckin' shirt.

As far as he was concerned, she could wear his shirts and nothing else, but he didn't suppose she'd find the idea too appealing once she was rested and feeling better.

Cade could help with the supply problem. His little brother was still living in Dallas, but made frequent weekend visits to the ranch. Cade had founded Langden Industries and was on his way to becoming a corporate powerhouse, so he handled most of the family's business interests.

Their parents had died within a year of each other. At that time, the ranch business had been deeply in the red, and inheritance taxes had nearly forced them into bankruptcy. So they'd allowed drilling for oil on the property. It had saved them financially. The following year, Cade had moved to Texas to attend college on a full scholarship. He had a talent for making money, so Trey let him do his thing.

The ranch was his domain. It took long hours of hard physical labor, every day, year-round, but he didn't mind. The land was his legacy. He planned to protect and nurture it for future generations of Langdens.

When the coffee finished brewing, he poured two cups, added sugar to Jillian's and carried them back to his bedroom. She was blinking sleepily as sunshine poured through the window and bathed her in its light.

"Do I smell coffee?" she mumbled.

Trey set both cups down on the stand and pulled a chair close to the bed so he could prop up his feet. "I hope you still take sugar," he said, making himself comfortable and reaching for his cup.

Jillian carefully pulled herself into a sitting position near the bedside stand and reached for the remaining mug of coffee. She took a sip, and then rested the mug in her lap while she took a good look at her host.

Trey's hair was thick, rumpled and as inky black as she remembered. His eyes were equally dark, the darkest black-brown eyes she'd ever seen. His face, with its high cheekbones, strong chin and sensuous mouth, might never be called pretty, but she'd always found it utterly fascinating.

His broad chest was bare except for a pelt of dark, curling hair that swirled down his flat stomach to disappear beneath his jeans. She'd never known any man who looked so good in jeans, and she'd always found his bare feet sexy.

God! How she'd missed him! Not for just the proud, healthy man that he was, but for all the other things that had made her fall hopelessly in love with him. She loved his strength and self-confidence, his devotion to his family, his home and his country. She loved him for his strong moral beliefs, and his willingness to stand up for those beliefs.

She loved the piercing honesty in his eyes, his quick-witted intelligence, his keen sense of humor and even the stubborn set of his chin. She'd missed their long hours of conversation—the disagreements and good-natured arguments. She'd missed the laughter, sharing and loving.

She'd thought she would die without him.

But it wouldn't do any good to give him a clue to her thoughts. It would be a long time, if ever, before they could discuss past mistakes. Jillian kept her comment brief. "You look good." she told him, knowing it was probably the biggest understatement of her life.

Trey had been studying her just as intently. Daylight made the dark shadows under her eyes more obvious. She was too thin and pale, but she was still damned sexy. In his bed, wearing nothing but his shirt, she was damned near irresistible. It made him defensive.

"You don't look too bad for someone who's been terrorized, shot and trucked across the country."

Jillian swallowed hard at the reminder of all the horror of her escape. Her eyes were filled with gratitude as they locked with his. "I'll never be able to thank you enough for helping me."

"Forget it." His tone was terse. He didn't want gratitude from her. "You said thanks. That's enough between friends, and you did say you wanted us to always be friends."

Jillian lowered her lashes and took a sip of her coffee. His cool tone and words answered questions that had plagued her since they'd gone their separate ways. She'd wondered if he would ever forgive her for accepting that first assignment, or if he'd ever really understood her decision. The answer was "no" to both. Right now, she didn't know if that was good or bad.

"I think what you did for me last night might have been a strain on any friendship." It had been arrogant on her part to ask for his help, but she'd been desperate. Her gaze locked with his again. "I know I was a lot of trouble."

"At least you were conscious and coherent."

The past few days had passed in a blur to Jillian. What she remembered most was the wonderful sense of security she'd felt once Trey had picked her up in his arms and carried her through his house.

"You were very kind and patient," she insisted, voice trembling with emotion.

Trey didn't want her to get weepy on him, so he decided to irritate her a little. "I didn't consider giving you a bath much of a hardship." His bold gaze swept over her shape beneath the covers.

Jillian knew he was trying to get a rise out of her, and he succeeded. Despite the intimacy of their past relationship, she felt shy with him. She lowered her gaze to her mug as a blush stole up her neck and face.

"No need to be embarrassed," he chided. "There's not one tiny inch of your body that I haven't seen and touched. It's been a while. I have a good memory, but I didn't mind a little refresher course."

Jillian's blush deepened and heat coursed through the rest of her body. His tone and words were meant to be provocative, and they were. They evoked memories of days and nights that ran together in the heat of passion. They reminded her of how many times he would reach for her, over and over again, as if he would never get enough of her love.

At the time, she'd been young and fairly innocent, on her own for the first time in her life. Sometimes his passion had threatened to smother her even though she had an equally passionate nature.

Trey Langden was a very virile, deeply sensual man whose possessiveness had both fascinated and intimidated her. They'd been intimate friends and insatiable lovers, but there hadn't been time for the slow building of trust their relationship had needed. Her inability to meet him in Dallas had probably destroyed what little faith he'd had left.

Had seeing and touching her left him as aroused and frustrated as it would have two years ago, or was he totally unaffected by her presence in his home and his bed? Did he have someone who gave him all the love he needed?

"It's been a long time," Jillian whispered. "We really don't know each other anymore. I hate being a nuisance. If there's somebody special in your life who'll resent my being here, I'll try to leave as soon as I'm a little stronger."

Trey had never heard her sound so humble. He didn't like it. He didn't want her feeling guilty, either. He didn't even want to care about what she was feeling. If he couldn't harden himself to her appealing vulnerability, he'd be suffering the same agonies of pain and disillusion that had nearly destroyed him two years ago.

"I don't have a live-in lover, if that's what you want to know. The ranch is pretty isolated. Women don't exactly pound down the doors and beg to share my bed."

Jillian knew he was mocking her, but any guilt she experienced was mild compared to the overwhelming relief she felt. She knew he had a healthy sexual appetite, yet she'd never been able to come to terms with the knowledge that another woman could easily fulfill his needs.

On the other hand, if he didn't have a lover, what might he expect from her? Would he view her plea for help as a signal that she wanted to renew their relationship?

"You're welcome to stay here as long as you want, with no strings attached," Trey declared roughly. Rising from the chair, he stepped closer to the bed, and held her steady gaze while he continued. "You don't have to worry about my attacking you or expecting favors." His tone grew harder. "You're the one who put an end to what we had, and I'm not going to try to stir a flame from cold ashes. If anything develops between us, it'll be purely physical."

His words shattered the last fragile hopes Jillian had been harboring and created a dull ache in her heart. The responsibility for any change in their relationship was on her shoulders, and she wasn't in any position to rectify the situation. Before she'd gotten involved with Jack Carnell's quest for justice, she'd been planning a joyous reconciliation, but the timing had been all wrong.

She'd missed Trey every day they'd been apart, but she didn't expect him to believe that under the circumstances. She'd never stopped loving him. No other man could ever compare. She'd met some wonderful, intriguing men in her travels, but none who touched her as deeply as Trey had. Now he was stuck with her until she was strong enough to fend for herself. It wasn't the way she'd envisioned their reunion.

Trey watched the conflicting emotions playing across her expressive features and decided he needed some breathing space. "I'm going to fix something to eat," he told her.

"Would you like some help?"

He cocked a brow. It took both hands and all her strength to lift her coffee mug. "I think I can handle it myself this time," he replied smoothly. "I won't be long."

Jillian watched him leave and collapsed against the pillows. He had good reason to be skeptical about her strength. She hated feeling so helpless, yet her arms trembled from the simplest task. There was nothing she could do until she regained some strength. She mentally vowed not to try her host's patience.

When Trey returned to the bedroom with their breakfast, he found Jillian still sitting up, but asleep. She opened her eyes and gave him a brief smile when he placed a tray-table across her lap.

Then she blinked in surprise at the enormous amount of food he'd cooked. "Are we hungry?"

"We're trying to rebuild our strength," he insisted.

"We must be trying to do it in one meal," she tossed back at him.

He began tackling his own plate of bacon, eggs and toast. "You need protein and lots of fluids."

"Is that why I have juice, milk and more coffee?

"This is breakfast and lunch."

"Well, that explains it," she said lightly. She was surprised, but pleased by the easy exchange of banter. It was one of the things she'd missed the most.

It was a slow process, but Jillian managed to eat half of her food. Then she handed her plate to him, and he finished the leftovers. It took her a little longer to get down all the liquids he insisted she needed.

"I'll have to spend the rest of the day in the bathroom," she complained good-naturedly when the last of her cups had been drained.

Trey rose from his chair in a slow, easy movement and gathered the dirty dishes. "Let me throw these in the dishwasher, and then I'll help you to the bathroom."

As soon as he left the room, Jillian eased herself to the side of the bed and swung her feet to the floor. She didn't want to depend on Trey every time she needed to go to the toilet. Unfortunately, her small spurt of independence was squashed when her legs refused to support her weight.

A few minutes later, Trey was back and had to control the desire to laugh out loud at the disgust on Jillian's face. He couldn't resist teasing.

"Not quite ready for a footrace?"

She gave him a tight smile. "Not quite. I think I might need a little help."

"Hang on to me however it's comfortable for you." He stepped close to the bed. "If I try to put an arm around you, I might hurt your side."

Jillian glanced at his bare chest, so close to her face. She could feel his heat and smell his musky, masculine scent. Even in her weakened state, the man had the power to inflame her senses. There was no avoiding the attraction. She grasped his muscled forearm and pulled herself upright. Then she clung to him until her head quit spinning.

Her legs felt stronger after she'd crossed the floor to the bathroom. She reached her hands to the door for support. "I think I can manage now," she insisted. "You wouldn't happen to have an extra toothbrush, would you?"

"Anything you need should be in the cabinet over the sink. I'll be right here until you're finished."

She had to do everything in slow motion, but felt better after brushing her teeth, combing her hair and splashing some water on her face.

When she reopened the door, Trey was waiting. He took hold of her arm until she was safely back in bed.

"Nap time," he told her.

Jillian would have argued if she'd had the energy. She decided to humor him and rest for a few minutes. Then she closed her eyes and sighed when her head sunk into the pillow. Within minutes she was asleep.

Chapter Three

Trey threw her clothes in the dryer and straightened the kitchen, then took a casserole from the freezer for their supper. Jillian was sleeping peacefully when he returned to the bedroom, so he decided to catch up on some paperwork.

His room was more like a suite. On one side was the bed and bath. The other side was furnished with a recliner and bookshelves, with an entertainment center in one corner. His desk, complete with computer system, occupied the other corner of the room.

The afternoon was spent updating the breeding files for his cattle. It was a chore he'd been avoiding, but needed to get finished. The only interruption he had was Jillian's bout of restlessness. When she started whimpering, tossing and turning, he held her and talked to her until she grew calm again.

He didn't like to think about the nightmares nagging at her subconscious. He wanted all the details of her brush with the criminal element, but had decided to wait until she was rested before plying her with questions. Maybe once he understood what she'd experienced, he could help her fight the demons.

The sun was starting to dip into the western sky when the ringing of the telephone broke the silence in the bedroom. Trey quickly reached for the receiver on his desk.

"Langden."

"It's Cade." Neither brother bothered much with pleasantries.

"You sound tense," Trey said as he took the opportunity to stretch his legs. "Is this call business or pleasure?"

"Neither," Cade informed him tersely. "I called because I just heard a news bulletin involving Jillian."

When Trey didn't immediately respond, Cade began to hurl questions at him. "Did you hear it, too?"

"Yeah."

"Do you know anything else about it?"

"Yeah."

"Is Jillian all right?"

"Yeah." The succinct response assured his brother that Jillian was close by and safe. A relieved sigh came over the line.

"Thank God. You can't talk about it?"

"No."

"Do you need anything?"

"Are you coming home this weekend?" Trey asked.

"I don't have any other plans."

"Then you might pick up some groceries before you head out to the ranch."

"Will do. Anything else?"

Jillian was going to need clothes, but Trey didn't want to say too much over the phone. "Nothing that can't wait."

"Okay, then, I'll see you Friday evening."

The connection was broken on both ends at the same time, with neither of them bothering to say goodbye. After replacing the receiver, Trey twirled his chair around to check on Jillian. She blinked at him sleepily.

"Did the phone wake you?"

"I guess," she said, struggling to sit up against the headboard. "But I feel like I've been asleep forever. What time is it?"·

He nodded to the clock beside the bed, and Jillian moaned when she saw that it was already past six.

"I guess I'm not very good company, am I?"

Trey shut down the computer and crossed the room before answering. "I needed the chance to catch up on some paperwork, anyway."

She gave him a smile. He really was the nicest man, even though he would deny it in an instant. "I'm glad your day wasn't totally wasted."

It occurred to Trey that he wouldn't consider a day spent with Jillian as wasted, whether or not he accomplished any work. It was an alarming realization. As soon as she was strong again, she was likely to leave.

"Paperwork makes me hungry," he declared, shoving the thought aside. "Supper's in the oven. Are you ready to eat?"

"I'd better make a trip to the bathroom first." Jillian slid to the side of the bed. "But this time I can manage all by myself."

Trey's lips twitched. Her independent nature must not have suffered any serious damage. He didn't argue, but stayed close enough to catch her if she lost her balance.

Jillian stood and took a minute to steady herself. Then she slowly covered the distance to the bathroom door. After grasping the handle, she turned and gave him a cheeky grin.

Her self-satisfaction pleased him, even though he didn't welcome emotional reactions to her every mood. "It's all that protein and fluid," he insisted.

Jillian closed the door, wondering if her small success was what sent a sudden thrill over her body, or if it was Trey's teasing.

He was still there, leaning against the doorjamb, when she exited the bathroom. She didn't refuse his assistance back to bed.

"Are we having supper in the kitchen?" she asked hopefully. Now that she was feeling a little stronger, she was anxious to explore Trey's home. "Right here," he said, allowing no argument. He helped her adjust the pillows so that she could sit upright, and then turned toward the door.

Jillian stalled his retreat. "Do you cook all your own meals? I thought you had a housekeeper."

Trey turned his gaze back to her. "My housekeeper's name is Delia Cooper, and she does most of the cooking. She made the casserole we're having for supper. I just stuck it in the oven."

"She was here today?"

"No, she's gone for a while, but she stocked the freezer before leaving."

"Will she be back soon?"

"That depends," he said, frowning at her line of questioning. "She went to Arizona to stay with her daughter who's having her first baby."

"You don't know how long she'll be gone?"

"No," he said, eyes narrowing. "Does it bother you to be alone in the house with me?"

"No," she declared firmly. What she really wanted to know was if there was anyone who might be shocked by her sudden appearance in Trey's bed. She didn't feel like explaining her situation, and she'd learned to be wary of strangers.

"What made you think I was afraid?"

"Maybe it was your inquisition."

Her eyes flashed. "I was just curious," she defended, not liking the intensity of Trey's expression. "I haven't been in a very sociable mood lately, that's all, and you know I have an insatiable curiosity."

They stared at each other for a long minute. Her words were a reminder of the brief time they'd lived together and learned to know each other so well. It was also a reminder of his insistence that her particular brand of curiosity usually led to trouble.

Jillian didn't want any reminders of past mistakes. "Weren't you going to get us something to eat?" she groused.

Trey was glad she didn't mind being alone with him and pleased by her show of spirit. He gave her a slight bow. "At your service, Ms. Brandt."

When he'd gone, she leaned her head against the pillows and sighed heavily. Then she berated herself for snapping at him. It wasn't his fault she'd gotten herself into such a mess. He was being incredibly patient, whether or not he resented having her here.

She couldn't help being curious about Trey's feelings. Had she totally crushed the love he'd once had for her? Was there a chance to rekindle a flame that had gone years without fuel? There was no doubting that the physical attraction was still strong, but had she destroyed all the finer feelings?

She was a little wary of how he might view their relationship, but she wasn't afraid to be alone with him. It amazed her that she could still trust anyone so completely. Would he ever trust her as unconditionally? Only time would tell, but she'd never been very patient.

Jillian managed to eat a good portion of her supper and offered to help with the dishes, but was refused. When he'd finished in the kitchen, Trey returned and pulled a chair close, using the bed for a footstool. He crossed his arms over his chest, and his expression grew serious.

"I think it's time to tell me why you decided to leave Miami without notifying the authorities."

Her gaze dropped from the intensity of his. She didn't want to talk about it, but she couldn't very well refuse him an explanation. It was difficult to describe her instinctive need to escape, but she slowly explained her reaction to Stroyer's whispered telephone conversation, the way he'd chased and shot her, the accident and her decision to hide in a truck.

"I knew I wouldn't be safe on my own in Miami, and I didn't know which, if any, authorities could be trusted. A truck with license plates from all the western states seemed the best solution."

"And you got lucky?"

Jillian nodded slowly. "I got really lucky. Butch and Joe Howe are independent drivers who share a rig. We were on the road for hours before they realized I was hiding, but then they were kind and understanding."

"What did you tell them?"

"The truth," she said. "I didn't give them names or all the facts, but I told them I was in serious danger. They believed me. They wanted to take me to a hospital, but they understood when I refused."

She was certain the truckers would have insisted if she hadn't sworn she was going to a man who would take care of her. She didn't mention that. Until she'd called Trey, she hadn't been sure he'd want anything to do with her.

Her fingers were plucking nervously at the bedclothes. Trey wondered if it upset her to talk about the trip or if there was something else she didn't want him to know.

"So they loaned you a shirt, gave you first aid and found you a ride to New Mexico?"

"They made lots of calls on the radio until they found someone they trusted who didn't mind bringing me the rest of the way."

"Who?"

Jillian hesitated. He wasn't going to like her answer. "All I know is his name was Donald. By the time I switched trucks, I was getting a little feverish."

She'd been totally at the mercy of strangers. Trey's teeth clenched at the thought of what could have happened to her. That she'd been put in such a position by a corrupt agent made him even more furious.

"Does anyone know where you are? Is there anyone you need to call or get in touch with?"

"No!" Jillian exclaimed hoarsely, and then calmed herself. "I made sure nobody knew exactly where I was going. All the truckers knew was Albuquerque, but they swore they wouldn't tell. I had to leave my cell phone at the safe house, but I wouldn't have used it anyway. I can't risk being traced. These people have powerful connections and a fortune to spend on tracking equipment."

Trey understood, but knew she couldn't hide forever. "Aren't there people who'll be concerned about you?"

Jillian didn't want to think about it. She knew she should contact Jack Carnell's editor and Lieutenant Mitchell at the FBI. She believed they could be trusted, but she wasn't ready to take chances.

When she didn't respond, Trey made a suggestion. "Cade's coming this weekend. If you want to write a couple letters, he could mail them from Dallas."

"Cade's coming?" Jillian hedged. She didn't want anybody to know she'd traveled west. Not even Cade.

"He heard the FBI bulletin."

"You told him I was here?"

"Not in so many words, but I'm sure he figured it out." His tone grew defensive. "Is that a problem?"

Jillian didn't want him to think she didn't trust Cade. It had nothing to do with trust. "I know I sound paranoid," she apologized. "But it's hard for most people to understand how powerful and vicious these criminals can be."

"Cade's careful. He's handled his share of greedy, unscrupulous people, and has an impressive security force."

Jillian managed a smile for him, resigning herself to the fact that Cade might also be putting himself in danger. She knew how proud Trey was of his brother, so she'd have to trust him, too. "I've heard he's become a real corporate dynamo. It will be nice to see him again."

"He's one of your biggest fans," said Trey, relaxing a little. "He's bought copies of every magazine that ever published your photos."

Jillian's eyes lit with pleasure. After she'd broken up with Trey, her work had been her salvation. She'd poured herself into it, body and soul. She was proud of what she'd accomplished.

"He really thinks I'm good?"

Trey didn't know how she could doubt the quality and popularity of her work. She'd won several awards. And he wasn't so petty that he resented her success. "He really thinks you're good."

Jillian noticed Trey didn't include his own praise, but she was sure he hadn't wanted to see every photo she'd ever sold. Even now, the mention of her work created a sudden tension between them. She knew he believed she'd chosen her career over marriage, but that wasn't the case. It had been his lack of faith in her that had torn them apart.

When an uncomfortable silence settled between them, Trey excused himself to fetch their meal. They ate with a minimum of conversation and then he carried their dishes back to the kitchen.

On his return, he said, "I need to spend some more time at the computer. Do you feel like taking a nap, or would you like to get up for a while?"

Jillian wanted to get out of bed. She knew if she didn't get some exercise, she would get more stiff and sore. With his help, she got up and moving. He insisted she wasn't ready to explore the whole house, but told her to make herself at home in his room. She slowly investigated while he went back to his desk.

The entertainment center offered a television, a stereo and several shelves of books. The TV didn't interest her. She'd never watched it much, and right now she didn't want any connection with the outside world.

She loved to read, but her eyes and attention span weren't at their best. It seemed like only a few minutes before her strength began to wane. So while Trey worked on the ranch's financial records, she played some country-western music and relaxed in the recliner.

Her side ached a little, but it wasn't nearly as painful as it had been yesterday. Nothing could be worse than the pounding her battered body had gotten while she was traveling across the country. She decided she was well on the way to recovery, even though her strength was limited. Her accommodations were a far cry better than any she'd had the past few weeks.

Trey's presence was an added bonus. Most of her attention was directed toward him. He was engrossed in work, so she had a good opportunity to study him.

His appearance hadn't changed much in two years, except to improve. His shoulders seemed broader, his whole body harder and leaner, but it suited him. Wearing nothing but low-slung jeans and a snug-fitting T-shirt, he was irresistibly sexy, and he never seemed to wear much else.

Her pulse fluttered as she soaked up the sight of him. She'd never forgotten the feel of his skin against hers, nor the way their bodies fit together so perfectly. It wasn't much of a surprise to realize that he could still stir the flames of desire in her, even when she was as weak as a kitten. He didn't have to do anything to make her aware of him. He just existed.

He was Trey Langden, her first and only love. She'd wondered if the burning attraction would lessen after years of separation. Now she knew. It hadn't. Two years of smoldering had just made it stronger and hotter.

Scolding herself for her thoughts, Jillian silently admitted she didn't have the emotional or physical energy for Trey's kind of loving right now, even if he was willing to accommodate her. She shifted her gaze from him and tried to concentrate on the lyrics of a love song, but her eyes and thoughts kept drifting back to the big man at the desk.

She'd phoned him and sent cards. He'd never refused her calls, but she'd always done most of the talking. He'd shared information about the ranch, but they'd never discussed their relationship. Then, when she'd dared to plan a reconciliation, she'd been the one who hadn't shown. He was bound to be furious about that.

She had seen Cade on occasion. Her parents were both dead, yet she still considered Dallas her hometown. She'd kept an apartment in Miami for the past two years, but tried to stop over in Texas when her work required a trip west.

Cade had told her the ranch was prospering and that Trey worked too hard. She'd gotten the impression that Cade wasn't any slouch when it came to work, either. She'd heard from other college classmates that Langden Industries was becoming quite a business empire.

She was glad the Langden brothers were finding satisfaction with their individual interests. They were both good, dependable men with big hearts.

They were the closest she came to having a family, even if she'd been estranged for some time now.

When Jillian caught herself dozing an hour or so later, she decided she could use a bath and change of clothes. Trey was stretching his stiff muscles and agreed it was time for a break. He helped her out of the recliner and found her a clean shirt to wear.

She settled for a sponge bath, promising herself a shower and shampoo in the morning. She was brushing her teeth when Trey knocked on the bathroom door and handed her the underwear he'd washed.

"When you're dressed, I want to look at your side," he told her. "Don't try to change the dressing yourself."

Despite his words of caution, Jillian managed to carefully remove the old bandage. She was pleased to see that the wound hadn't seeped at all. It was still ugly, but it was healing well.

She hated sleeping in a bra and panties, yet she didn't want Trey to think she was totally wanton. The bra wasn't any problem, but bending to step into the panties brought unexpected pain and dizziness when she stood upright again.

She'd just regained her balance when Trey entered the bathroom after a sharp knock. "I forgot you might have trouble with the underwear," he said, taking in her discomfort at a glance.

"It was tricky, but I persevered," she teased. Her sense of humor had been her salvation in lots of sticky situations.

She would have liked to shield herself with a towel, but she had both hands on the sink to steady herself. Under the circumstances, it was silly to feel so modest, yet she couldn't control the blush that crept up her face.

Trey couldn't control the way his blood raced at the sight of her. The silk underthings enhanced rather than hid her womanly curves. The tumble of gold hair on her shoulders and the abundance of bare skin were an aphrodisiac he didn't want or need. The swift, violent surge of desire made his tone harsher than he intended. "I told you not to change the bandage."

Jillian was appalled by the sudden sting of tears in her eyes and the way her lips trembled, delaying any response she might have made. Her nerves were more frayed than she'd realized. She knew he wasn't really upset about the bandage. He was just concerned and tense. She was the basket case.

Turning from his watchful gaze, she took her time slipping into the borrowed shirt.

Trey dragged a hand through his hair in frustration. He hadn't meant to snarl at her, and he sure as hell hadn't wanted to upset her. Her shimmering eyes and quivering lips made him feel like a first-class bastard.

"I only took off the old bandage," Jillian explained when she'd regained her composure. "I'd appreciate help with a clean one."

He grabbed the supplies he'd need. He didn't attempt to touch her, but stayed within reach. "Why don't you stretch out on the bed?"

Jillian was rapidly running out of energy. She realized that she'd wasted her efforts buttoning the shirt because he still had to have access to her wound.

A weary sigh escaped her when she was once again flat on her back in bed. "I can't believe how easily I get tired." Her arms were at her sides and felt too heavy to lift.

"You probably lost a lot of blood," Trey said. He sat on the edge of the bed and unfastened the shirt buttons for her. "If you'd gone to the hospital, they'd probably have given you more blood. Without it, it'll take some time to rebuild your own supply."

Jillian groaned in disgust. "Do you suppose I could just drink some blood and get it over with quickly?"

Trey admired her ability to find humor in the situation. Her quick wit had always delighted him, but he wasn't in the mood for it now. "I'm afraid I don't have an extra pint sitting around."

"I don't suppose cow blood counts, does it?"

"No."

His clipped response dampened Jillian's playful mood and silence fell between them again. Trey smoothed cream on her side and replaced the bandage. "It looks better. You shouldn't need to cover it at all when it dries up some more."

"I'm taking a shower tomorrow no matter what. I don't see how it can hurt to keep it clean."

"I don't think there's much chance of infection now," he replied, hoping she didn't notice how unsteady his hands were when he refastened the buttons over the tempting curves of her breasts. As soon as he had her decently covered again, he put some distance between them.

"Thank you," she murmured softly.

Trey just grunted and took the medical supplies back to the bathroom. When he returned to her side, her eyes were closed. He pulled the covers over her and switched off the light next to the bed. He needed to talk to Wayne, so he pulled a heavier shirt from the closet and headed toward the door. He was ready to leave when Jillian's anxious words halted him.

"Trey? Are you leaving?"

"I'm going outside to talk to my foreman."

"Will you be long?"

"An hour, at the most."

"Aren't you sleepy?" she asked as a delaying tactic.

"I'm getting tired, but I probably won't go to bed for a couple of hours." It would take him that long to get the rampaging desire under control again.

"Will you be coming back in here?"

Trey thought he knew what she was really asking. "Do you mean this room and this bed?"

"Yes."

"I'll be sleeping with you." His tone brooked no argument. "I'll try not to bump your side during the night."

Jillian's husky voice expressed relief. "You won't bother me," she assured him, then added in a sleepy whisper, "I like having you with me."

The softly spoken words cut through him like a knife. He'd been prepared to argue if she tried to keep him out of his own bed. The truth was that she wanted him as close as he wanted her. The problem was that her need was based in fear, and his need went a whole lot deeper.

"I won't be long," he assured her as he headed out the door. He figured she'd sleep while he was gone, and he'd be back before her nightmares began.

His bed was a king-size one, but when he climbed in it later that night, he carefully shifted as close to Jillian as he could get. She was sleeping on her stomach with her right side toward the edge of the bed, so he pressed himself close against her left side and draped one arm across her hips.

She felt deliciously warm and smelled sweetly feminine. His body reacted swiftly to the feel of her; his blood heated, raced through every vein in his body and pooled between his legs. He'd have to be dead not to respond to Jillian. The arousal was unwelcome, but it was better than the indifference he'd felt whenever he'd considered assuaging his hunger with other women. He just didn't want anyone but her.

He'd waited most of his life for the right woman. Once he'd found her, he'd never wanted anyone else, but Jillian hadn't wanted him as much. She'd been full of youthful enthusiasm for her career. She hadn't understood how he could be so jealous of her working with an old boyfriend.

Maybe he had overreacted, but only because he'd loved her so passionately. He'd tried to see her point of view, but his heart had never accepted all the arguments and explanations. He'd finally come to the conclusion that she just hadn't loved him as much as he'd loved her. His pride had taken a beating and their separation had been hell. Now he was more than ready to give his body to her, but he was never going to trust her again with his heart and soul.

Trey eventually fell asleep, but awakened once at the sound of Jillian's whimpered cries. His gut twisted at the thought of the continued nightmares. All he could do was hold her and quietly swear that she was safe now.

Chapter Four

Thursday was spent in much the same way as Wednesday. Trey stayed close to Jillian while she rested and regained her strength. She was still confined to the bedroom, but she could move more freely and without much pain.

When she was sleeping he told himself that she was no more than a very desirable houseguest. But when she was awake—when she looked at him with her beautiful eyes or spoke his name—he was bombarded with unwelcome emotion he didn't care to analyze. He tried to convince himself that the feelings were nothing more than lust.

They were careful not to discuss sensitive subjects. Trey avoided talking whenever possible, keeping his responses to a bare minimum. He didn't want a renewal of the rapport they'd shared in the past, nor would he risk being emotionally seduced.

He didn't get much sleep. By Friday morning, he needed to escape the mounting tension caused by the close proximity with Jillian. Holding her and sleeping with her body tight against his own was playing havoc with his hormones. He needed an outlet for the stress and physical frustration.

Spending most of the day working himself into exhaustion in the barns and ranch yard helped. He was careful not to drift too far from the house and made several trips inside to ensure Jillian was all right. He fixed breakfast and lunch, shared them with her, and then ordered her to rest while he spent the afternoon working with livestock.

Cade arrived in the early evening, and Trey helped him carry groceries into the house. They put everything away, and then Cade started supper while Trey got cleaned up. Jillian was sleeping when he entered the bedroom, so he quietly stripped, showered and pulled on a clean pair of jeans and a denim shirt.

"I took some steaks out for supper," Cade said as Trey rejoined him. He'd already set three places at the table. "They're under the broiler and should be ready in about fifteen minutes. I bought baked potatoes and salad at the grocery's salad bar. We just have to nuke the potatoes."

Trey nodded, pulled beers from the refrigerator for both of them and set out a glass for Jillian. She liked beer, but she needed milk to build her strength.

"How is she?" Cade wasn't surprised that she'd sought refuge at the ranch. She didn't have any family to turn to. "The reports weren't specific, and I didn't want to make waves until I talked to you."

Trey leaned against the kitchen sink and faced the door to the hallway. Cade sat down at the table and sipped his beer, but his gaze never wavered from his brother's intense expression.

"She's had a bad scare. Physically, she's healing, but she's still in a lot of danger."

"Emotionally?"

"That, and the fact that somebody wants her dead."

"Gardova."

Trey's eyes narrowed. "How much do you know?"

"Just that she's the government's only witness in the murder trial against him. When she disappeared, his lawyers started screaming that they didn't have enough evidence to keep him in jail, that the photos weren't clear enough. The judge released him on a ten-million-dollar bond."

Trey swore viciously, and then downed the rest of his beer. Gardova was out of jail. He would be relentless in his search for Jillian.

"He's being watched every minute so that he doesn't get a chance to skip the country, but my contacts heard that he's upped the price on Jillian's head to two million."

The news slammed into Trey and staggered his breath. He should have known there'd be a contract on her life, but he hadn't thought about it. Every slimy hit man and bounty hunter in the world would be hunting her. Her paranoia about being found started to make more sense.

"Did you hear anything about where he thinks she's hiding?"

Cade shook his head. "All Gardova and the FBI know is that she was last seen in Miami. Word is they're all damned frustrated. The FBI agent who was assigned to protect her says she was abducted by Gardova's people. My contacts say the drug baron doesn't have a clue to where she is, but he's frantic to find her."

"Which FBI agent said she was abducted?"

"Name of Stroyer."

"Jillian said he got hit by a car."

"Broke both his legs. He's laid up in the hospital in traction, but he says he saw two men force her into a car. There's evidence he shot at them."

Trey's mouth twisted derisively. "The only one he shot at was Jillian. He was chasing her, and when she didn't stop, he shot her in the back. One of his bullets grazed her right side, from back to front."

Cade's hand clenched around the beer can, nearly crushing it. "The agent shot Jillian?" he snarled.

"Right."

His brother's spate of obscenities reiterated Trey's opinion of a man who would shoot anybody in the back, especially a defenseless woman.

"You're sure she's all right?"

"The wound is healing, but she lost a lot of blood, and she's a long way from all right," Trey responded. "How did you get so much information without making waves?"

"Steven has a friend on Miami's vice squad." Steven Tanner was the Langden Industries' security chief. "The detective hates Gardova and isn't too fond of the Feds, but he keeps a close watch on anything that happens in his jurisdiction."

"There's no way he could trace Jillian through you?"

Cade shook his head. "Steven says his friend's one of the best. He didn't ask questions. Even if he finds out I want information, it won't make a difference. Jill and I were college buddies. That's common knowledge. Very few people know about your relationship with her."

Trey nodded. He trusted his brother's judgment and knew he wouldn't do anything to endanger Jillian.

"How did she get out here?" Cade asked.

Trey explained how she'd hitched a ride with truckers. "Does Langden Industries have any need for trucking services?"

"Occasionally, and I have friends who are always looking for reliable transportation for their products."

"Butch and Joe Howe are independents. I'd like to make sure they get all the work they can handle."

Cade nodded in understanding. Trey took care of his own and anyone who helped him take care of his own. "I'll find out where their base is and spread the word that they're people who can be trusted."

"Thanks." Trey wished he could personally thank the truckers, but he wasn't likely to get the chance. He got another beer from the refrigerator and returned to his position facing the door.

He saw Jillian heading down the hallway toward the kitchen. Their gazes locked, and she gave him a smile that made his pulse race. Her hair was clean, shiny and bouncing on her shoulders. She was dressed in his favorite blue flannel shirt. The tails fell to mid-thigh, exposing long, bare legs. The soft, thin fabric did little to conceal her enticing feminine curves.

Jillian was feeling much stronger after three days of rest and Trey's tender care. She still got tired easily, but she'd managed to explore Trey's home between naps. He still wouldn't let her do the cooking, but she liked watching him wherever he was. As she entered the kitchen, she headed straight to him. She'd missed him today because he'd spent more time outdoors. Feeling bold, and a little reckless, she stopped in front of him, stretched on tiptoe and placed a light kiss on his lips.

Trey stiffened, and Cade noisily cleared his throat behind her. The unexpected sound startled Jillian. She screamed and threw her body sideways, slamming her sore side against the countertop. Pain exploded through her, making her stomach roll and her knees buckle.

Trey's strong arms caught her before she could fall. He wrapped his arms around her shoulders and pulled her close to his chest, offering badly needed support. Jillian sagged against him, dragging in long gulps of air until the fear and pain subsided.

"Damn, Jillian, I'm sorry," Cade apologized gruffly. Her frightened, defensive reaction had brought him out of his chair. He moved closer to gently touch her arm. "I didn't mean to scare you."

After taking a few more deep breaths, she turned her face toward him and offered a shaky smile. "Don't worry about it," she insisted huskily. "You just took me by surprise. It's not your fault that I'm a basket case."

The brothers exchanged worried looks. Jillian had always been fearless; always ready for a challenge. She'd never been the nervous, jumpy type. They had to wonder how much the events of the past few months had changed her.

"Did you hurt yourself?"

Trey eased his grip on her as he felt her strength return. When she was standing alone, they both glanced toward her right side.

"Let me see if you hit it hard enough to reopen the wound," said Trey.

She hadn't put on a new bandage after her shower today, so all she had to do was raise the hem of the shirt and expose her side. The gash was still an angry red. Her flesh was varying shades of black, blue and sickly green from breast to waist.

Cade's breath hissed out when he got a look at the wound. He wasn't shy about using a few X-rated words.

"It's not as bad as it looks," Jillian assured him, turning toward Trey to show him that no damage had been done. "It's much better, but the bruises are still ugly."

"A federal agent did this to you?"

Jillian's gaze flew to Trey.

"Cade learned that Stroyer is alive," he told her, making her aware of his brother's deeper knowledge of the situation. "He has two broken legs and is telling his superiors that the shots he fired were at someone who abducted you."

She stepped away from both men and moved toward the table. "He's a liar."

Trey held out a chair for her until she was comfortably seated. He didn't think she needed to rehash the whole thing right now, so he silently motioned Cade to drop the subject. Then he turned his attention to the steaks while his brother warmed potatoes in the microwave. The two men worked in a perfect harmony that came from years of fending for themselves and sharing chores.

Jillian loved watching them. They were alike in so many ways, yet very different. They both stood at six feet, were tanned, lean and muscled, but Trey was darker, with coal-black hair and impossibly dark eyes that mirrored his passionate nature.

Cade had sable hair and whiskey-colored eyes that glittered with arrogant amusement, a wicked trait that often concealed his intense nature. He was one of the most handsome men she'd ever known. In college, she, and a majority of the other women, had found him incredibly attractive.

Then she'd met his big brother and realized the attraction for her classmate was mild compared to the impact Trey made on her senses. He wasn't quite as pretty, but he was devastating. She'd fallen fast and hard.

As they worked, Jillian took the opportunity to study them and their surroundings. The kitchen didn't provide much of a masculine background for them. It was big, homey, comfortable, and decorated with a woman's touch. The decor was a popular country blue combined with natural wood cabinets and furniture. She could tell that Mrs. Cooper had had a hand in the decorating.

The windows over the sink gave a broad view of the ranch yard beyond the porch. The three doorways opened to the porch, the pantry and the inside hallway. Despite a few frills, it was a natural setting for the two competent bachelors.

During their meal, the conversation stayed general. The men exchanged news and discussed business, occasionally asking Jillian for an opinion. She responded when spoken to, but was content to eat and listen without saying much. It was a rare pleasure to have her two favorite men together.

Her side was still throbbing a little, so she didn't argue when ordered to sit still while they cleared the table and loaded the dishwasher. Darkness had fallen by the time the kitchen was cleaned.

Trey suggested they take their coffee to the living room. He led the way, built a fire in the hearth and then joined Jillian on the soft leather sofa. Cade turned on a lamp and sat across from them in a matching easy chair.

Jillian loved the living room, especially with the fire burning brightly. It was exactly what she'd imagined when she'd wondered about Trey's home. The room had a Southwest decor with a beamed ceiling and shiny hardwood floors covered by hand-braided rugs. Wall hangings and crocheted afghans added brilliant splashes of color to the tan hues of the furniture. The overall effect was warm, inviting and aesthetically pleasing.

Aside from appreciating the room's comforting beauty, Jillian felt warm and safe in the heart of Trey's home. It had been a long time since she'd felt really safe, and it was amazing how much she'd missed that basic quality of life. She didn't think she'd ever want to leave the ranch.

Trey thought about all the times he'd imagined having Jillian here, by his side. The reality was bittersweet; their situation was anything but ideal.

There was no sense in further delaying the discussion they'd avoided during supper. "Cade learned that Gardova was released from jail," he told her, knowing there was no easy way to break the news.

Shock sent an uncontrollable shudder through Jillian, shattering her newfound sense of security. Her hands began to tremble, so she slowly leaned over to place her cup on the coffee table.

"When and why?" she asked in a hoarse tone.

Cade explained about his contacts, about Gardova's bid for freedom and the fact that the FBI needed more than photographs to take the case to court.

"I find that hard to believe," Jillian argued. "Anybody who's seen the photographs would find that hard to believe. Maybe there was another mysterious accident in the FBI's evidence room."

"Not that I know of," he said.

"What did you do with the negatives?" Trey asked. "You said you didn't escape the safe house with anything but your wallet and Stroyer's coat and hat."

Her eyes widened at his question. She'd forgotten about the negatives. "I sent them to Langden Industries in care of Cade," she said, turning to him. "I thought they'd be safer at a corporate headquarters than anywhere personal I might stash them."

"I wondered about the mysterious envelope and your instructions to hide it. At least, until I heard about the Gardova case," the younger man said, rising from his chair and heading from the room. "I brought it with me. It's in my briefcase."

In a few minutes, he returned with a photo-mailer envelope, and held it out to Jillian. She shuddered at the sight, not even wanting to touch it. At her nod, Trey took it. He opened the mailer and pulled out several strips of negatives, then lifted them toward the light of the lamp.

Jillian's chest grew tight. She didn't have to look at the negatives. The gruesome images printed on the film were indelibly printed on her brain. No matter what she did or where she went, the images haunted her.

While she and Jack Carnell had been holed up in that dark, dank warehouse, they had watched the cold-blooded torture and murder of a man. As soon as they'd felt safe to leave, she'd lost the contents of her stomach. She'd done the same when she'd made the reprints.

Trey's jaw clenched and every muscle in his body hardened into knots as he viewed the negatives. He'd seen the same kind of horror when he'd been in the service, but the fact that Jillian had witnessed such atrocities made him burn with anger.

The man he assumed to be Juan Gardova was dressed in an expensive suit. The background was dark, so he couldn't get a clear image of the drug lord's face. That's probably why the defense lawyers had managed to get him freed on bond.

Two big, burly thugs had beaten a fourth man, slashed him with knives and tortured him in more ways than most people could imagine. The photos gave a clear picture of the man begging for mercy, falling unconscious, being revived and then brutally tortured again.

It was no wonder Jillian had nightmares. The photographs were vivid enough, but she'd witnessed the actual crime. The memories would be seared into her brain, heightened by sights, sounds and smells. On top of that, she would have known that any attempt to intervene would mean certain death.

He passed the negatives to Cade and watched all the color wash out of his face. His features grew grim, eyes hard, as he studied the evidence.

Trey's eyes were equally hard. "Show those pictures to any jury in the country and you could get the death penalty," he ground out harshly. "Why the hell did they let Gardova out of jail?"

"Maybe the FBI's evidence team can't positively identify Gardova," said Cade. "Or maybe they want something else from him."

"A few more murders?" Trey retorted as he carefully returned the negatives to the protective package.

"Who knows?" Cade rose, took the envelope and crossed the room. He shifted a large painting that hid a wall safe, then locked the envelope inside and returned the painting to its proper position. As he moved back across the room, he tried to second-guess the authorities.

"Maybe they have round-the-clock surveillance on him and think he can lead them to Jillian."

"Not likely." Jillian spoke, her tone and expression totally devoid of emotion. "If he knew where I was, I'd be as dead as Jack Carnell."

Both men watched her closely, trying to comprehend and come to terms with what she'd experienced in the past few months. She'd suffered more than a gunshot wound and loss of faith in the justice system. The severe emotional trauma was more debilitating. They glanced at each other, expressions equally fierce.

"Don't you think they'll put Gardova back in jail once the proper authorities learn that you're still alive?"

"No!" Jillian shouted harshly, and then calmed herself with visible effort. She shifted her gaze to the fire. "I don't want anyone to know anything about me."

"We're not going to advertise your location, Jillian," Trey soothed, reaching out a hand to stroke her arm. "But Cade can use his Dallas office as a go-between for you. You can get messages to anybody you need to contact."

"I don't need to contact anyone," she insisted stubbornly. "Nobody needs to know if I'm dead or alive. You're the only two people in the world I can trust."

"There has to be someone," Cade insisted. "What about close friends? A roommate or a newspaper editor who's above bribery?"

Jillian was shaking her head vigorously, sending her hair dancing back and forth across her shoulders. She had tucked her feet beneath her and was gradually curling into a ball in the corner of the sofa. She remained adamant.

"I have colleagues and college friends I keep in touch with, but I certainly wouldn't involve any of them in this mess. There's nobody."

"What about the people Jack Carnell worked with?" Trey asked. "Do you think Stroyer was responsible for his death? Was Stroyer the only agent on the take, or do you think more FBI operatives were involved? Isn't there anyone you've met in the agency that you feel can be trusted?"

They watched a myriad of expressions flicker across Jillian's face. She seemed to give the questions thought, mentally reviewing the choices. Then

61

she hardened herself again. She wasn't willing to trust anyone, and she didn't appear willing to cooperate.

Jillian finally spoke. "Jack's editor knew what we'd done. Jack trusted him, but Jack was murdered. I don't know anything about the man."

"Then he's too much of a risk," Trey declared. "What about the authorities?"

Jillian shifted her gaze from his searching eyes." There's a Lieutenant Mitchell with the FBI who seemed to be genuinely concerned with my welfare. I trusted him, but he assigned Stroyer to watch me."

Her gaze flashed from one man to the other. She knew there was a price on her head. "I still can't comprehend the fact that someone thinks my death is worth a million dollars."

"Two million," Cade automatically corrected her.

Her eyes widened in shock and her face went white. Trey swore, and Cade quickly apologized. "God, I'm sorry, Jill. I shouldn't have said that."

"Don't worry about it," she told him in a tight voice. "I should be kept up-to-date on my face value."

"It might not be bad news," Trey reasoned. "The FBI will know Gardova isn't behind your disappearance if he's upped the price on your head. Maybe they've got their doubts about Stroyer, and are waiting to see if there's any contact between the two men."

"Stroyer will be spending the next few weeks in a hospital under constant surveillance," Cade said. "He won't risk contact with Gardova, and he won't be going anywhere with half his body in a cast."

"You're not going to let them get away with murder, are you?" Trey asked Jillian, his tone softly challenging.

It was obvious that she was the only person who could bring both Gardova and Stroyer to justice, but it was the first time he'd suggested that she needed to act on her knowledge.

Both men expected the question to rouse her anger, to put her on the defensive and elicit a spirited response, but her eyes remained dull with disillusionment.

"They've already gotten away with it," she stated flatly. "Nothing I can do will bring Jack back or stop the violence. I'm done trying."

"You have the power to stop Gardova, and if you don't tell the truth about Stroyer, he'll keep his rank and tenure with the FBI. A lot of other innocent people could be at risk," Trey reminded her.

Jillian steadily returned his gaze, but no spark of concern entered her eyes, making it clear that she wasn't going to change her mind or discuss the matter any further.

Trey stared at her for a long, silent moment, his expression concerned, his gaze penetrating. His own rigid moral code made it hard to accept her attitude, but her apathy was understandable. He was certain she'd change her mind once she'd had some time to heal and felt safe again.

"My security people are well trained and completely trustworthy. Is there anything you want me to have collected for you from Miami?" Cade broke the tense silence by asking. "They could pick up some of your personal belongings, and I could bring them out next weekend."

Jillian gazed at him with a resigned expression. Her voice was toneless. "I don't have any personal belongings anymore."

The statement brought more tension to the room. The men watched her with curious, expectant expressions until she finally explained.

"After I testified against Gardova, my apartment was trashed. Every article of clothing, piece of furniture and keepsake was either smashed or slashed to ribbons. The vandals were very thorough. There was nothing that could be salvaged."

The grim admission stunned her companions, but not as much as her totally unemotional description of the violation.

"Your darkroom and portfolio?" Cade asked, knowing that she valued her work above all other possessions.

"Everything was destroyed," Jillian reiterated without blinking an eye. "The only thing I had left was one camera and the clothes on my back. I bought a few replacement items, but I had to leave them behind at the safe house."

The sound she made was a mockery of laughter. "I guess that officially makes me a homeless person."

"What about all the antiques and furniture you kept from your parents' house in Texas?" Trey asked. "Was that at your apartment in Miami?"

"No, thank God. It's stored in Dallas. Ironically, I have plenty of money and great credit, but I don't dare touch a penny of it. Any activity on my accounts would be reported and traced before I had the cash in hand."

"Well, as long as your credit's good," Cade teased, trying to lighten the atmosphere, "Langden Industries can float you a loan. Just tell me what you need, and I'll see that it's here in a week."

"Thanks," she replied, offering him a weak smile. "I'll think about it."

Trey had been aching to touch her all evening. He'd missed her today, more than he cared to admit. Even though he'd spent some time with her, he hadn't felt her close since waking this morning.

He reached for her without thinking, and without a word, Jillian uncurled and closed the distance between them. His arms gently enfolded her, and she curled up in his lap with her head resting on his chest.

Trey's body tightened with overwhelming need—the need to comfort, to battle her demons, to chase away her fears, to protect and possess her. The need was primal and brutal, emotional as well as physical. It was tearing him apart.

Even though Jillian let him hold her, she didn't completely relax. He wanted her total, unequivocal trust. He wanted her to let him share the fear and pain.

He wanted her to open up and let it all out—to scream, cry, or rant and rage at the injustices she'd suffered. Her eyes remained dry, her temper rigidly controlled, her exuberance stifled.

The most joyful and optimistic woman he'd ever known seemed totally devoid of emotion. It wasn't healthy. She couldn't survive this way, but he didn't know how to help her. His gaze met Cade's, both registering deep concern.

"Time," his brother mouthed silently.

Trey nodded. It would take time for Jillian's emotional wounds to heal, more time than for the physical wounds. He had to find the patience and strength to help her, even if it meant losing part of himself in the process. She'd already lost too much.

When the men started talking business again, Jillian stirred in Trey's lap. She wasn't really sleepy after her late nap, but she felt a sudden, intense need to be alone. Discussing the horrors she'd experienced in Miami made her want to isolate herself, even from the men she most trusted.

She knew they had plenty to discuss, anyway, so she slowly eased herself from Trey's arms. "If you two will excuse me, I think I'll call it a night. Thanks for dinner. It was delicious. I'll see you in the morning."

Trey reluctantly released her. Two pairs of worried eyes watched her leave the room. When she was out of earshot, Cade spoke to his brother in a low growl. "The bastards have to pay."

Trey nodded in agreement, not surprised his brother shared his feelings on the subject. "You'll have to be careful. Find out everything you can about this Lieutenant Mitchell. He may be our only hope. Until we find out who we can trust, I don't want anyone to know Jillian's alive."

Cade nodded in agreement. "Steven's working on it, and I'll keep you informed."

Renewed fury vibrated through Trey at the thought of Jillian facing the destruction of everything she owned. His eyes blazed. His hands were clenched into fists, and his muscles knotted with impotent rage.

"As soon as that bastard Stroyer is out of the hospital, I want him locked in jail," he snarled in a voice raw with emotion. "Find out all you can about the agent Gardova murdered and check into his background."

"I'll do everything I can," Cade promised. "Stroyer's superiors might be suspicious, but he's got a clean record, and they can't do anything without Jillian's testimony."

"She'll testify. You know how she feels about any kind of injustice."

"I know how she used to feel," Cade corrected.

"She hasn't changed," Trey argued hotly. "She's just in hiding. She'll come out of it and demand that Stroyer pay for his treachery."

"I hope you're right."

The brothers' eyes met. They both hoped Jillian would recover from the terror and betrayal she'd experienced. Right now, she was just a shell of her former self.

"I'll get some help with shopping and bring Jillian a few clothes when I come next weekend. Do you have any idea what she needs and what sizes she wears?"

"I checked everything when I did laundry," Trey said as he tried to control his anger. "I'll make a list of sizes. Just buy some things she can wear around here. I don't think she'll be leaving the ranch for a while."

"Do you want me to hire extra help so that you can spend more time with her?"

"At this point, I don't know if I can stand spending more time with her," he confessed raggedly. Jillian was an earthy, passionate woman. The attraction between them was as fierce as ever. The sparks had grown steadily hotter whenever their gazes locked or their bodies accidentally brushed.

He was willing and more than able to meet her physical needs, but he'd sworn that she would have to make the first move. He couldn't stand the waiting much longer. He felt like a time bomb ready to explode. Every tick of the clock brought him closer to detonation. If Jillian didn't give him some sort of sign soon, he would go out of his mind.

Cade watched the play of emotion on his brother's face and knew that he and Jillian were still going through a rough time, mentally, physically and emotionally. Even though he believed they loved each other, nothing between them seemed to have been resolved. Maybe time and proximity would help.

Chapter Five

It was well after midnight when the two brothers finally said goodnight and headed for their separate bedrooms. Trey had relaxed in Cade's company, but the minute he saw Jillian lying in his bed, his body grew tense again. His need for her was a relentless ache.

He quietly stripped and headed for the bathroom, but the first thing he noticed upon entering was her lacy panties and bra hanging over the towel rack to dry. She'd obviously rinsed them out in the sink, which meant she was just as obviously without them right now.

Knowing she was naked under his shirt wasn't going to make sleeping any easier tonight. He took a quick, cold shower, trying to ease the discomfort of his desire, yet knowing the effect wouldn't last long. He didn't bother to put on anything but clean briefs after he was dried and ready for bed. Sleeping nearly nude against Jillian's warmth was an exquisite kind of torture.

She'd left a small lamp burning. Trey turned it off, then opened the drapes and allowed moonlight to flood the room. When his eyes adjusted to the dim lighting, he moved to the left side of the bed. Jillian was lying near the center.

Moonbeams danced on the golden hair splayed across the pillowcase. The sight of the tumbled, satin tresses and her lovely features negated any relief he'd found in the cold shower. His pulse surged in reaction.

She turned her face toward him when he pulled back the sheets, and he realized she was awake. He hoped she wouldn't be upset by the sight of his arousal. There was no disguising it, but he stood perfectly still until he could be sure she wasn't alarmed.

"Having trouble sleeping?"

She shook her head from side to side, her jeweled gaze fastening on him like a warm caress. "I dozed for a little while."

Her sultry, sexy tone shivered over Trey, heating his blood and sizzling along his nerves.

Jillian's eyes were accustomed to the darkness and his big body was bathed in moonlight. Her hungry gaze slid slowly over his gloriously masculine form. He was the most beautiful man she'd ever seen, and the sight of him made her quiver with long-suppressed desires.

He'd slept with her and held her close every night since she'd arrived. Trey was a sensual, virile man, and she'd been aware of every inch of his hard body and his tightly leashed restraint. She knew he must be aching badly, but he hadn't pressured her or made the slightest demand. He was more than beautiful, he was a prince among men—her white knight, her protector and trusted friend.

Until tonight, she hadn't had the strength or courage to face her own burning need for his loving. Now she was aching, too. She wanted him with a desperation that had been intensified by two years of separation.

"Do you want me to turn on the television or radio?" he asked, trying to block out his physical needs and put her needs before his own. He knew once they'd made love, there would be no stopping.

She shook her head again, not wanting anything but Trey. Her gaze locked with his while she reached out a hand and touched his bare thigh. She heard his sharply indrawn breath and felt the muscles quiver beneath her stroking fingers.

"Jillian." His breath poured out in an agonized groan, his tone a ragged combination of wanting and warning.

Her courage faltered and her fingers stilled. She wondered if he disapproved of her familiarity. "Would you rather I didn't touch you?" she asked in a soft, hesitant voice.

Trey groaned and pressed a hand over hers on his thigh. His fingers tightened, urging her to touch him more boldly. Then he was pulling her hand to the part of him that had a persistent ache. "No, don't stop."

Relief washed over Jillian. She hadn't been aware of holding her breath, but it hissed out of her lungs on a shaky sigh. Trey wanted to make love, and she wanted it, too. She'd never been more certain about anything in her life.

Her caressing fingers slid up his thigh until she cupped the softness between his legs. She heard him groan deep in his throat while she explored the different shapes and textures of his masculinity.

His whole body clenched in desire. Blood rushed to his head and throbbed in his groin. The touch of her soft hands seared him to the soul. He shut his eyes and locked his jaw. His hands knotted into fists at his sides, and he had to concentrate on control.

Part of him was so soft, and part was so hard. Part was hair roughened and part was satin smooth. Jillian had forgotten the incredible, exciting differences. She was enthralled by the feel of him, and wanted to rediscover the incredible joy she'd found with him in the past.

Trey endured her explorations until his legs began to tremble. Then he dragged her hand to his lips, bending a knee to the bed for support. He kissed her fingers, one by one, and then planted a hot, wet kiss in her palm.

"I can't stand your sweet touch this time," he told her roughly. "You'll have to let me do all the touching."

Jillian growled in disagreement and slid both hands up his furry chest and over smooth shoulders as he leaned down to her. She silently coaxed him to join her in bed. Her fingers kneaded the bulging tendons in his neck as he shifted closer.

Trey braced his hands on either side of her head and lowered his face to hers. His tongue darted out to deftly trace the curves of her lips, and the contact sent white-hot lightning coursing through both of them.

Becky Barker

Jillian's arms tugged him closer and her lips parted invitingly as she sucked his tongue deeply into her mouth. A shudder of exquisite pleasure ripped through her, and she felt a matching response in Trey's body as he eased more of his weight over her.

Their lips locked fiercely while their tongues dueled and danced with primitive pleasure. They tasted, stroked and suckled, unable to get close enough. When forced to draw in air, their lips roved hungrily over each other's faces, kissing eyes, cheeks, chins, and then moving back to mouths.

The needs of their bodies were momentarily forgotten as they strained to deepen their kisses, striving to make up for the two long years they'd been parted. Each successive kiss was longer, deeper, wetter, until they were both gasping for air.

"You go to my head!" Trey whispered in a shaking voice as he scattered hot kisses down her throat to the pulse pounding in her neck.

Jillian's breath rumbled from her lungs as his mouth fastened on her sensitive flesh and sucked greedily. She made an inarticulate sound of hunger and dragged his mouth back to hers for another savagely arousing kiss.

When Trey finally tore his mouth from hers, he slid downward, leaving a trail of damp kisses across her chin, neck and chest. The buttons of the shirt she wore were swiftly unfastened so that he could continue his downward trail of kisses. He stopped at her navel and rose to capture her lips for one more heady kiss.

Trey gradually eased the shirt off her shoulders, and they swallowed each other's moans of pleasure when he lowered himself to the cushioned fullness of her breasts. Jillian's arms locked around his waist as his chest rubbed her nipples to pebbled hardness.

She moaned and began to writhe beneath him, wanting and needing more. His mouth made a slow foray down her throat and neck and over one silky breast until his lips found a tightly puckered nipple. He touched it with the tip of his tongue and felt her quiver violently.

She made a whimpering sound that made his blood boil. He drew her nipple into his mouth and sucked hungrily, using his tongue and teeth until

70

the fat nubbin was diamond hard, and Jillian's whimpers turned to deep, sexy moans. Then he replaced his mouth with his thumb while he gave equal time and attention to the other nipple.

Jillian's fingers clenched and unclenched in the thickness of his hair. She thought she would go crazy from the sweet, prolonged torture of his hand and mouth on her breasts. Having both nipples so thoroughly adored at the same time was almost too much to bear.

Heat spiraled from her breasts to her womb and a heavy, throbbing ache settled deep within her. She shifted restlessly on the bed. Trey had been on his knees, but he pressed his body closer and their legs tangled. Jillian strained toward his hardness and arched her hips against him demandingly.

"Trey, please." she exclaimed huskily.

"Tell me what you want," he demanded, keeping his hands on her breasts as he lifted his head to gaze into her turbulent emerald eyes.

"I want you!" Her voice was vibrant with emotion. "All of you!"

Another rough sound tore from his lips as they locked with hers again. His tongue plunged deeply, then retreated, then plunged again in an ancient rhythm of love. "Is that what you want?" he finally rasped.

"Yes, yes," she pleaded.

"I don't want to hurt your side."

Jillian wasn't concerned about her injury. Any discomfort would be insignificant compared to the pleasure she knew he could give her. "You won't hurt me."

Trey was nearing the limits of his control. He had to hope she was right. He reached to the bedside stand and removed a package from the drawer while stripping off his briefs. His hands trembled as he struggled with protection.

Jillian was pleased that he'd remembered. When they'd been together in the past, she'd taken birth control pills, but she'd quit taking them when they'd parted. Now, with her life in such turmoil, they needed to be careful. She didn't have the emotional strength to worry about carrying a child.

His next move was back to her breasts. When he renewed his assault on her nipples, she forgot everything but the need to have him inside her.

Trey slid a hand between their bodies to the soft mound of curls at the junction of her legs. His fingers gently stroked her as his legs nudged hers farther apart.

Jillian opened herself fully to him. She had no reservations about settling his weight between her thighs. His fingers were creating a searing heat at the very core of her femininity while his mouth continued to suck her nipples to aching hardness. The sensations made her mindless with excitement. She could barely catch her breath.

"Trey! Please! Please! Please!"

"Tell me how much you've missed me," he grated against her lips as he positioned himself more fully along her body. His voice shook with the force of his desire. "Tell me how much you want me."

"More than you'll ever know!" She undulated her hips against his straining hardness. "I want you more than you'll ever know!"

Trey doubted it. His need for her was like a whip flaying him for prolonging the tension, yet he was desperate to make her need as great.

"Tell me," his voice rumbled with urgency. "Make me believe."

"I'm so empty." She clutched his head between her hands. "So empty," she insisted while scattering swift, hard kisses across his face. "I've been so empty for so long."

The breathless admission shattered what was left of Trey's control, and he joined their bodies with one slow, sure stroke. Jillian's breath caught on a sob as he entered her, and he went still.

"Am I hurting you?" he asked hoarsely, exerting brutal control over the desire that racked his body, trying to give her time to adjust to his possession.

Her head thrashed back and forth on the pillow. "No, no, no," she assured him in a voice vibrant with emotion. He was harder, thicker and hotter than she remembered, but the feeling was incredible. "It just feels so good, so very good."

A shudder quaked through him. "You're so hot and tight. Even sweeter than I remembered."

She'd been a virgin when they'd met. Trey was her first and only lover. She'd missed him more than she could ever explain. She was a sensual woman, but she'd never wanted anyone but him.

Trey's eyes were closed and a moan ripped from his throat. The gripping tightness of her body was dragging him into a maelstrom of pleasure.

"Mine," he mumbled possessively against her lips. Then his mouth slid down her throat, across her breast and clamped on a fat, hard nipple. He was trapped by the softness of her thighs as she wrapped her legs around his hips and urged him closer. Finally he surrendered to the savage desire pulsing hotly through his veins.

His thrusts increased in speed and intensity as their passion soared. The tension heightened until Jillian cried out with pleasure, her body clenching around his in release. The rippling contractions of her muscles swiftly brought him to a release that ripped up his spine and shuddered over his whole body.

He collapsed against her briefly, but found the strength to lift most of his weight off her chest. Propped on his forearms, he rested his face in the curve of her neck and fought for each scorching breath. Their bodies were slick and soaked with sweat. Their lungs were tortured, their limbs trembled. Trey finally found the strength to roll to his side, pulling Jillian into the cradle of his arms. She turned on her left side and grunted when his arms slid over her right side.

"Damn, I'm sorry," he whispered hoarsely. "I forgot about your wound."

Jillian smiled and pressed a kiss against his neck. Her voice was husky, too, and warm with intimacy. "So did I," she confessed, even though her side was throbbing again. "You have that kind of effect on me."

Trey's slow smile was full of masculine satisfaction. "I'm glad," he murmured against her lips.

He hugged her close until their bodies had cooled and their breathing had regulated. They gradually relaxed, but neither of them wanted to sleep, so they weren't quiet long. Their hands were busy caressing, soothing, and then exciting one another again. Trey rolled to his right side and switched on a bedside lamp, then rolled back to her.

They blinked, and then focused on each other. His gaze searched hers. "I want to make love again," he told her quietly, easing her onto her back. "But this time I want to see every inch of you and watch you go up in flames. Think you're strong enough?"

His eyes quickly rekindled the flames within Jillian. Anticipation sang through her veins. With just a few words and those dark eyes, he'd managed to excite her all over again. It made her weak with need, yet stronger than she'd felt in months.

"I think I can cope," she teased, her eyes dancing with warmth and wicked delight.

"I hope so," he insisted as he lowered himself slowly over her body. "Because I have two years of hunger to satisfy."

Jillian caught her breath, wondering if he'd actually missed her as much as she'd missed him. "Tonight?" she dared to taunt.

"Tonight...tomorrow...tomorrow night...the next day...the next night," Trey told her through a series of warm, wet kisses.

He spent the next hour relearning every curve and sensitive inch of her body. By the time he was done exploring, Jillian was twisting restlessly on the bed and begging him to relieve the ache he'd created. He wasn't shy about giving in to her demand.

Exhaustion finally claimed them in the early hours of the morning. They slept soundly, wrapped in each other's arms. The sun was pouring through the window when they were finally awakened by the intercom. Trey reached for the switch and groaned as Cade's voice came into the room.

"Hey, are you guys going to stay in bed all day? What about breakfast? I cooked bacon two hours ago, and it's still sitting here on the stove."

Trey's gaze locked with Jillian's. His body was already stirring against hers in bold demand. When she shifted closer and rubbed herself against his thighs, he dragged in a ragged breath.

"Leave the bacon," he told his brother. "We'll eat it later."

Cade's laugh was a short bark of amusement. "Does that mean you're not ready to come out of the bedroom?"

"Take care of my work for a while," was Trey's only response. The click of the intercom announced the end to his conversation.

Jillian was blushing and the heat in her cheeks fascinated him. He brushed a finger down her face. "I didn't mean to embarrass you, but Cade's not stupid."

"I know. I don't really mind." Most of her life, she'd been sexually repressed compared to her contemporaries, but that had changed when she'd met Trey. She'd never had any inhibitions where he was concerned.

"You don't care if he knows we're making love?"

Jillian added a sexy smile to her blush. "I don't care who knows," she murmured, threading her fingers through his hair and drawing his face closer.

Trey's groan was low as he gave in to temptation without resistance. He'd waited too long, wanted too much and might never be completely sated. The ranch and his brother would survive without him for a few more hours.

ॐ

In the kitchen, Cade stared at the intercom for a second and then grinned broadly. He grabbed a handful of bacon and headed out of the house.

Wayne Reilly met him at the door of the horse barn. The tall, burly man was smoothing wayward locks of hair before cramming his hat on a rapidly balding head. His voice always reminded Cade of sandpaper.

"Is the boss gonna stay holed up in the house all day?" the foreman wanted to know.

"Could be," Cade told him after swallowing the last mouthful of bacon. "He's got company."

"So he said." Wayne thought it must be pretty strange company 'cause the boss was sure actin' strange.

"His company is female," Cade explained. "She's been sick, and he's taking care of her. She's a special lady, but she's having some trouble, and Trey needs to spend a lot of time with her."

The big man nodded, thinking the lady must be real special. His boss hadn't wanted anything to do with women for a couple a years.

"I want you to hire a few more hands to help for a while," continued Cade. "Trey's going to be spending a lot of time with Jillian, and it might not hurt to hire an extra couple men just to keep an eye on the perimeters of the ranch."

"I'll try, but help is hard to come by sometimes. Does the lady have somebody huntin' her?"

Cade wasn't worried about sharing information with the foreman. Reilly was the most closemouthed man he'd ever known. He'd worked on the ranch for more than twenty years and was fiercely loyal to the Langdens.

"She witnessed a murder, and some powerful people are offering a lot of money to anyone who can find her. I don't want anybody within miles of the house that you don't personally recognize. Nobody knows she's here, so I'm not expecting trouble, but warn Trey about strangers."

"I'll keep my eyes and ears open," the foreman promised. "All the guys on the payroll right now are regulars, and newcomers stick out like a sore thumb."

"That's what I'm counting on," said Cade. "Just make sure any new hands are local, or get in touch with me and I can run a check on their backgrounds. Let Trey know if anything strikes you as unusual."

Wayne's nod of agreement was as good as his word.

"Now, what needs to be done today?" asked Cade.

"I'm tryin' to get the barns cleaned before all the horses start foalin'"

Cade grimaced. Trey had started breeding horses a few years back and the operation was growing steadily. There were lots of pregnant horses, and they'd need plenty of clean stalls now that they were foaling.

"Great. I always manage to offer a hand when the stalls need mucking."

The foreman just laughed, handed him a pitchfork and headed into the first barn.

ഇരുഭ

Inside the house, the sun sparkled over Jillian's naked body as Trey lifted her into his arms and carried her to the bathroom. He set her on her feet long enough to adjust the water and then drew her into the shower with him.

She closed her eyes as water poured over her, but Trey kept his gaze trained on her upturned face. He studied each of her delicate features, rediscovering and memorizing them as the water trailed over her creamy skin.

Her hair became saturated, turned dark gold and fell past the curves of her shoulders. It was a lot longer than it had been the last time he'd seen her, but just as smooth and sleek. She was thinner, yet more shapely.

He cupped her breasts in his hands and watched in fascination as the spray made her nipples tighten into hard knots. The temptation was too great. He lowered his head to lick moisture from one tight bud, then the other.

Jillian moaned and clutched his head between her hands, holding him as fire rushed through her veins. She couldn't get enough of his loving. She never grew tired of having his mouth on her.

"You make me feel totally wanton," she admitted huskily.

"I like you wanton," he murmured, his lips sliding up her neck to capture her mouth.

They shared a long, deep, satisfying kiss. Then Trey reached for the shampoo and began to wash her hair. While he concentrated on that, Jillian took a bar of soap and leisurely rubbed it across his broad shoulders and chest.

By the time they were both clean and shampooed, their bodies had once again been coupled in passion, and they were temporarily sated. Weary with exhaustion, they managed to get dry, brush hair and teeth, then fall into bed for some much-needed sleep.

Chapter Six

The following week, April made an entrance with brilliant sunshine and milder temperatures. Horses and cattle started dropping their young, and the ranch staff was kept busy seeing to the care of all the new additions.

Cade was back in Dallas, and Trey had no choice but to spend most of his waking hours working. His nights were spent making love to Jillian, so he was forced to function on very little rest. The lack of sleep should have made him tense and irritable, but had the reverse effect. He felt stronger, healthier and happier than he'd felt in years. Knowing that Jillian would be waiting in the house at lunch time and at night gave him the energy and momentum to work long hours without complaint.

He tried not to dwell on the reasons for his deep satisfaction. It was easier to credit his feelings of contentment and well-being to great sex. He refused to consider the future beyond each night when he'd have her in his arms again.

Jillian grew stronger each day. The tenderness and bruising of her wound had diminished, and she was getting plenty of rest. Trey kept her awake most nights, but she slept late each morning, waking in time to shower, dress and prepare lunch.

The sunshine beckoned to her more every day. Spring had always been her favorite season, and the terrors she'd experienced halfway across the country were forced more deeply into her subconscious. Her fears began to pale in comparison to the renewal of life on the ranch. By Thursday, she was tempted to stray out-of-doors for the first time.

Having come to that decision, she dressed in her only pair of jeans and her trucker T-shirt. The neon green didn't look bad on her, mused Jillian as she brushed her hair in front of the bathroom mirror. She was pale, but the shirt added color without making her skin look pasty.

Her hair had gotten darker over the winter. It was easily bleached by the sun, and she normally spent as much time as possible in sunny climates. This year had been different, so her hair had less natural streaking.

It was getting long, she thought as she pulled the brush past her shoulders. No attempts to curl the thick mass had ever been completely successful. Her hair was straight and heavy, falling in a curtain from a center part. The only choice she had in styles was the graduated lengths she'd had cut to frame her face.

She'd never allowed it to get really long, because she'd never wanted to take the time to care for long hair. Now, she just might let it grow. Trey seemed to like it longer. It wasn't as if she were too busy or even working.

When thoughts of her work surfaced, she quickly forced them aside and concentrated on the present. She didn't need to work. She had no desire to stray from the ranch and no need for money.

She didn't even have a camera. That knowledge slipped past the shell she'd erected to protect her emotions, and she allowed herself a moment of grief. For most of her life, her cameras had been her best friends and constant companions. Now she didn't even own one, and she had nothing to photograph. It didn't matter anymore, Jillian assured herself, turning from her image and heading for the kitchen.

She'd been occupying her time by taking care of Trey's home and doing basic chores such as cooking and laundry. At first he'd objected, but she'd assured him that she wouldn't do anything she didn't really feel like doing.

Mrs. Cooper, the housekeeper, had called to say she couldn't return for a couple more weeks. Jillian knew this was the busiest time of the year on the ranch, so she felt good about helping in the house.

Trey was a big eater, and she'd started fixing big meals for him. She wasn't a great cook, but her skills improved with practice, and he ate without complaint whatever she prepared.

"Jillian!" he shouted as he came indoors for lunch. It was his way of letting her know she was no longer alone in the house.

He always entered the house through the porch off the kitchen, and Jillian had gotten into the habit of meeting him at the door. She smiled as he stamped dirt off his boots and tossed his hat toward a rack. Her pulse accelerated at the sight of his dark eyes, rugged features and tangled hair.

"Been busy?" she asked, trying to contain her need to be in his arms.

Trey enjoyed the bright welcome in her eyes. Her smile tied his stomach in knots. Her poorly disguised impatience made his blood churn. He ignored her question and dragged her into his arms.

Jillian pressed herself close to him, locked her fingers in his hair and opened her mouth for his urgent, searing kiss. He felt hard and warm. He smelled like fresh air and sunshine. He tasted like a man—her man.

Trey took his time kissing her. His tongue stroked the roof of her mouth, the smooth ridges of her teeth and the hidden softness inside her cheeks. His breath caught when she sucked greedily at his tongue, then demanded equal time and thrust her tongue into his mouth to do her own exploring. A shudder ripped through him as he claimed her tongue and sucked it deeply into his mouth, savoring the honeyed sweetness.

His hands convulsively stroked the firm curves of her backside as one kiss melted into another, then another. Every hour they were apart seemed like an eternity, so they tried to compensate with kisses and caresses. When it was necessary to catch their breath, Trey finally released Jillian's mouth and rested his forehead against hers.

"Miss me this morning?" he asked, his voice suddenly gruff with emotion.

"I always miss you." She ran her fingers through his hair to smooth the ridges made by his hat.

He always missed her, too. His fingers gripped her hips and pulled her close to the hardness of his erection. He slowly rocked her back and forth against his straining flesh in an attempt to ease the ache the taste and feel of her always created.

"You'd better eat before your lunch is ruined," Jillian said without making any effort to shift out of his arms.

"Whatever it is, it smells good." He didn't want to let her go, but knew he had to before his desire got completely out of control. He ran his hands over her hips, up her ribs and to her breasts.

"You've got on an awful lot of clothes today." The jeans, shirt and bra prevented him from feeling soft, firm flesh. In the past few days, she hadn't bothered with anything except his shirts.

"I thought I might go outside for a while this afternoon," she explained as he gradually released her, "and I didn't want to shock your staff."

Trey gave her a rakish grin, pleased that she finally felt well and safe enough to leave the security of the house. "I'd have to carry a big stick and beat off the men."

She returned his grin. "You don't think my green neon will be too much for them, do you?"

"It might be blinding if it reflects the sun."

Her grin widened. "I'll be careful not to get too close to anybody with sensitive eyes."

"I'll make sure none of them get too close to you," he assured her, turning to the sink to wash his hands. "If I catch anyone looking too long or too much, I'll order them to the farthest boundaries of the ranch."

Jillian smiled as she served their lunch. Trey's declaration didn't surprise her. She didn't doubt that he would resent any man who took an interest in her. After all, that had been the basis of their breakup two years earlier.

"Cade's going to bring you a few clothes when he comes this weekend," Trey said. "You'll have some variety, but I'm going to hate everything he brings. I like reaching for you and finding soft, warm flesh."

His tone and the wicked gleam in his eyes brought a blush to Jillian's cheeks. Heat suffused her body. Some of it could be contributed to how much she liked having his hands on her bare skin.

"You're getting spoiled." She shifted her gaze from the devilish glint in his. "You can't spend the rest of your life with a naked woman at your fingertips all the time."

"You're destroying my fantasies." Her blush and teasing delighted Trey. She was slowly opening up to him in more ways than the physical.

"You're letting your food get cold."

"Is that a hint for me to keep my lecherous thoughts to myself?" He held out a chair for her, and then sat beside her at the table.

"At least until you've eaten." she chastised, sounding maternal until spoiling the effect with her next words. "You work hard and you need a lot of nutrition to maintain your stamina. I'm very selfishly concerned."

Trey threw back his head and laughed. The occasional glimpses of the old, playful Jillian made him feel young, carefree and capable of tackling the world. He'd missed her blind optimism, her enthusiasm for life and her wicked sense of humor.

His laughter rippled over Jillian like the slide of silk. It made her feel feminine, sexy, and gloriously alive. She loved making him happy. He did work long, hard hours, and it felt good to help him relax.

When they'd finished their meal, Trey helped her load the dishwasher and found her a lightweight jacket to wear. He followed her out of the house and began to describe the ranch property.

"The house is shaped in an L," he explained, his voice almost failing him when Jillian tilted her face to the sun and let its heat caress her lovely features.

He cleared his throat and continued. "There's a long, open porch on the far west side of the house. The patio and a pool are protected by the inside curve of the building, and the ranch yard stretches out to this side."

Jillian opened her eyes and focused on the barns, outbuildings and fenced areas where horses grazed on the lush green grass. She realized that she'd been here for more than a week without even knowing what the exterior of the house looked like. The thought was a little unnerving.

She'd made a career of observing everything around her with an artist's eye, and she'd been seriously remiss in learning about her present surroundings. Over the past couple of years, she'd spent countless hours imagining how the Langden ranch would look. Now she wanted to know how well her imagination compared with the reality.

"We have two barns, an equipment garage and smaller buildings for maintenance and storage," Trey told her while measuring his stride to her slower pace. "The barns are used as stables and to store hay."

"What about all the land surrounded by redwood fence?" Jillian asked.

"The ones close to the barns are corrals," he replied. "We use them for the horses and to confine cattle when we're branding, cutting or loading. All the pastureland is surrounded by board fences. We use regular fencing for outlying crop areas."

"Do you raise many crops?"

"Mostly hay and other grains for the livestock," he explained, "but not much for sale unless we have more than we can use."

They walked about a hundred yards down a gradual slope before the grass gave way to graveled drive and bare dirt areas around the barns. Vehicles of all sizes and shapes were scattered around the area. There were men working at various jobs, but only one came to greet them.

"Jillian, I'd like you to meet my foreman, Wayne Reilly. He's been running this place since I was a teenager."

The older man tipped his hat and gave her a nod. She cautiously studied his rough features, and he remained still until she'd decided to offer her hand.

"Nice to meet you, Mr. Reilly." Her hand was completely engulfed by his, but he didn't hold it long enough to make her panic.

"Nice to meet you, miss, but I can't remember anybody ever callin' me Mr. Reilly. It's just Wayne to most folks."

"And I'm Jillian," she supplied, giving him a smile that rivaled the sunshine for warmth and had melted hearts all over the world. Wayne's heart was no exception.

He'd met plenty of people who pretended to care about others, who smiled, but didn't give a damn about anybody but themselves. Trey's lady friend was somebody who really cared. It was in her eyes. He returned her smile and flashed an approving glance at his boss.

"You need anything, don't hesitate to holler," the foreman insisted.

"Thank you. I appreciate that, Wayne. I'm just learning my way around today."

"There's plenty to see," he agreed. Then he told Trey, "If you're gonna stay out here, I'll head to the north pasture and check on the new calves out there."

"I'll take care of things here."

When Reilly was out of hearing range, Trey turned narrowed eyes on Jillian. "Well," he drawled, crossing his arms over his chest. "I wouldn't have thought that Wayne, a crusty old bachelor, could be charmed with just a smile, but you managed it somehow. Did you see him give me that nod of approval? He obviously appreciates my taste in women."

Jillian crossed her arms over her chest to mimic him and haughtily lifted one brow. "Women," she queried, "as in plural?"

"Woman," Trey growled and reached for her. He cupped the back of her head and drew her close enough to plant a long, hard kiss on her mouth.

It was irrational, but when she smiled at other men, however innocently, he felt compelled to stake some kind of claim. He needed reassurance. It annoyed him, but the possessiveness hadn't lessened in their years of separation.

Jillian understood his need. She'd wondered if it would be the same this time, or if he'd deny his possessive tendencies. "Feel better now?" she challenged softly as their lips parted.

Trey's eyes flashed darkly. He'd feel better if he could bury himself in her warmth and keep the rest of the world at bay. Instead of answering her sassy question, he grabbed her hand. "Come on. I'll show you the babies."

She followed him around the corner of the barn to a large corral. Several mares were grazing with their newborns at their sides. The sight of the long-legged, wobbly little creatures made her gasp with pleasure. She immediately reached both of her hands to her right side.

Trey's eyes narrowed with concern. "What happened? Did you hurt yourself?"

For an instant, Jillian could only stare at him with a blank expression. Then she relaxed and crossed her arms over the top rung of the fence, leaning on it for support.

"I didn't hurt myself," she assured him, keeping her eyes on the horses. "I just reached for my camera and realized it's not on my shoulder. It's been an extension of my body for so long that I was shocked for a minute."

Shocked, exposed and hurt. Trey was willing to bet she felt completely naked without her camera. It had always been her ticket through any gate, her eye on the world, her passport to excitement. Her camera had been her best friend.

He leaned against the fence beside her and watched the horses. "It would be nice to have a few shots of the mares with their young. I've been thinking about putting together a sales brochure featuring some of my breeding stock. I haven't taken the time to do it, but you could do it sometime if you're interested."

Jillian didn't comment, but she mentally stored the suggestion to consider later. Her mind's eye automatically focused on prospective angles and frames. One chestnut mare was outlined by a blue sky and distant mountains. Her offspring was unsteady on its feet, but diligently searching under her belly.

The light and color were perfectly balanced. The sun was behind Jillian's right shoulder at a good angle. It would make a clear, beautiful picture. She shook her head to rid it of details and images.

"The scenery out here is gorgeous," she commented, surveying pastures that rose into heavy woodlands and distant mountains. Trees and grass were already budding and green.

"In another week or two, everything will be in full bloom," he told her.

She nodded in agreement, then turned her attention back to the foal that was trying to nurse while its mother kept moving. "How old are the babies?"

"Most of these are only a couple days old. When they get bigger and stronger, we'll move them farther from the barns. They'll nurse for several months."

The persistent little colt finally managed to grasp hold of his mother and began nursing with vigor. Jillian watched as he tugged fiercely on his mother's body and she was filled with an innocent wonder at the simple beauty of life. Too often it was taken for granted.

Trey watched her face light up with an inner beauty that he couldn't quite put a name to. Whatever it was, it touched him too deeply, and he didn't want to explore it. He wouldn't allow himself to get totally wrapped up in her again.

"I've got to get back to work. Do you want to tag along or explore on your own?"

Jillian turned toward him, wondering what had prompted his gruff question. She didn't want to be any trouble. "I'd rather stay with you, if you don't mind."

"I don't mind," he said, turning on a heel and heading back to the barn. She followed more slowly and made herself a promise not to be a burden.

For the rest of the afternoon, she watched Trey do the work of four men. He rarely slowed down and seemed to be everywhere. Men shouted at him from all corners of the ranch, using radios for the most distant areas. He issued orders and answered questions while loading hay on wagons, cleaning out stalls and transferring hundred-pound bags of seed from storage buildings to feeding bins.

No job seemed too big or small, and he didn't do anything at a slow pace, yet Jillian still got the impression that he was moving slower than normal so that she could keep up with him. He rarely took a break, and the only time he rested was when he was crooning to a horse.

By late afternoon, she was exhausted from just watching Trey. She'd brought him several cold drinks throughout the day, but decided it was time to start supper so the poor man could replace some of the energy he'd burned.

When he finally came to the house for his evening meal, Trey informed her that he had to go back to the barn for part of the evening. He had a horse due to deliver her first foal and wanted to keep an eye on her in case she had trouble or needed the veterinarian.

She decided to go, too. "Do you mind if I watch? I've never seen a horse born."

Her comment surprised and pleased Trey. There was a time when he'd looked forward to showing her all the aspects of ranch life. Since then, he'd often wondered how he would react if she were bored or disgusted by the dirty, unglamorous work on the ranch. There was no time like the present to have the questions answered.

He knew he didn't have to put in so many long hours anymore. He could afford more help these days, but it had become a habit to push himself to exhaustion. Right now, there was more work than manpower. He couldn't cut his share of the load until extra help was hired, but he liked having Jillian by his side.

"Will I be a bother?" she asked when he took so long in responding to her question. "Is the mare really nervous?"

"No. You're no bother, and the mare'll be too busy to worry about who's watching. Are you sure you're not doing too much? You were busy all afternoon."

Jillian laughed. "I'm sure. I felt like a real bum today while I watched everyone else working so hard. All I did was stick a pot roast and potatoes in the oven."

Trey rose from the table and planted a smacking kiss on her forehead. "It was delicious and much appreciated. I hate to eat and run out on you, but I'd like to head to the barn if you don't mind clearing the dishes."

"No problem," she assured him. "I'll be out as soon as I'm finished."

"Okay, don't forget a coat. It's still pretty cool in the evenings."

Jillian's gaze followed him out of the house. He'd grabbed his hat, but hadn't donned a coat as he'd instructed her to do. She doubted if he got cold. He never stopped moving long enough to feel the chill.

By the time she had the kitchen clean and headed outdoors, the moon was high in the sky. Just like earlier in the day, everywhere she looked she saw potential material for exquisite photos. Despite her efforts to ignore her calling, the colors and scenery all around her appealed to her highly developed visual senses.

The title "Moon over the Mountains" jumped into her mind. One of her favorite aspects of photography was titling individual projects. Sometimes she had to see the photo before deciding what to call it, but sometimes the name came to her first, urging her to get the image on film.

She shoved the thoughts of her work to the back of her mind as she entered the birthing barn where Trey's mare was in labor.

"Anybody home?" she called.

"Back here," he replied, motioning to her from the far end of the stable.

Jillian shed her coat and hung it on a hook inside the barn door. The building still held the warmth of the sun and smelled of fresh hay. The lighting was good, so she had no trouble making her way to where Trey and Wayne were kneeling beside the heavily breathing horse.

"Is she all right?" Jillian asked in alarm.

"She's okay, just getting close to her time," Wayne explained.

"She panicked a little earlier, but she's calmed down some," Trey added. "The contractions are strong and everything looks good."

"What's her name?"

"Rosie River," said Wayne. "This is her first."

Jillian stepped over a low railing and knelt down near the horse's head. Trey and Wayne were rubbing the mare's stomach and flanks, so she stroked her nose and began talking to her in what she hoped was a soothing tone.

The three of them watched as the horse's body heaved with contractions, forcing the smaller body farther through the birth canal. When Trey could see the foal's head and knew the foal's position was normal, they all stepped back to let the mare finish the delivery.

He wrapped an arm around Jillian's shoulders and tugged her close while they witnessed the miracle of birth. She didn't realize she was holding her breath until the wet, squirming body had escaped the water bag and the mare was on her feet tending to her baby.

"It's a colt," Wayne announced after a brief check of the animal.

The mare snorted and the newborn struggled to its feet. Jillian laughed softly. The little guy's head looked too big and his legs seemed far too long for his short body. It took him several attempts to master the art of standing.

When he'd accomplished his objective, Wayne used a soft cloth to help his mother clean him. Jillian looked up at Trey, smiling with pleasure. His head dipped and his mouth closed over hers. The kiss was soft and tender, a down payment on the wealth of kisses he would give her later.

She slid an arm around his waist and hugged him. "This is what you need on film."

"Snapshots wouldn't do it justice."

"You could videotape a birth."

"Why?"

She shrugged. "I don't know. I'm sure it's been done hundreds of times, but you could keep the videos for prospective buyers who want a record of their horse's birth. Or you could use the tapes to teach new employees about the process."

"A training tool?"

She shrugged again. "At least that way you and Wayne wouldn't be the only two people on the ranch qualified as midwives," she teased.

Wayne grunted, exiting the mare's stall. "I've been called a lot a things over the years, but midwife ain't one of 'em. I think it's time I took this poor old tired body to bed before the insults get any worse."

His grumbling was followed by their laughter.

"I'll take care of things now," Trey told the foreman. "I'm just going to watch a while longer. Then I'm calling it a night."

"I'll check on her early tomorrow," said Wayne.

Trey cleaned soiled hay from the stall and replaced it with fresh bedding. Jillian refilled the mare's feed and water troughs, and then he secured the rails of the stall.

Next, he arranged some bales of hay beside the enclosure and dragged Jillian down on the makeshift seat. He leaned against the wall with his legs outstretched and pulled her onto his lap. For a while, they were content to relax and watch the mother and baby get to know each other.

"Do you have to do anything else for them?"

"If the mare shows any signs of refusing him or he doesn't learn to nurse right, we'll have to worry about getting him fed, but I think they'll be okay."

"Just let nature take its course?" she suggested, idly stroking the arm he had resting across her stomach.

"Some horse breeders like to take care of everything for the animal, but I don't like to interfere unless there's a problem."

"Makes sense to me."

Much like the foal Jillian had watched earlier in the day, this little guy started hunting for food as soon as he was steady on his feet. His nose brushed his mother's belly, and he snorted while searching.

"How does he know where to look?" she wondered aloud.

"The same way as most babies, I guess," Trey said, sinking his face in her soft hair, and then nibbling on her ear. "He just finds a warm body and starts rooting around."

Jillian laughed, her eyes shining as she shifted to lock gazes with him. "Just root around, huh?"

His eyes sparkled sensuously. He slowly turned her in his arms, then slid a hand under her T-shirt and pulled it up so that he could bury his face against her bare stomach. She giggled and squirmed as his hot mouth roamed over the ticklish flesh.

"Is this rooting?" she said on a gasp, combing her fingers through his hair and clutching the thick strands.

He found the fastener on her bra and unclipped it. "This is a hungry man searching for sustenance." His tone became muffled by her skin.

"Sustenance, huh?" She lost herself in the sweet sensuality of his caresses.

"Necessity of life," he explained, continuing his search over the outer edges of her breasts.

She was stretched across his lap, waiting impatiently for his seeking mouth to find its target. "Trey!" she cried in frustration.

"I'm still rooting."

Unable to stand a second more of his teasing, she guided his mouth to the throbbing peak of her breast.

"Here?" he asked, flicking one of her nipples with the tip of his tongue.

Jillian moaned and arched her back. He knew how to touch her until she was wild for his mouth. "Yes, there."

"Here, too?" he teased her, lashing the other nipple. He slid one hand between her legs and began to stroke her through her jeans.

"Trey! I'll get even for this!"

She felt his smile against the swollen fullness of her breast. An instant later he was drawing her nipple deeply into his mouth and creating an even greater ache.

Jillian squirmed and rocked her hips against the hardness of his. "Let's go to the house."

"I'm busy," he insisted, shifting his attention from one tight nipple to the other. When he suckled it, she began to whimper.

"House. Bed."

Her impatience inflamed him. "I can't walk." His tone went just as hoarse.

Jillian caught her breath on a sob. "Then you'd better behave until we're both capable of functioning again."

He didn't want to behave. He'd been burning with need all day. He wanted her here and now. "Ever made love in the hay?"

She shook her head. "Sounds brazen and scratchy."

"It is," he assured her. He licked a taut nipple and moaned against her breast when her hand slid to the crotch of his jeans. He was so hard, throbbing and ready to explode. His voice was gruff. "You could avoid the painful part if you straddle my lap and ride me."

The idea sent heat spiraling through Jillian and filled her with wanting. She reached for his belt buckle with unsteady fingers. The action triggered a hasty struggle to get clothing out of their way. Then Trey pulled her back onto his lap until flesh met bare flesh and she'd sheathed him within her velvet heat.

Chapter Seven

Dawn on Friday found Trey and Jillian awake, dressed and ready to start the day. They'd gotten a good night's sleep and had eaten breakfast by the time the sun started to shine through the windows. She had washed her only set of clothes and was wearing her jeans with one of his shirts knotted at the waist.

He'd gone to another part of the house when she insisted on cleaning the kitchen. She was mentally planning menus and taking meat from the freezer for the rest of the day when he reentered the room, carrying a small black case.

"This was Mom's," he said, handing her the camera. "It's old, but it should still work. If you tell me what kind of film you need, I'll call Cade and ask him to bring some."

Jillian took the camera from the case and studied it while fighting back a sudden rush of tears. It was good to feel the camera in her hands, but Trey's thoughtfulness made an even bigger impact. It made her feel weepy. She doubted if he could understand how much the gesture meant to her. He had plenty of reason to resent her obsession with cameras, yet he was apparently more concerned that she be happy and content.

"It takes 35 mm film, and I like to use 400 speed." She forced the words past a tightly clogged throat.

He frowned, took the camera from her hands and set it on the table. "I wouldn't have given it to you if I'd known it would upset you. I just thought you might like to take some pictures."

She stepped close to him, wrapped her arms around his neck and dragged his head down for a long, hard kiss.

"Thank you," she whispered, releasing him. "I have been missing my camera, and I appreciate the loan."

"You're not going to get upset every time you use it?"

Jillian shook her head vigorously. "Only this once," she promised with a smile.

Trey's lips curved in a crooked grin when he realized it was his gesture, not the camera that prompted her tears. "Women!" he muttered in exasperation.

"Woman," she corrected, earning another sexy, masculine grin.

"Do you need some help with the food?" he asked.

"I'm almost finished."

"Then I'll call Cade now." He headed for his bedroom.

"It's still early," she yelled after him.

"If he's not awake, I'll be his alarm today," he yelled back.

Cade was awake and alert. He listened to his brother's request for film and made a note to order plenty. Then he shared his own news. "I was going to call you this morning. I heard some disturbing things at a party last night and thought you'd better know about it."

"What kind of disturbing things?"

"There was a stranger in Dallas this week asking a lot of questions about Jillian. He showed up at the hotel where we were having a reunion with some college classmates. He flashed a badge and passed himself off as an FBI agent. Once I heard about it, I went searching for him. I didn't have any luck, but I sent word around that Jillian was in danger. Everybody who was there will be more careful now, but this guy might already know about the two of you."

Trey swore under his breath. That's all they needed right now. Jillian was just starting to feel safe. If someone had learned about her friendship with both Langdens, it wouldn't be hard to trace them to the ranch. With a two-million-dollar contract on her life, there could be several bounty hunters looking for her. They had to beef up their security.

"Did anyone get a look at this guy?"

"He took Carla Grady out for cocktails. Whoever he is, he did his homework. Carla always was the biggest blabbermouth of the class, and she's not too dependable after a few drinks."

"But she can identify him?"

"She said he was kinda cute, but average. Not too tall, not too short. Thin, but not too thin. Light brown hair and green eyes. That was her description. It could fit half the men in the country," Cade said in disgust.

"It's better than nothing. You don't think of professional hit men as being average."

"I can't get out there until sometime tomorrow," Cade added. "Steven's coming with me, and we're bringing a few men we can trust to watch the place."

"Good idea. I'll take some extra precautions today. Just let me know if you hear anything else."

"Do you want me to run a check on known hit men?"

"I'll take care of it. I have an old army buddy who still works for Uncle Sam. I'll give him a call and see what I can find out."

"Okay, I'll see you later."

The two men hung up, and Trey immediately dialed the number of Jim Kregg's office in Washington, where it was already midmorning. He frowned when he heard a recorded message.

"Jim, this is Trey Langden." Before he'd had a chance to leave his phone number, a familiar voice came over the line.

"Hey, Trey, that really you?"

"Hey, it's really me, G-man." A wealth of affection accompanied the old nickname.

Kregg's tone was equally warm. "God, it's good to hear your voice, Langden. It's been too long. You in D.C.?"

"No, I'm at home."

"Then I don't suppose this is a long-overdue social call," he surmised, his tone more brisk. "What's up?"

Trey didn't bother with pleasantries. "I need some help. I have a friend who made an enemy of a Florida drug lord, name of Juan Gardova. There's a big price on her head, and I need some information about professional hit men."

Jim whistled softly. "Damn, that would be the Brandt woman. She made the national news last night. She a friend?"

"Right." Trey wasn't pleased to hear of Jillian's increased notoriety.

"She's with you?"

"I know where she is." He trusted Kregg. The two of them had worked together in army intelligence and had formed a lasting, unshakable bond. Still, he didn't want to be too specific on the phone.

"I don't suppose you want anybody to know."

"Nobody, but my brother heard about a stranger asking questions in Dallas. I thought you might tell me who to watch out for."

Kregg didn't hesitate.

"We've been on the lookout for a couple men we think might have entered the country in the past few days. One's named Benny Orson—he was last seen in Lisbon boarding a plane for the U.S. The other is Harold Germaine. We think he was responsible for a hit in South America, but we lost track of him. Two million is enough to get either of them interested."

"What do they look like?"

"Our photos aren't too clear, but we know Orson is less than five feet tall, almost bald and has dark, Mediterranean looks. Germaine is harder. He looks like your average, nondescript Caucasian."

"Caucasian?" Trey asked. "Brown hair, green eyes, average height and weight?"

"Sounds right." Kregg's tone sharpened. "Have you seen him?"

"I haven't, but that description fits the guy Cade said was asking so many questions."

"He's a nasty one. From what we know about him, he moves into an area and goes unnoticed for a while. He zeroes in on his target, strikes fast and is gone without anyone remembering exactly what he looked like."

Damn, Trey didn't like the sound of it.

"Do you have a fax machine?"

"Yeah. Can you send a picture of him?"

"It's not too good, but it'll give you something to work with." He took Trey's fax number and began sending a transmission on a separate line.

"Where did your brother see Germaine?"

"Dallas, but we figure he found out about the ranch," Trey explained. His forehead creased in a frown as he watched the picture coming across the fax machine.

"Mind if I send a couple men out your way?"

"Don't send them unless you trust them with your life. We've already had trouble with some dirty feds. Cade and Steven are bringing some extra help tomorrow."

"I can't leave Washington right now, but I'll send two men out there today. Their names are Monroe and Howard, and there's nothing average about either of them. I'll have them call you as soon as they get into Albuquerque and wait for instructions."

"Have 'em bring their Western gear, and I'll put 'em on the payroll."

Kregg chuckled. "Not a bad idea. Just be careful about hiring anyone average looking."

"I'll keep that in mind. Thanks for everything. I owe you."

"Uh-uh, I'm the one who owes you. You covered my tail plenty of times," Kregg insisted.

Trey ignored the reminder. "You know you have a standing invitation to visit."

"I just might do that sometime soon."

"Sure you will. The nearest town is half an hour away, has only one stop light and no frills. It'll be a cold day in hell before you find your way out here."

The comment brought chuckles from both men. Kregg was a city boy from head to toe, and Trey was just as much country. They'd been firm friends, but when their tour of duty had ended, they'd happily gone back to their own corners of the world.

"Keep me posted."

"Will do."

After hanging up the phone, Trey tore the photo off the fax, folded it and tucked it in his shirt pocket. Wayne was going to town to interview prospective employees later in the morning. He wanted to make sure his foreman recognized Germaine if he showed his face.

"I've got to get to work," he told Jillian when he returned to the kitchen. He didn't want her to know anything about the hit man, but he didn't want to let her out of his sight for long, either. "What are you planning to do today?"

"Couldn't I help you?"

"Like how?"

She shrugged. "I don't know. Surely there's something I can do. Everyone else seems to have so much work. Couldn't I feed the horses or clean stalls?"

Her offer to help pleased Trey. He didn't want her doing anything too strenuous, but she looked a lot healthier after spending yesterday in the air and sunshine.

"I promise I won't overexert myself. I'll rest when I get tired and take a lot of breaks," she insisted.

Her beautiful, beguiling eyes held him mesmerized for a minute. His chest tightened, and he realized with an unwelcome jolt that there was little he'd refuse her when she smiled at him like that. He wasn't particularly comfortable with the knowledge.

"I could use some help hauling stuff to a couple fields where we're planting crops," he suggested. "I need somebody to run errands around the ranch, but you'd have to drive a truck with a standard transmission."

"I can drive a stick shift, and I don't mind learning my way around if you don't mind taking the time to show me."

Her sincerity swayed his decision. "Then let's go," he said, taking her arm. They grabbed a jacket for her on the porch, and then headed outside. After a brief, private conversation with Wayne, Trey picked one of the smaller trucks for Jillian to drive.

Showing her the ranch was a special pleasure for him. He'd often thought about having her by his side and sharing the rare beauty of his land. The two of them didn't get a lot of work done, but her enthusiasm and delight over the next few hours made him especially proud.

They covered a lot of territory during the morning so that she could learn the lay of the land. He let her drive while he directed, and they checked on various projects he'd been too busy to supervise since her arrival. Trey was especially watchful for anything or anybody out of the ordinary, but they didn't encounter any trouble.

"The west section of the ranch is best seen on horseback," he explained as they drove back to the ranch after delivering seed to a hay field. "When you're stronger, we'll tackle the foothills and lower mountain ranges."

"I'd like that," said Jillian. She'd always enjoyed riding and she loved sharing time with him. She also wanted to learn all about his beloved land.

When they reached the ranch yard, she pulled to a stop beside one of the outbuildings and shut off the truck's engine. A sigh escaped her as she turned to him. "I never realized it took so much energy to sit in a vehicle and shift gears."

"You've done more than drive this morning," he said, turning more fully toward her. He brushed a strand of hair off her cheek, and his gaze was tender as it locked with hers. "You're good company and a good chauffeur, but maybe you'd better call it a day."

Jillian grimaced. She didn't want to be confined to the house when there was so much happening outdoors, but she was feeling pretty weary. Her strength wasn't returning as fast as she'd like.

"I'll fix lunch and then poke around the barns this afternoon. Maybe Rosie and the baby would like company."

The mention of the mare brought a sexy gleam to Trey's eyes. "It's a good thing horses can't talk or Rosie would be gossiping about the way you attacked me last night."

She couldn't help but blush at the reminder of how abandoned she'd been when they'd made love in the barn. Trey delighted in teasing her about her lack of inhibitions when she was with him. He'd encouraged her to be bold, and she had been. The results made pretty erotic memories.

"I can't believe we were so brazen. Anyone could have walked in and seen us."

"What can I say?" he taunted, eyes glinting with mischief. "I lose my head when I start touching you."

Her eyes widened and searched his. He'd meant it as a joke, but his tone had dropped an octave, suggesting there was some truth behind the words.

"You always could make me lose my head," she whispered softly, reaching out a finger to stroke his cheek. Then her tone grew more serious. "I used to be a little afraid of the power you had over me."

The confession stunned Trey. He'd never imagined she might be frightened by the intensity of their desire for each other. Even though she'd been a virgin when they met, she'd always responded to him with passionate fervor. The thought that she might have been scared by his attentions came as an unpleasant shock.

"Why didn't you tell me the sex bothered you?" he demanded tersely. He'd always thought the physical side of their relationship was perfect for both of them. Her admission injured more than his pride. It hurt; it created doubts about his perception of their relationship, and that made him angry.

Jillian turned more fully toward him and splayed her hands on his chest, loving the hard warmth of him. A frown touched her brow when she felt him stiffen. She hadn't meant to offend him or create tension between them.

"I'm not, and never have been, afraid of making love with you," she assured him. "What I meant was that I knew I could easily have become dependent on you, and that scared me. I was at a stage when I thought personal independence was one of the most important things in life."

"I thought it was your career," he groused. As much as he resented ranking second best in her life, that was preferable to being someone who frightened or intimidated her.

Since Jillian had arrived at the ranch, they'd avoided discussion of the reasons for their separation. She knew Trey had felt cheated and was bitter, but she wished he could understand how she'd felt at the time. Then maybe he could really forgive her.

"There was so much more involved than a career decision," she tried to explain.

He didn't want to hear excuses. "Forget it. It's past and better forgotten." He shifted out of her reach, got out of the truck and slammed the door. Then he rounded the vehicle and opened her door.

Jillian didn't have much choice but to climb from the truck. She thanked him politely, but he turned his back on her.

"I'll be in for lunch as soon as I see if Wayne is back from town."

She sighed as she watched him cross the barnyard. Then she turned and slowly headed for the house. His rejection stung, despite the fact that she understood his sensitivity on the subject. He might insist they forget what happened, but he obviously hadn't forgotten or forgiven.

She knew they needed to come to terms with the past before they could ever hope for a future, yet he obviously wasn't ready to discuss the matter. All she could do was wait until he was willing to listen.

Lunch was a quick, quiet meal. Trey was withdrawn and barely took the time to eat before going back to work. Jillian missed his kisses and the conversation they normally shared. She tried not to be depressed by his attitude, but she couldn't help feeling rejected. She promised herself to wait a long time before broaching the subject of their past again. After loading the dishwasher, she started a pot of chili for supper. It could simmer all day without requiring a lot of attention.

Trey's temper simmered while he worked. He was angry with Jillian for reminding him of the pain and rejection he'd suffered. What made him even angrier was having to admit that he might have behaved like an insensitive jerk. He'd never considered the fact that she might have found him intimidating back then.

Had he actually driven her away with his sexual demands? She'd been an innocent, and he'd been insatiable. He didn't doubt that she'd enjoyed their loving as much as he had. She'd been a willing participant, but had their passion been more than she was prepared to handle?

He was a passionate man. That he couldn't deny or change, even if he wanted to. Jillian was the most incredibly sensual woman he'd ever met. Desire had always raged between them, but had they neglected all other aspects of their relationship to fulfill the physical needs?

What the hell did he care? He'd already wasted too much energy by caring too much. He wouldn't be so susceptible this time. She'd destroyed his desire for a wife, family and lifetime commitment. All he wanted now was to enjoy what she could offer for as long as she offered it. This time his heart wasn't involved. It was just a physical thing. He could take it or leave it.

His traitorous body grew hard just thinking about how much he enjoyed taking. Last night, she'd been wild and uninhibited, making love to him until he'd nearly lost his mind with pleasure. His body pulsed with heated rushes of blood every time he thought about it.

Sweet satisfaction. That's what he wanted from a relationship with Jillian. When the heat of their passion eventually cooled, she'd leave again. That's how it had to be, he argued mentally, but it didn't improve his temper.

Things went from bad to worse when Wayne returned from town. Trey was forking clean hay into horse stalls when the foreman found him.

"Bad news, boss."

"What is it?" asked Trey as he finished his chore and set aside the pitchfork.

"One of the guys who came for an interview bears a strong resemblance to that picture you showed me. His hair's shorter, and he don't have a mustache, but I'd bet a week's pay that it's the same guy."

Trey's jaw clenched. He hadn't expected the hit man to trace them so fast. He'd thought he had another day or so, at the very least. Cade and Steven were coming tomorrow and Kregg's men might be within hours of the ranch, but he couldn't depend on any of them right now.

"What did you do?"

"I did just like you told me. There were three men who wanted jobs, and I hired 'em all. They just have to show up here at six in the morning."

They'd decided to hire everyone who applied for the job at the ranch. That way the hit man wouldn't realize his identity had been discovered. Trey hoped it would give them a slight edge when dealing with him.

"I don't suppose he'll wait until morning," he growled, thinking aloud.

"I reckon I wouldn't if I was in a mind to sneak up on somebody," Wayne said. "Now that he knows where to find the Langden ranch, he'll be makin' his move."

"The government men should be in Albuquerque by now. I'll call and have them head straight out here. You call Cade and tell him to get here as soon as possible. Bring the hands you can spare closer to the house, warn them about danger and see who wants to help. Make sure they're armed and show them the picture of Germaine. I'm guessing this guy will make his way out here tonight, check our security and try to get a glimpse of Jillian."

"You gonna warn her?"

"I don't want to. She's had a long day, so she should be tired enough to go to bed early and sleep soundly. I know she won't risk talking to strangers. She wouldn't even answer the door if somebody knocked."

"At least we know he's comin'," Wayne said. "He don't know we're wise to him and layin' a trap, so maybe we can take him by surprise. I'll get busy alertin' the men and then we'll watch all roads leadin' to the house."

103

"Just tell them this guy's ruthless and probably a weapons expert, so nobody takes unnecessary risks. I'll have Kregg's men stop at the main gate, then radio you. You can direct them here, and we'll coordinate things from the barn."

"You want me to post men all around the house?"

"As close as you can get without alarming Jillian. I don't want to leave her alone, so I'll stay inside and keep checking with you through the intercom."

Trey and Wayne both moved to the tack room that served as a small office in the barn. He used the phone to return a call from Kregg's men, who'd arrived in Albuquerque. He told them to head to the ranch and watch for Germaine along the way.

Howard, who was doing the talking for the pair, said, "Kregg forgot to tell you that Germaine prefers a .45 with a silencer at close range. He's good with a rifle at long range, but he won't be likely to try that since your ranch is isolated. Not unless Brandt is traveling all over the ranch."

"She has been," Trey said. "But she's in the house for the night, and she'll stay there until we get this guy."

"We'll be there as soon as we can make it. We've rented a white pickup truck, and we think Germaine is driving a black Jeep. Is there anyplace close to the ranch where he could park and continue on foot?"

"The whole west side of the property is heavy with cover and the house is nestled in a natural barrier of mountains and forest," explained Trey. "It's harder to get to from the road, but that's the route I'd use if I wanted to stay hidden."

"Right," Howard agreed. "We'll assume Germaine is coming the long way. Monroe and I will come straight in from the road. Do you want us to approach the house?"

Trey explained that he was trying to keep Jillian from being alarmed, so he wanted everyone to check in with Wayne at the barn. Once procedures were agreed upon, he said goodbye to Howard and called his brother to update him. Cade told him that he, Steven and two other men would be at the ranch within hours.

After hanging up the phone a second time, Trey turned to his foreman. "Well, that's the best we can do right now. Help's on the way. We'll just have to be careful until they get here."

"We got the advantage," Wayne said. "He won't know we're setting a trap."

"Let's hope he walks into it without a firefight and without scaring the hell out of Jillian."

The sunlight was fading when Trey finally went to the house for supper. He hadn't shaken his concern about their earlier conversation, but he didn't want any strain between him and Jillian tonight. He needed to keep her close and have her cooperation, so he decided to forget their earlier disagreement and act as though nothing unusual had passed between them.

"Mmm…smells good in here. I haven't had chili for a long time."

She was standing at the stove and flashed him a surprised glance. Their gazes met, hers searching for any sign of residual anger in him. Finding none, a silent truce was declared.

"Cade's not coming?"

"He had some business, so he might be really late. We've got new hands arriving, too, so don't get upset if you hear a lot of activity outside. Wayne'll take care of everything."

Jillian nodded, thinking Trey was especially thoughtful to try to allay her fears. She'd met most of the ranch hands and felt safe on the ranch due to its isolation and distance from the horrors she'd experienced. The nightmares hadn't ceased, but they were becoming less frequent. Thanks to him, she was finding some peace.

After they'd eaten supper, Trey took a quick shower while Jillian cleaned the kitchen. When she took her turn in the bathroom, he moved swiftly through the house, locking all the windows and outside doors, and then pulling curtains closed. He shut off the lights and lit a fire in the living room fireplace, having decided to stay out of the bedroom and on the east side of the house. He was tossing cushions from the sofa to the floor when she finally caught up with him.

Jillian raised her brows. "It looks like you might be planning a seduction here, Mr. Langden," she commented lightly.

She was wearing another of his shirts, and nothing else. When she lifted her arms to brush her hair, the thin fabric molded to her damp skin, outlining the fullness of her breasts and teasing him with shadowed curves while baring long, sexy legs. His pulse quickened.

"Is that what it looks like, Ms. Brandt?"

"All you need is a little mood music," she suggested, moving farther into the room. "Something soft and romantic."

Trey's tone was rough velvet. "And a willing woman," he added. His eyes glittered in the semidarkness, flirting and challenging her to join him.

Her breath caught in her chest, and her body tingled with an anticipation she was determined to resist. He was dressed in nothing but soft, formfitting jeans. His chest was broad and bare. He was a walking, talking, breathing temptation.

She didn't know what to expect from him this evening. He'd been quiet and brooding during lunch, then deliberately casual at supper. She couldn't help but wonder if his mood swing was directly related to their physical relationship.

Had he coldheartedly decided to forget their earlier argument and humor her? Did he want to share an intimate, romantic evening with her, or did he just want sex? He was a virile man. She was well aware of his stamina and seemingly insatiable desire. Would he understand if she didn't feel completely comfortable with him tonight? She didn't know if he really wanted her, or if any willing woman would do.

The fire looked inviting, so Jillian crossed in front of him and eased herself to the cushions on the floor. It was a relief to sit. She was exhausted. She'd skipped her nap today and was really beat, but hated to admit it.

He sat down with her and pulled her between his legs, then relieved her of the hairbrush. With gentle strokes, he finished untangling her heavy hair and brushed it until it was almost dry. The silence for the next few minutes was broken only by the whisper of their breathing, the crackling of the fire and the soft sounds of the brush.

Trey loved her hair—the thickness and silky texture was a pleasure to feel against his skin. It shone with a warmth and vitality that was very much a part of her. He loved brushing it, touching it, burying his fingers and face in it.

She loved having him brush her hair. It felt heavenly, and Trey seemed to enjoy it, too. Tonight, though, it was too soothing and much too relaxing. A deep moan of pleasure escaped her as she closed her eyes and leaned more fully against him.

He put down the brush and wrapped his arms around her to pull her closer, then burrowed his face beneath her hair to find her nape with his lips. She smelled clean and sweet and womanly. She felt soft and warm and incredibly sexy. Desire slammed into him as he pressed kisses on her still-moist skin.

His unrelenting hunger for her annoyed him. He didn't welcome this savage need. She was the only woman who could make him a slave to passion, and he resented the intensity of it as much as he thrived on it. He couldn't be near her without wanting her.

Letting her back into his life was probably the worst mistake he'd ever made. When they were together, the desire they shared seemed to have a life of its own. He couldn't deny it any more than he could have denied her plea for help. There was no ignoring the facts.

But he couldn't risk losing himself in her sweetness right now, not even for a brief time. He'd noticed how weary she was, and knew she'd overdone it today. Her wound didn't give her trouble now, but her strength hadn't fully returned. She was tired and needed sleep. He needed to stay awake and alert.

He'd placed the cushions directly in front of the sofa to hide them in the shadows of the room. The heavier furniture was behind them so they couldn't be seen from any of the windows. Stretching full-length, he pulled Jillian snugly into the curve of his body. Nothing and no one could get to her except through him, and he intended to keep it that way.

"You pushed yourself a little too much, today, didn't you?" he asked, his mouth close to her ear.

Jillian involuntarily tilted her head up and back so that he could have better access to the sensitive curve of her neck. "I have to get out of the habit of napping all day," she told him, stifling a yawn.

"You might be stronger, but I don't want you to make yourself sick again," he insisted, caressing her tender flesh with warm lips.

"Yes, sir."

"You still need plenty of rest."

"Yes, sir."

Trey dragged his mouth from the tempting sweetness of her skin. He reached to the sofa for an afghan and pulled it over them, then tucked his arms under her breasts and hugged her. "You must be exhausted if you're being so agreeable," he commented in a low tone. "Better get some sleep."

"Yes, sir," Jillian mumbled a third time as she nestled closer to him.

She felt the strength of his arousal pressing against her backside and experienced a thrill of feminine satisfaction. His body's involuntary reaction assured her that she hadn't killed his desire by daring to mention their past.

The hard strength of his body comforted her as nothing else could do. She felt a pang of guilt for her lack of energy, but was immensely relieved that he wasn't expecting a night of wild, passionate loving. Maybe he cared more than he realized. Maybe there was hope. She started to speak.

"Rest," Trey reiterated. "It's been a long day and you overdid it with all that shifting. You're worn out and need sleep."

In just a few minutes, the slow, steady sound of her breathing convinced him that she'd fallen asleep. It wasn't much past eleven, and he wasn't expecting any trouble until the early hours of the morning, so he allowed himself the pleasure of holding her for more than an hour. By then, the hunger of his body had subsided to a comfortable warmth.

When he finally untangled their bodies, he gently shifted Jillian so that she was tucked between the protection of the sofa and another pile of cushions. The fire had died to ashes, so there was no light to illuminate the living room if somebody should get close enough to search.

He didn't intend to let anyone that close. If Germaine got by the men protecting the house, he'd take him down himself. Guns were familiar weapons in this part of the country. His dad had taught him to use and respect their power, and he'd honed his skills in the military.

Trey made a trip to the bedroom to pull on a shirt and his spare boots. An intercom call to Wayne assured him that all was quiet on the property, so he went next to the gun case. Once armed with his favorite rifle, he walked through the darkened house to ensure that everything was as he'd left it.

Cade's bedroom faced the west side of the house, so he spent several minutes in there, peering out the cracks in the drapes to survey the area beyond the window. There was a wide stretch of yard between the house and the first trees of the forest, separated only by a shrub-lined patio. It was partially illuminated by the ranch's powerful night-lights, but darkly shadowed by the cloudy, moonless night.

According to Wayne, Howard and Monroe had arrived. They were scouring the woods to the west. The foreman had sent one man to the front gate to watch for unfamiliar vehicles. Several other men were guarding strategic points around the property. All Trey had to do was make sure nobody got inside the house.

It was fortunate that most professional hit men worked alone. At least Trey's men didn't have to worry about a divided effort. There wasn't much chance that one lone man could get past their defenses, especially not one who was unfamiliar with the terrain around the ranch.

If Germaine came near enough to realize they were waiting for him, he might turn tail and run. Those types of men didn't want any witnesses to their crimes. They survived and succeeded by making themselves invisible, by slithering and striking like snakes.

Convinced all was quiet on the west side, Trey moved quietly through the rest of the house and then returned to the living room. Jillian was still sleeping peacefully, so he sat in an easy chair and laid the rifle across his lap.

As the minutes ticked slowly, his thoughts bounced from the potential physical threat of a professional killer to the certain emotional threat of the beautiful woman who'd reentered his life. His gut-level concern for her safety reinforced her increasing importance in his life. He'd fight for anyone under his protection, but he'd die for her.

He didn't want to open himself to more pain and rejection. He wanted to dismiss the tender feelings she inspired, but it was getting harder all the time. He'd never forgive himself if anything happened to her, and he didn't want to consider life without her again. It was better not to think about the future at all.

As the night crept by, Trey's ears became attuned to every small sound. He made regular trips through the house and checked in with Wayne every half hour. All the men on guard had been supplied with radios and were reporting to the foreman, so he knew they were all awake and alert.

By 3:00 a.m. he was growing more tense. The early hours of the morning were when defenses were at their lowest; therefore, victims were more susceptible to an attack. Gut instinct told him Germaine was near and preparing to make his move.

Jillian hadn't stirred all night, and Trey was glad she slept soundly. He was fairly sure Germaine would try to sneak in from the west, so he had Wayne come and keep an eye on her while he made his way to Cade's room and slipped out the patio doors.

Ray Clark, one of his longtime employees, was beside him within seconds. "What's up?" the other man whispered.

"I'll take the watch out here for a while. Wayne is in the house. I need you to take over for him in the barn."

Clark nodded his understanding and quietly slipped into the shadows, making his way around the corner of the house and out of sight.

Trey crouched down behind an evergreen shrub and peered into the darkness, watching for any unnatural shifting of shadows. He knew every tree and rock that bordered his property, and strained to distinguish anything out of place.

Within half an hour, he caught sight of a man moving stealthily through the smaller trees at the edge of the woods. Both of Kregg's men were big and broad shouldered and this intruder was much smaller in stature. They'd planned well, and their quarry was in sight.

Trey noiselessly slid the magazine into the rifle and flipped the safety.

Once he was forced to leave the cover of the trees, Germaine dropped to the ground. He began to inch his way across the grass on his stomach, just like the snake Trey had compared him to. His progress was slow, but steady, revealing that he had no concern he might be crawling straight into a trap.

Another cautiously moving shape materialized at the edge of the woods. This man was much taller and broader. Trey knew it was one of Kregg's men. Good. Germaine's line of retreat was blocked. The trap was gradually being sprung without him being any the wiser.

Trey waited until the hit man was almost to the house and completely exposed. Then he rose far enough above the shrubbery to take careful aim. In a low growl, he warned the man to halt.

"You're surrounded, Germaine. Give it up."

His target reacted swiftly, rolling to his feet and bringing his gun up to fire.

Trey didn't hear the shot, but felt a rush of air as the bullet passed by him. Then he fired. Germaine had started dodging wildly to avoid being hit, but the bullet caught his leg. He grunted and stumbled, then swung his arm around to fire again.

Several shots rang out simultaneously. Germaine's gun flew out of his hand and his legs collapsed beneath him. He grasped his thigh and fell to the ground with a groan of pain as another bullet made contact.

Trey didn't think the man was mortally wounded and doubted that he was totally unarmed, so he was slow to leave his cover. He approached Germaine with caution.

Monroe started across the grassy expanse of yard, identified himself as an agent of the federal government and warned Germaine not to try anything stupid or they'd kill him on the spot. Still, there was no knowing whether the murderer preferred death to capture. Trey's eyes were trained on the fallen man, and he watched as his hand slipped from his wounded thigh to the top of his boot. The action was barely perceptible, but he saw it.

"Don't make a move unless you want to lose your fingers," he snarled. Then to Monroe, "His left boot."

Trey moved closer and kept his rifle trained on the hit man while Monroe jerked his arms behind him and secured them with handcuffs. Next, he pulled off the gunman's boots, confiscating a small-caliber gun and a switchblade. Howard joined them and used another pair of cuffs on Germaine's ankles.

"That should do it," said Monroe.

"You have the right to remain silent," chanted Howard, reading the prisoner his rights while the circle of armed men around him grew. Even in the darkness of night, it was obvious that the hit man's face was totally devoid of expression, and he didn't utter a word.

The relative quiet of the night was shattered by the sound of an approaching helicopter. It took everybody but Trey by surprise. "My brother's security chief pilots one," he explained. "That will be them. He'll have to land it on this side of the house."

"Germaine's been hit in both legs, so we could use a lift to the nearest hospital," Monroe said, having checked the prisoner for injury. "Howard can escort him while I tie up the loose ends here."

Over the sound of the helicopter came a shout from the house. Wayne called that Jillian was waking, and Trey turned immediately to go to her.

"I could hear gunfire," Wayne explained as Trey entered the house.

"We got him."

"She hasn't woke up, but I think all the noise is makin' her restless. She started moanin' in her sleep, and I wasn't sure what to do."

"I'll take care of her. Cade and Steven are landing. I'll be back out as soon as she's settled again."

Wayne relieved him of the rifle and locked the patio doors while Trey moved to the living room. Jillian was sitting up in a tangle of blanket and cushions. He sat beside her and scooped her into his arms, realizing that she was softly sobbing.

His chest tightened at the desolate sound. He was used to the nightmares, but not her crying. He couldn't stand it. "Hush, baby, you're all right. I've got you, and nobody's going to hurt you," he swore fiercely.

"I heard guns," she rasped, clutching his shirt and burying her face against his chest. "I heard him shooting at me."

"No, sweetheart, no. It was just a bad dream," he whispered roughly. The relentless demons she faced hurt him as much as her. Her pain cut him to the quick. He felt her tears dampening his shirt, and ached to destroy all her fears. She didn't need to know the whole truth right now.

"You're right here with me. We're on the ranch. You're safe."

"Trey?" Jillian murmured from a semiconscious state between waking and sleeping.

"I'm right here, baby," he continued to whisper in a gentle, soothing tone. He held her and slowly rocked her until she quieted and the tension began to drain from her body. Then he eased them both to the floor where he could pull her more fully against his body, shielding her with his size and strength.

"Bad dream," she mumbled against his neck as she instinctively snuggled closer.

"Just a bad, bad dream," he agreed.

Her hair was a tangle of satin, and Trey smoothed it over her shoulders with fingers that weren't quite steady. He continued to stroke her until both their hearts had stopped racing and her breathing was even.

She was asleep again within minutes, but Trey didn't hurry to let go of her. The sounds of the helicopter were muted in the house, but he heard it coming in for a landing. He held his hands close to Jillian's ears to muffle the sounds until it had landed and the engine had been killed. He assumed they were loading Germaine into the craft, but knew they wouldn't take off again until he joined them. Still, he was reluctant to leave Jillian.

A few minutes later, Wayne quietly entered the room and took a seat across from the sofa. Trey forced himself to release his sleeping lady. He eased out of her arms and tucked the blanket around her again, then rose to his feet. With a nod to the other man, he left the room.

Cade met him at the kitchen door and they walked back out to the barnyard where the copter had landed. Monroe had done some first aid on Germaine's wounds and was getting him settled in the aircraft. Howard was preparing to take off again with Steven.

"I'll ride with Steven to Albuquerque. When we get back, Steven can get a couple guard trailers set up on the property," explained Cade.

"We'll take care of the tough guy," said Howard. "Kregg is going to be one happy man to have this one, and I don't expect you'll have any more unpleasant guests. The contract has been canceled."

"What?" asked Trey and Cade in unison.

"We got a call from Kregg right before leaving Albuquerque. The bodies of Gardova and his two closest lieutenants were dumped outside FBI headquarters in Miami. He was killed by the Valdez organization, the ruling cartel now. They wanted to make a statement. Kregg said it wasn't a pretty statement, but it made an impact."

"So there's no price on Jillian's head?" asked Cade.

"Nope. She's got celebrity status now. Gardova's problems with the government gave Valdez's people the opportunity to take down their biggest rival. Valdez would probably crucify anyone who tried to collect on that contract."

"Hear that, Germaine?" Howard taunted as he fastened his seat belt. "It was all for nothing. You're the only one who has to pay for this job."

His declaration generated a quiet, but lively conversation among the ranch hands. By now, they had a fairly good idea what was happening. The doors of the helicopter were secured and the engine roared to life. Men stepped out of the way as the blades began to whirl.

Monroe waved to Howard and Steven as the aircraft slowly cleared the ground. It hovered briefly, and then turned east to limit the amount of noise that could be heard in the house.

Monroe then told Trey he'd keep in touch and hitched a ride to where he'd left his truck. Germaine's Jeep had been disabled, so plans were made to have it taken back to the rental agency.

Trey thanked all his men and told them he didn't want Jillian or anyone outside the ranch to get wind of what had happened. He promised them a bonus in their next paycheck and sent them back to their quarters. It would be dawn soon; none of them would get much rest, but they all considered the rare hours of excitement worth a few lost hours of sleep.

By the time he went into the house, everything was quiet and back to normal. He thanked Wayne, and they agreed to try to get a couple hours of sleep.

After carrying Jillian to his room and laying her on the bed, he stripped and joined her. As he pulled her into his arms, he pressed his flesh against the warmth of hers. He needed her close, needed to feel the beat of her heart against his own, needed to reassure himself that she was okay.

Jillian stirred and squirmed against him in a sensually enticing rhythm that shattered the rigid control he'd maintained throughout the long night. Her hands caressed him with arousing effectiveness. Without words, but with a language all their own, they communicated their needs. She invited, and he accepted. Then they slept.

∞ℂℂ

It was early evening on Saturday before Cade returned to the ranch. He'd hired two new hands to add to the two Wayne had hired. Trey had given most of the other men the weekend off, so the extra manpower was needed.

The Langdens spent the day helping the new men learn their way around the property and discussing duties. By early evening, they were satisfied that everyone was settling in nicely, and they headed to the house to unload the nonperishable supplies Cade had brought.

"Mmm…" said Cade as they carried boxes and suitcases through the kitchen. "It smells like pot roast."

"That's what Jillian has in the oven. She's been doing most of the cooking," Trey said. He took suitcases to his bedroom and returned to help Cade unload boxes.

"Was she aware of anything that went on last night?"

"The gunshots woke her, but she still has nightmares, so I convinced her that's all it was. She'll have to know eventually, but she didn't bring up the subject, and I didn't say anything yet."

"Germaine was patched up at the hospital and whisked off to D.C.," Cade informed him. "He won't be a threat to anybody for quite a while."

"Glad to hear it," Trey said. "Did you get Jillian's film? She's been feeling stronger and wants to take some shots around here."

"Right here." Cade pointed to a box. "I got her a whole case. I figured she probably goes through a roll pretty fast. What about developing? Have you thought about fixing a darkroom here at the house?"

"No," Trey said. He'd had too many other things on his mind. "I just dug out the old camera yesterday. I don't know what supplies she'd need for developing. You'll have to ask her."

Cade was having a hard time reading his brother's mood. He sounded annoyed. "You're the one who asked me to get some film," he reminded him. "Do you object to Jillian's photography or a darkroom?"

Trey shook his head. "No. There's plenty of space in this house, and she's getting restless. She wants to help, but she's not completely recovered."

"From the wound?"

"It's pretty much healed, but she lost a lot of blood. It's going to take time."

Cade nodded. It would take a lot of time for Jillian to recover from all her wounds, physical and emotional.

Trey got them both a cold beer. "Did you find out anything else about Gardova?"

"Steven's contact confirmed what Howard said last night. Gardova is dead and there's no longer a contract on Jillian's head. Has she mentioned anything about contacting the authorities? About letting them know she's alive?"

"Nothing."

"Do you think she'll testify against Stroyer once she's had time to fully recover?"

Trey's gaze met his brother's. He practically snarled a response. "I don't know. She's just beginning to smile again. I don't want her upset."

Cade threw up his hands in mock surrender. There was no pleasing his brother. "I won't say a word," he insisted. "I like seeing her smile, too. We can all pretend it never happened, but that won't make it go away."

Trey sighed wearily and raked a hand through his hair. "I know we can't avoid the issue for much longer. I'll tell her Gardova's dead and about the hit man, then see how she reacts. Maybe if we just give her a little more time, she'll decide to testify."

"Agreed. Now how about supper? The smell of that beef is making my mouth water."

Trey managed a grin. "Set the table, and I'll go find Jillian."

"Deal," said Cade.

Trey left the house and headed for the barn. When he entered the building, he nearly collided with Wayne. The foreman put a finger to his lips and pointed in the direction of Rosie's stall.

Jillian was sound asleep. Trey found her curled up on the bales of hay where they'd made love. She was using a jacket for a pillow, and her hair was splayed across it like a golden fan. Her legs were tucked close to her stomach. She looked young, innocent and so lovely that his heart constricted. It had been only a few hours since he'd seen her, yet he'd missed her. He let his eyes drink in the sight of her before touching her shoulder.

"Hey, sleepyhead," he said, and then cleared his throat of its sudden huskiness. The wave of emotion angered him. "It's time to wake up."

Her lashes fluttered and her brilliant green gaze focused on Trey. Her smile was for him alone—wide, warm, and intimate. He needed to hold her. He didn't want to think about how much; he just wanted to do it. Scooping her into his arms was the fastest way to accomplish his objective. He sat on the bale of hay and cradled her in his lap.

"I have news about Gardova," he told her while she was still relaxed from sleep. She stiffened and grew more tense, but didn't interrupt while he explained all that had transpired.

When he was finished, there was a short silence. Then Jillian spoke softly. "Gardova's really dead?"

He assured her it was true.

A few minutes of silence passed as she considered the turn of events. "A hit man actually tracked me here?" she asked with a catch in her voice. All her muscles and nerves seemed to desert her at once and she was thankful for Trey's strong arms. The knowledge that she might have brought death and destruction to his home made her physically ill.

Trey didn't like her feeling vulnerable while under his protection, and he didn't want her feeling responsible for bringing danger to his ranch. But he didn't want any secrets between them, either.

"We were ready for him.'"

"Did you...?"

"He's alive, but he's wanted for other crimes, so he'll be locked away for a long time."

"When?" Jillian asked next.

"Last night."

"That's why you let me go to sleep in the living room?" Then she remembered the sound of gunshots. "It wasn't just a bad dream, was it?"

"No, but it's over now." He rose and lifted her in his arms to put an end to the discussion.

"You're sure about Gardova?"

"There's no doubt. He and two of his top men were executed. The contract on you has been canceled and you're probably the heroine now instead of the hunted."

Jillian shook her head, her eyes wide with confusion. "It seems hard to believe."

"Believe it," Trey commanded.

He didn't want her dwelling on what might have been. In an attempt at distraction, he pressed his mouth to hers for a long, seductive kiss. She was a little slow to respond, but then she tightened her grip on his neck and returned his kiss with searing hunger. After a few minutes of passionate kissing and promises for more later, Trey finally carried her to the house.

Chapter Eight

"Thank you," she managed to say politely when he deposited her in a chair at the kitchen table. She noticed their guest and smiled for him. "Hi, Cade."

"Hi, yourself," he replied. "I'm playing waiter tonight. Just sit still, and I'll serve."

Jillian didn't argue. She was still a little numb, but she wasn't ready to consider all the ramifications of Gardova's death. All she cared about was being with Trey, and she was determined not to dwell on anything else.

Trey took a chair opposite her, and Cade handed them plates heaped with beef, potatoes, and carrots. When he took his own seat, he glanced from one of them to the other, frowning. The tension between them was thick.

His brother caught his eye and shook his head, warning him not to ask what was wrong. Cade's eyes lit with understanding when he realized that Jillian had just learned about recent happenings.

"I'm starved," he said. "I hope you'll both forgive me if I dig in."

"Just eat and forget about conversation," said Trey.

Cade took his advice. The rest of their meal was eaten with a minimum of small talk. Dessert was an apple pie purchased from a bakery in Albuquerque.

Jillian didn't have much of an appetite. She ate sparingly, but felt stuffed. "I have to get up and move around a little," she told them after dessert. "You guys sit still and let me clean the kitchen."

She didn't get any arguments. The men each helped themselves to a second slice of pie, and Jillian poured them cups of coffee before starting to clear the table.

"The new hired hands seem to have settled in," Cade said when his appetite was finally satisfied. "I don't figure you'll need all four of them, but somebody usually quits after they've collected a couple paychecks."

"We can use all of them right now."

"The two I hired had good references. Wayne said the two he hired are trustworthy, but not apt to stay very long."

"Things will slow down soon," Trey reminded him.

Jillian liked listening to the men discuss the ranch business. They worked without the constant power struggles some siblings experienced. She washed and dried dishes just to keep herself busy while their conversation moved from new employees, to breeding stock and then to upcoming tax returns.

When she was finished, she hung the dish towel up to dry and turned back to the table. Her artist's eye immediately focused on the sharp contrasts between brothers, and the basic similarities. Trey was dressed in his usual faded jeans and cotton shirt. Cade was wearing expensive, designer slacks and a silk shirt, yet both men shared striking physical similarities.

She wanted to capture them on film. The desire was so strong and unexpected that it stunned her. The urgency of her need was much worse than the earlier desire to take outdoor shots. She felt almost desperate to capture their images, and she didn't welcome the painful rush of feelings. Caring about anything too much was a risk. Her heart's desire always seemed to come at too high a cost. She'd traded Trey's love for a career, and look where it had gotten her.

Curling her hands into tight balls, she willed away the nagging urges. She wasn't aware that the Langdens' conversation had ceased or that they'd turned concerned gazes on her, until Trey's voice broke into her troubled thoughts.

"Jillian? You okay?" he asked after she'd ignored his first effort to gain her attention. He didn't like the strained look that had settled over her features.

She blinked, forcing herself to relax and summon a smile. "I'm fine," she assured them quickly, feeling foolish and unwilling to air her real concerns. "I think I just ate too much and feel like a zombie." The excuse was lame, but the best she could manage.

"Well, sit down," Cade said. "Relax a little bit."

She felt an almost suffocating need to get out of the room. "If you'll excuse me, I think I'll go take a shower," she said, turning to the hallway door.

"Cade brought you some clothes," Trey told her, halting her flight. "Everything's in suitcases. I put them in the bedroom."

Jillian managed a more sincere smile for Cade. "Thanks. I imagine everyone's getting tired of my one outfit. I know I am."

"Don't thank me. Sallie did all the shopping. I figured she'd have a better idea of what you might need."

"Sallie?"

"My secretary."

His comment served as a perfect distraction for Jillian. She gazed at him in amazement. "Your secretary is willing to do your shopping for you?"

"Not hardly," Cade admitted. "She's a real stickler for office decorum, but she made an exception when I told her it would be a favor for Trey."

"She's particularly fond of Trey?" Jillian queried testily.

Cade's brows rose. Trey grinned devilishly, making her realize how sharp her question had sounded. She strove for a less proprietary tone. "Did Sallie know who she was buying the clothes for?"

"I just told her you were a friend of my brother," Cade explained, grinning. "I don't think she has any romantic interest in him, but she likes him. And since it wasn't a personal favor for me, she was happy to help."

"Well, please thank her for me," Jillian replied. "I appreciate her time and trouble."

"Will do. She told me to bring back anything that doesn't fit or that you don't like. She can make exchanges and returns."

Jillian agreed and turned toward the door again, then hesitated. "How much do I owe you?"

"I don't have a clue," Cade admitted. "Sallie charged everything to Trey's credit card."

"Trey?" She directed her query at him.

"I'll let you know when I get the bills." He had no intention of letting her repay him, but he didn't want to argue about it.

Jillian wanted to argue that she wasn't a complete charity case, but she knew it would be a waste of time. She made a mental note to discuss the subject after she'd estimated how much money had been spent on her.

"I got some film, too, and Trey and I were discussing a darkroom. Would it be too complicated to convert a small bedroom or a big closet here in the house?"

The question took her by surprise. She hadn't even considered the possibility. Her gaze flew to Trey. He'd loaned her a camera, but did he really want her involved with photography? Would he resent her working in his home?

"I hadn't given it any thought," she said.

"You had one in your apartment in Miami, didn't you?"

The mention of Miami made her stiffen. A chill swept over her. She didn't want any reminders of that dark, cruel world she'd barely escaped with her life.

"It was just a small closet," she told them. Her mind's eye conjured an image of the tiny space. The last time she'd seen it, there was nothing left but a ravaged shell. Everything she'd worked on for months, hundreds of yards of irreplaceable film, had been viciously destroyed. She couldn't think about it.

"Is it hard to set up a darkroom?" Cade asked again.

"Could the supplies be purchased in Albuquerque?" Trey asked, hating the wounded look that had flashed in her eyes. He realized he would do

123

anything in his power to provide her with the things that were most important to her.

"I imagine they could be purchased locally or online, but I don't want you going to a lot of trouble and expense."

"Why?" Cade prodded. "Are you planning on leaving here soon?"

"No!" Jillian paled and her gaze shot to Trey again. "You don't want me to leave, do you?"

"No." Trey didn't elaborate, but his tone was firm, and he glared at his brother for deliberately baiting her. "We just want to make sure you have everything here you want or need. If you'd like a darkroom, I'll see how soon one can be furnished."

"I'll have to think about it," she hedged, unsure of what she wanted. "I haven't even taken a photograph for weeks. I may not need a darkroom."

"It can wait," Trey said. "Why don't you join us in the living room after your shower?"

"All right." She gave them a smile that didn't quite reach her eyes. "I won't be too long."

He watched her walk down the hall, and then turned angry eyes on his brother. "Why the hell are you badgering her? You know she doesn't have anywhere else to go."

"I just wondered if she was giving any thought to what happens next," Cade answered defensively. "She has to make some hard decisions."

Trey rose from the table and started to pace the room in agitation. He hated seeing that panicked and haunted look in Jillian's eyes. He didn't like to think about his own panic at the thought of her leaving.

"She's only been here a little over a week, and she's recovering from a gunshot wound," he grumbled. "She's just started to come out of shock, and you have to upset her all over again."

"Sorry," said Cade. "I want what's best for her, but I'm not sure the two of you are capable of making a rational decision."

Trey pinned him with dark, accusing eyes. "What the hell is that supposed to mean?"

"I think you'd keep her here on any terms. She wants to hide forever. It won't work, for either of you."

"You're accusing me of taking advantage of the situation? Of her vulnerability?" Trey's tone rose with his temper. "You think I want her to spend the rest of her life being so scared she won't step foot off my property?" he charged. "What kind of a selfish bastard do you think I am?"

"Hell, Trey, that wasn't what I meant," Cade argued. "I know you love her and want to protect her."

"I don't love her!" he bit out harshly, then dragged in a rough breath and raked a hand through his hair in frustration. "I want her, and she wants me. We need each other right now. That's it. No devious schemes or ulterior motives, just basic human need."

Cade didn't voice his skepticism, but he knew his brother was living in a fool's paradise if he didn't think his emotions were involved. He was more concerned about the long-term problems they'd be inviting if they weren't honest about their needs. Trey was right about Jillian, though. It was obviously too soon to pressure her about returning to Florida to testify.

"I'll try not to mention Miami the rest of the weekend," he assured his big brother. "I'll leave it up to you to decide when she's ready to face reality again."

Face reality. Trey didn't like the suggestion that Jillian would be satisfied with a make-believe existence. She might be emotionally and physically fearful right now, but she had plenty of reason. Once she was stronger and had regained some emotional security, she would regain her fierce desire to right the wrong that had been done.

℘℧

When Jillian had finished with her shower, she wrapped herself in a large bath towel and started looking through the suitcases Trey had put on the bed.

She found several pairs of jeans, shoes, shirts, a sweat suit and a couple of dresses. There were sets of lacy underwear in a rainbow of colors, three gorgeous silk nightgowns and a white satin robe with matching slippers.

The sizes all looked right and everything was made of the finest quality or had a designer label. Cade's secretary has great taste, she thought as she slowly unpacked the clothing. This was no low-price collection.

Inside a cosmetic case, she found a blow dryer, some basic cosmetics and a variety of toiletries. Sallie had also included feminine hygiene products, and Jillian mentally thanked her for her thoughtfulness.

Her period was due soon, and she was always regular, but hadn't given a thought to the basic necessities. Sallie had saved her the embarrassment of asking one of the men to buy such personal items. Even though she and Trey shared an intimate relationship, it wasn't the same as being married or feeling completely comfortable with the subject.

She had to wonder now if they'd ever be married. Trey didn't hesitate to show his desire for her body, but he was very careful not to reveal his inner emotions to her. Their lovemaking might be passionate, yet he never really lost control as he had when they'd first met. He always managed to keep an emotional distance between them.

Could he learn to love her again, or had she destroyed any possibility of a long-term commitment from him? Could she teach him the importance of having unquestionable faith in the one you loved? What would she have to do?

Sighing, she realized that only time would tell. Maybe in time, and with a lot of loving, he could learn to care for her the way he had before their traumatic argument and separation. Time was her only hope, but she had plenty to spare.

Her fingers caressed the silk nightgowns. The tags had been removed and everything looked freshly washed, so she folded them and put them in a drawer. One gown was a particularly striking shade of teal green. She lifted it and held it against her body, then decided to try it on. Tossing the towel aside, she slid the silk over her head and let it glide down her body.

The cool fabric felt good against her skin. Her body was incredibly sensitive after days and nights filled with Trey's amorous attentions. The gown was soft and hugged her curves without being tight. Sheer lace cupped her breasts in a perfect fit, with the lace extending into narrow straps across each shoulder.

She wondered what Trey would think of her new nightwear. If he liked it enough, maybe he'd forget that he'd been annoyed with her earlier in the day. She didn't want him to worry about the past or be hurt by the memories.

There was a full-length mirror in his wardrobe, so she stood in front of it and studied her reflection. Her hair was damp from the shower. She lifted it high on her head with both hands, and then turned from side to side to see how the gown fit from several angles.

Trey chose that minute to enter the bedroom. His mouth opened to speak, but he abruptly snapped it shut. The sight of her stole his breath and made him completely forget what he'd been going to say.

She gave him a tentative smile and lowered her arms. "What do you think?" she asked, turning toward him.

He closed the door and leaned against it while searching for words to describe how beautiful she was. He decided there was no way to express what he felt when he looked at her. His eyes adored her, and his tone was gruff with emotion.

"I like it." He moved toward her.

Jillian's smile widened. She didn't need flowery compliments. The light in his eyes told her what she needed to know.

"Cade's secretary has great taste," she insisted, her nerves singing with awareness as he came closer. "I need to thank her for her thoughtfulness."

Trey stopped an arm's length from her. He savored her alluring beauty with heavy-lidded eyes. He could smell her fresh, sweet scent, and his body reacted instantly, but he didn't touch her.

Jillian was the first to reach out. She splayed a hand on his chest and stepped close to him. "Thank you for giving Sallie permission to shop for me. I love your shirts, but I really like this silk, too."

127

Trey put an arm around her waist and tugged her lower body against his. With the index finger of his other hand, he slowly traced the swirling pattern of lace cupping her breasts. He didn't touch her nipples, but they pebbled and stabbed against the fabric in wanton demand for attention. His eyes darkened at the instant, involuntary invitation.

"Cade and I wondered what was keeping you," he told her in a barely audible tone. "I'm glad I came to check."

His fingers caused heat to lick at her nerve endings. His body was hard and straining against her stomach, making Jillian intensely aware of her effect on him.

"I was putting away the clothes," she explained.

The unsteadiness of her voice made him smile. He liked knowing his touch inflamed her. Especially since the sight, scent and feel of her created a turbulent reaction of his senses. He kept his gaze locked with hers as he enveloped one breast with his hand and gently kneaded. She moaned softly, and her eyelids drooped. A flush spread across her cheeks. He felt her nipple thrusting against his palm. When she quivered in his arms, a groan rumbled from deep in his chest.

"You're so beautiful," he whispered, knowing the word didn't begin to describe the depth of her sensuality and desirability. Would he ever get enough of her?

His lips brushed the warmth of her cheeks, and then slid to the satin skin at the base of her throat. He felt the erratic pounding of her pulse, and his blood pulsed through his veins in a fevered rush.

"Trey." She murmured his name in a husky tone that scolded, yet praised. "You're making me weak."

Her breathy admission stroked his ego. His mouth grew more urgent, sucking her neck until she trembled and leaned heavily against him for support. He thrust his hips against her in urgent demand.

"Cade's waiting," Jillian managed to remind him.

"I want you. Right here, right now." His brother could wait; he didn't know if he could.

Jillian lifted her face and opened her mouth as his lips sought hers for a hot, hungry kiss. He slid one knee between her legs, shoving it high into the juncture of her body and simultaneously pulling her closer until her feet left the floor and she was riding his thigh. Then he drank the rush of breath from her mouth, and groaned as he felt the muscles of her thighs clenching around his.

Jillian dragged her mouth from his and gasped for breath, then buried her face in the curve of his neck as her body quivered in his arms. Trey experienced a rush of guilt at her vulnerability. They hadn't been alone for two minutes before he'd deliberately started arousing her.

Was he being a total jerk? Was he putting his own needs above all else? "I didn't come in here to seduce you," he swore roughly, trying to excuse his actions. "I just can't seem to look at you without wanting."

His words and hot breath scorched her ear. She tightened her arms around his neck. She couldn't think of anything but the way he made her feel when she was pressed against his hard body.

He held her close and fought to control his rampaging desire. Restraint was difficult with her soft, quivering body in his arms, but he fought a tough battle. He was dirty and needed a shower. The loving could wait until they were both comfortable in bed, and he could make it really good for her.

He gradually lowered her feet to the floor and loosened his hold on her while stroking her back in what he hoped was a soothing fashion. He hadn't meant to tease. He'd never practiced much restraint around Jillian, but maybe it was time he learned how to do it.

When they were both calmer, he eased some space between their bodies. "Cade's waiting." He repeated her earlier reminder, his eyes still dark with passion as they locked with hers. "Why don't you get dressed and go keep him company while I take a shower?"

Jillian stepped out of his arms and searched his face. His eyes assured her that he wanted her, but that he wanted to wait. She smiled with relief, and then teased, "You don't think I should model my nightgown for him?"

Trey's eyes flared. "Hell, no," he bit out gruffly.

"He might be intrigued by his secretary's taste in lingerie."

"No doubt. Did she send anything that covers you from neck to ankle?" he asked as he began to unbutton his shirt.

"A nice lavender sweat suit."

"Is it baggy and shapeless?"

She turned back to the dresser, shaking her head in resignation. "Go take a shower."

Trey obeyed the gentle command, but went into the bathroom, grumbling about women's fashions. Jillian stripped off the nightgown and laid it across the foot of the bed. She stepped into lacy panties and then the fleece-lined sweat suit. A pretty, raised pattern on the front of the shirt kept it from defining the shape of her bare breasts. It wasn't too revealing, and the fleece felt soft and warm.

Other than having a few creases, it was neat and comfortable. It wasn't the least bit baggy, but it did cover her from neck to ankle. She slid her feet into her new slippers and left the bedroom. As she walked down the hallway, she heard voices, but then realized that Cade was watching television. She hadn't watched TV since she'd arrived at the ranch. While at the safe house, there'd been little else to do, but she'd quickly tired of the regular programming.

Cade was reclining in an easy chair with the television's remote control in one hand and a beer in the other. He gave her a smile when she entered the room, then continued to flip from station to station.

"Is there anything you'd like to watch?" he asked as she eased herself into one corner of the sofa.

"Nope."

"Did Trey get lost?"

"He's taking a shower."

Cade settled on a station with a sitcom, and then gave Jillian his attention.

"The sweat suit looks nice on you. Do you like the things Sallie sent?"

"I didn't try on all the clothes, but the sizes look good, and your secretary has excellent taste."

"She always does everything well. She's damned near perfect," he said with a hint of annoyance. "I didn't doubt that she'd know what to buy."

She wondered if he had a problem with his secretary's competency. "Please thank her for me. She must have taken a lot of time with the shopping, and she was very thoughtful to include some extra things I might need."

"Write her a note, and I'll deliver it on Monday."

Jillian frowned. She couldn't write a note without signing it, and she didn't want to make personal contact with anyone beyond the ranch. "I'd rather you just convey my thanks."

His brows drew together in a frown. He responded in a tone that was gentle, but firm. "Sallie isn't a threat to you, Jillian. You can't keep hiding forever."

He expected his words to spur anger. Instead, her face lost all expression. "I'll never feel safe again," she declared flatly.

He decided to try persuasion. "There are a lot of good, trustworthy officials who would do everything possible to protect you."

"That's what Jack Carnell believed. Even after he was killed, I still believed. I don't believe anymore."

"You're letting them win, Jillian, the bad guys," he argued gently. "You're letting crime and injustice triumph over the law and basic human rights. You were always the most ardent defender of justice and the American way. Two wrongs don't make a right. Stroyer shot you. He knew about the other murders. He and any accomplices have to be brought to justice."

His earnest plea was met with dead silence. She steadily returned his intense regard, but she didn't respond with so much as a blink of an eye. Cade reluctantly accepted the fact that he was wasting his time. She still wasn't ready to listen to reason.

The sitcom suddenly held great appeal to Jillian. She shifted her attention to the television screen, not wanting to hear or consider Cade's arguments. She wasn't the same naive, optimistic schoolgirl he thought he knew so well. She'd changed. She'd been forced to change. She'd put her life on the line, had it shattered and nearly lost it. Never again. She was with Trey now, and starting to feel whole for the first time in endless months. She had a second chance at his love. She wouldn't risk that happiness twice.

One sitcom was over and another was beginning before she spoke again. She didn't look at Cade. Her tone was emotionless, but the words came straight from her heart.

"I love Trey more than I love life itself. I was a fool to walk away from him once, but I won't do it again. He may never forgive me for the past, but as long as he wants me, in any capacity, I'm staying with him.

"All the drug lords and crooked cops in the world aren't worth one minute of his time," she continued, still staring at the television screen. "I can't right all the world's wrongs. It took me a while, and I learned that lesson the hard way, but I learned it well."

It pleased him that she felt the need to explain herself. It was a step in the right direction. He knew she couldn't live the rest of her life in uncertainty, but she obviously thought Trey was the answer to all her problems.

"I won't insult you by saying I understand how you feel," he told her while studying her beautiful, frozen features, "but you might consider Trey's feelings on the subject. How can he ever be sure it's him you want, not just a refuge?"

Jillian's eyes flashed angrily as she turned to him. "Are you suggesting that Trey won't ever be able to trust me if I don't go to the FBI and testify against Stroyer?"

The emerald fire in her eyes encouraged him. Apparently his brother's love was something she was willing to fight for. "How would you feel if the situation were reversed? Would you ever be completely sure of his motives?"

Jillian didn't respond. She refused to think about Cade's questions and determinedly focused her attention on the comedy on TV. He didn't say anything else, and the room grew quiet except for the television. The second half-hour show was nearly over before Trey joined them, juggling three plates holding pieces of pie.

"Here," he told Jillian, handing her a plate. He gave one to Cade and then sat beside her on the sofa.

"I was beginning to think you'd fallen asleep in the shower," she said before taking a bite.

"I had to make a few phone calls to prospective horse buyers," he explained. "Then I went to the kitchen for a drink, saw the leftover pie and decided we needed a snack."

"I was just thinking about this pie," said Cade, "but I was too lazy to go get it."

"Glad to be of service." Trey helped himself to a forkful of the dessert.

For the next few minutes, the three of them exchanged small talk while they ate, and Trey noticed that neither Jillian nor his brother wanted to look him directly in the eyes. He wondered what they'd been discussing before he came into the room. When she volunteered to take then dirty plates to the kitchen, he got the opportunity to ask.

"You promised you weren't going to say anything else to upset her," Trey reminded, leveling a cool stare at his brother. "What have you two been talking about?"

"I promised not to mention Miami, and I didn't."

"Then what did you say to make her so tense?"

Cade gave him an edited version. "I told her to write a thank-you note for Sallie. She thinks that constitutes a security risk."

"That's it?"

"She's not willing to take even the slightest risk."

Trey already knew that. Cade wasn't telling him the whole story, but Jillian returned to the room and the subject was dropped. He held out his arms, and she curled up in his lap, slipping her arms around his waist and resting her head on his shoulder. After a few minutes, she began to relax.

Trey was relieved to feel some of the tension drain from her body. She felt good as her soft curves molded to the harder contours of his body. It didn't take long for him to realize that she wasn't wearing a bra under the sweatshirt.

His interest in the late news broadcast wasn't as avid as his imagination when he considered the possibility that she wasn't wearing anything at all under the sweat suit. He splayed a hand on the soft skin at the back of her waist and let it slowly rove beneath elastic.

Jillian rested her cheek against Trey's broad, bare chest. His usual attire for relaxing was a pair of worn jeans and nothing else. She thoroughly approved. She liked the feel of springy hair and hard, warm flesh. His hand was caressing her in a slow, soothing motion. His heart beat steadily beneath her ear. She forgot the television, Cade's disturbing suggestions and everything but the blessed contentment she found in her lover's arms.

Trey's legs were propped on the coffee table. He rested his chin on the top of her head, inhaling the fresh, womanly scent of her hair. Jillian was soft and warm in his arms. It was a far cry from the way he'd spent his evenings before she'd arrived.

He didn't need alcohol to numb his senses or put him to sleep now. He didn't even need sleep when he had Jillian by his side. How long could he hope for it to last? How long could they ignore the outside world? Was she really obligated to testify against Stroyer? If and when she left, would she return?

Would she have come to him if she hadn't been desperate? That was the biggest question. The only way to know for sure was to let her go again and see if she returned. Trey didn't want to think about it. He couldn't let her go yet, and he wouldn't consider letting her leave until he was absolutely certain she would be safe. Stroyer would be laid up for at least another four weeks. Maybe then they could consider the options of having her return to Miami. Until then, he intended to enjoy having her with him.

When the news was over, Cade tuned in to a late-night talk show, and Trey caught himself dozing. Jillian had fallen asleep in his arms, so he decided it was time to head for bed. After a word of good night to his brother, he rose from the sofa and carried her to the bedroom. By the time he'd closed the door behind him, they were both awake and very aware of each other. Trey let Jillian's feet slide to the floor, but he kept his arms around her. Her arms stayed locked about his neck.

"I've been wondering if you're wearing anything under that sweat suit," he murmured against her ear.

"Not much," she replied drowsily, rubbing against him like a sinuous cat.

He moaned softly and slid both hands up her rib cage to cup her breasts. Her nipples instantly reacted to his touch, and his mouth trapped her inarticulate sound of pleasure. Their tongues dueled in delight. He took his time removing her clothes, enjoying every minute of undressing her. Then he carried her to bed and made slow, painstaking love to her.

They fell asleep in each other's arms, but a few hours later, Jillian began to toss and turn as her dreams gradually evolved into nightmares.

At first, her restlessness didn't wake Trey. Then the horrors in her subconscious escalated, making her tremble with fear.

She sat straight up in bed and released a blood-curdling scream that echoed in the silence of the house. Trey's arms encircled her, but she fought him, continuing to scream. "No! No! No!"

"It's all right, baby," he whispered roughly, calming her enough to wrap her in the blankets and draw her close to his chest. "It's just a dream. Just a bad dream."

He rocked her gently, continuing to offer her comfort with words and his tight embrace.

"It was so real." Jillian's tone was raw with fear. "So real," she whispered hoarsely. The nightmare was familiar. She regularly relived the horror she'd witnessed in Miami, but this time Trey's face had taken the place of the undercover cop who'd been tortured and murdered. It was more than she could bear. Another shudder ripped through her body.

"It was a nightmare. You're safe. I'm not going to let anything happen to you," he promised huskily.

After a sharp knock on the door, it swung open and Cade flipped on the light. "What happened?" he demanded, focusing on the couple in the bed. "I thought I heard Jillian scream."

"A nightmare," Trey explained succinctly.

Cade frowned. His brother's expression was enough to heighten his concern. "Does she have many of them?"

"At first it was every time she slept. It's gotten better, but tonight must have been a bad one."

The younger man rubbed his face with both hands. He wondered if his discussion with Jillian had increased her fears. "I'm really sorry if I triggered this." He hadn't meant to traumatize her. "Should I call a doctor?"

"No." Jillian responded to his question. She gently withdrew from Trey's arms and tugged the blankets up to her chin. "I don't need a doctor," she insisted, dry-eyed. She managed to get her emotions under rigid control.

"Maybe a therapist could help," Cade suggested.

She just shook her head in rejection of the idea. The nightmares plagued her, but she didn't want to trust anyone with the information locked inside her head. She wasn't trusting any strangers.

"I'm sorry I woke you," she told both men, then lay back in bed. "The dream shouldn't reoccur tonight."

The brothers exchanged looks. There was little they could do but go back to sleep.

"Goodnight," said Trey.

"See you in the morning," Cade said as he turned off the light and closed the door.

Trey leaned over Jillian and threaded the fingers of one hand through her hair while stroking her cheek with the fingers of his other hand. He desperately wanted to ease her pain, but he didn't know how to help her. He knew the nightmares scared her to death, yet she never talked about them. The silent sobs last night had been only a brief, unconscious release of tension.

He wasn't a psychologist, but he knew it wasn't good for her to keep so much destructive emotion bottled up inside of her. "Want to tell me about it?" he coaxed.

She shivered. There was no way she could discuss the nightmare with him. How could you tell someone that your mind just conjured up their torture and death?

"Jillian?" he prodded gently.

"I can't," she whispered, closing her eyes against the dark concern in his. She didn't want his sympathy and compassion. She didn't want anything but his love. She wouldn't allow the torment she suffered to intrude on their secure little world.

Trey brushed a thumb across her cheek. She'd closed her eyes to shut him out and it hurt, but he couldn't force her confidence. He touched his lips to hers. "Anytime you feel like talking about it, I'm willing to listen," he promised softly.

His tenderness made her feel weepy, but no tears formed to cleanse her of the pain and fear. She would never be able to accept his offer. The only way she could survive was to bury the emotions too deeply to resurrect.

ℰℭ

Sunday passed without further discussion of Jillian's predicament. She spent a great deal of time following Trey around the ranch and taking pictures. With a camera in her hands, she felt almost normal. She was learning her way around the property and began to feel as though she were helping with some of the work load.

Each of the ranch hands was introduced to Jillian as she worked among them. None of them were very talkative, but they treated her with respect and were quick to help her if she had a question or a problem. By the time evening arrived, they had become accustomed to the constant clicking of her camera. No one escaped the focus of her lens.

Cade had Sunday dinner on the ranch, and then flew back to Dallas with Steven in the helicopter. Jillian and Trey finished work for the day at a relatively early hour and headed for the shower, then bed.

She had her back to him when he climbed into bed, but that didn't stop Trey from sliding close to her and enveloping her in his arms. She tensed a little when he drew her against his body, and panic slammed into him. Why didn't she want him close to her? She'd never rejected his touch. Was she growing tired of his constant demands?

Fear kept him from asking, but he tried to help her relax by gently stroking her thigh and hip closest to him. Sliding his hand beneath the hem of her gown, he stoked upward and encountered the lacy edge of underwear.

"What's this?" he asked.

"Underwear," she mumbled, half embarrassed and half amused. "Commonly known as panties."

Trey braced himself. His tone was low and carefully measured. "Are they a subtle hint that you don't want me touching you?"

The question took her by surprise. She hadn't meant to offend him. Turning onto her back, she studied his face in the dim light. "What makes you think that?"

"You don't usually wear panties to bed."

"I don't like to," she admitted, "but at certain times of the month, I have to."

"Certain times..." he wondered aloud. Then understanding gradually dawned. "Oh," he muttered, "is it that time of the month?"

She nodded, wondering how he would take the news. It would put a temporary crimp in their love life.

Trey visibly relaxed. He was glad she had a practical, rather than emotional, reason for rejecting his touch. "That's a relief," he told her.

Jillian stiffened. She supposed he was relieved that she hadn't conceived a child. "Were you afraid I might be pregnant? We've been insatiable and taken a couple of risks."

She'd completely misunderstood his reaction. He felt her emotional withdrawal and tried to explain himself better. "That's not what I meant," he insisted. Her misconception made it easier for him to express his real fears. "I'm just glad you weren't hinting that you're tired of sex."

Her eyes widened in surprise. She couldn't imagine Trey being insecure about the physical aspect of their relationship, but apparently he was. She hoped he hadn't gotten the wrong impression when she'd told him that she'd been a little overwhelmed by his loving in the past.

His vulnerability gave her a glimmer of hope for their future. She was equally vulnerable where he was concerned. Grasping one of his hands, she carried it to her mouth for a kiss. "I'm never going to get tired of making love with you," she promised softly. "I live for your touch and the time we spend together."

Trey's heart raced at the sincerity of her tone, and the coiled tension slowly drained from his body. He propped his head on one hand, watching her intently as he splayed the other on her abdomen.

"Do you hurt?" he asked, gently rubbing her stomach.

His caring tone warmed her. "A little."

"Can I get you anything? Pain pills?"

"I already took a couple aspirin," she said.

Trey didn't have much experience with this type of thing. "Do you need anything? Stuff from the drugstore?"

She smiled at him. Neither of them had a lot of practice in the area of communication, but they seemed to be doing all right. "Sallie was thoughtful enough to send a few supplies. I won't need anything this month."

He slid his hand up her body to caress her arm, shoulder and neck. "Sallie's a nice lady."

Happy to wallow in his tenderness, she asked for more information. "Tell me about her," she said. "Cade seemed a little annoyed when I suggested his secretary had great taste."

His grin was wicked as it flashed between the moonlight and shadows. "She's one of the few women who can't be swayed by Cade's charm. She annoys the hell out of him, but she's damned good at her job and more of an assistant than a secretary. He can't find anything she's not good at. She doesn't give him a clue about her personal life, yet she helps him juggle his personal and professional schedules. It drives him crazy."

"Cade needs a friend and lover who can love him for the person inside the gorgeous facade."

Trey growled low in his throat and leaned fully over her. He propped his arms on either side of her head, and his tone dropped an octave. "You think Cade's gorgeous?"

She held his gaze as his head dipped and their breaths mingled. "I used to think he was the most attractive man in the world," she teased, eyes sparkling, "but then I met his big brother."

Taking his face in her hands, she let her gaze roam over his beloved features. "He can't hold a candle to you," she whispered huskily. "I missed you so much."

Pride kept him from asking why she hadn't come to him if she'd missed him so much. Instead, he asked the question that had tormented him for two years. "Did you meet plenty of men willing to take my place?"

She outlined his lips with one finger. "There were times when I thought I'd die with wanting," she admitted gruffly. "Times when I wanted someone to hold me, kiss me, love me. But no one else would do. I only wanted you."

He caught her finger between his teeth, and then caressed it with his tongue. His throat was too tight to push a word past it. He wanted to believe she was telling the truth, but it was too good to be true. She may not have had sex with anyone else, but there had to have been men who hounded her.

"Have there been lots of women?" she asked when he didn't immediately comment.

Trey's eyes narrowed. Was she jealous? She'd always claimed to be as possessive as he was, but he doubted it. "Does it really matter?" he asked, not ready to admit that her rejection had left him numb for two years.

"It matters," she replied softly, "but it doesn't change the way I feel about you. I never expected you to live like a monk."

"A monk would have found my life pretty dull," he said, brushing a kiss across her lips.

His admission prompted a confession from her. "We hadn't been parted for a month before I was ready to come running back to you, you know." She watched his eyes narrow in disbelief. "I'd just finished my first major assignment and instead of feeling suitably elated, I mostly felt lonely. I decided to call you and beg you to let me come to New Mexico."

Trey had gone very still. His eyes bored into hers and his vocal cords barely functioned. "What stopped you?"

"Nothing. I did call, but you always seemed so distant. The last couple times I called, your housekeeper said you were on dates. I got mad, even if I had no reason or right to. I imagined you with other women, and I decided you weren't missing me half as much as I was missing you."

Trey groaned, wondering if a little bad timing had added years to their separation. "There were no other serious relationships. Just casual dates. And you never left a number where you could be reached."

She knew it was time to explain how she'd felt back then. He might never accept her reasoning, but she wanted to try and make him understand. "I guess I lost the courage, and I was a little ashamed of my dependence on you. I'd spent most of my life preparing for a career and waiting for the chance to spread my wings. My friends used to say I'd throw it all away when the right man came along, but I never believed it. Then you came along. I guess it was hard to accept the fact that I *would* give it all up for you."

"So you stayed away for two years to prove that nobody had the power to change your mind?" he asked, his tone harsh.

Jillian searched his face, looking for a clue to what he was feeling. "It was never really about my career or need for independence," she insisted firmly. "It was a matter of trust. You said you were supportive of my career, but then you objected to the first big assignment I was offered. You didn't trust me. You turned into a jealous tyrant and said some pretty terrible things. You were just as guilty as I was for the breakup."

"You didn't have to accept an assignment from an old lover!"

"You know he wasn't my lover. You know you were my first and only lover," she countered, tightening her hold on him when he started to shift away.

"I have a little pride, too," she insisted. "What was I supposed to do? Did you think I should come crawling back and beg your forgiveness when you were the one who told me to get lost?"

"You know I didn't mean it."

"I know we both lost our tempers. And I know I'm the one who finally came crawling back. I'm the one who called and begged to see you."

"Then didn't show," he snarled, remembering the humiliation of waiting all those hours in a hotel room...waiting in vain and getting more furious by the minute.

"I wanted to!" she cried softly. "I really wanted to come to Dallas. That was not my fault. January was when all hell broke loose on the Gardova case. I couldn't keep our date."

"You could have called."

"I didn't want you involved."

"I'm involved now."

"Because I ended up crawling to you anyway."

Trey heaved a heavy sigh. The debate was a waste of time. The past was dead.

"You didn't exactly come of your own free will. You were desperate," he reminded grimly. "What do you plan to do next? Have you given the situation more thought now that Gardova is dead?"

Jillian didn't want to respond. She'd felt some relief at the knowledge that the drug lord could no longer hurt her, but it would be a long time before she completely recovered from the whole nightmare. Her intention was to suppress any thoughts of murder and violence. This was the first time Trey had mentioned the future, but the questions weren't ones she wanted to answer.

"Gardova's death doesn't change how I feel. I don't want to think about anything but spending time with you."

"Does that mean you've decided to let me make all your decisions for you? Are you ready to give up your independence and trust me?"

She knew it was hard for him to believe, but she was willing to let him take control of her life. She'd made a miserable mess of it so far. All she knew was that she didn't want to think about a future without him.

"I just want to stay here with you."

"You're satisfied to let the rest of the world think you're dead?" he challenged, cupping her face in his palm. "You know you can't deny the truth much longer. You needed a refuge, and I'm glad you came to me, but you can't plan a future without facing the past."

Her jaw tightened. Was he suggesting that she had to go back to Miami and testify before she'd be welcome in his home on a long-term basis? Did he think she was unworthy of his love until she'd done her civic duty? Was his old-fashioned code of ethics being challenged by her refusal to cooperate with the authorities?

"Are you issuing me an ultimatum?" she demanded, pulling free of his touch.

"No," he said without elaborating. Then he asked, "Can you let me make the decisions for you without considering me a threat? Do you trust me to protect you and do what's best for you?"

"Of course I trust you. You're welcome to make all my decisions because I'm sick and tired of being independent. I'm not willing to risk more mistakes and maybe my life."

She sounded sincere, but he knew as soon as her self-confidence returned, her independent nature would also resurface. All he could do was take care of her until then.

"Something has to be done about Stroyer," he reminded her, knowing she wasn't going to like it.

Jillian caught a quick breath and her mouth went dry. Her heart pounded so heavily that it hurt. She just couldn't think about facing Stroyer.

Something inside of her went numb with fear every time she thought of returning to Miami.

"He's still recuperating," Trey explained, "so he'll be laid up in the hospital a few weeks. But you're the only one who can bring him to justice."

"No." Jillian put her hands over her ears. Her thoughts and emotions were in total chaos. She'd been afraid for so long. She'd seen so much injustice that she couldn't imagine righting all the wrongs, and she didn't even want to try. She refused to consider leaving here and going back to face all the horror.

He gently pried her hands from her ears. "I didn't say you have to do anything right now," he assured her softly. "Just let me worry about it."

She let her hands drop and gave him an unblinking stare. Something inside of her went cold and dead every time she thought about returning to Miami.

"Do you trust me enough? Will you let me worry about making the decisions for a while?" Trey asked once more.

She didn't verbally respond, but slowly nodded her head in agreement.

"Good," he said. It wasn't the rousing vote of approval he'd hoped for, but it was a beginning. He dropped a kiss on her mouth and shifted to her side.

"Now we'd better get some sleep. I have buyers coming early tomorrow to look at some horses. Do you want to meet them?"

She wasn't quite ready to accept normalcy in her life again. She'd been wary too long. "I'd rather not meet anyone else right now. I can help Wayne or work inside while you talk to the buyers."

Trey hadn't expected her to welcome strangers. "You're sure you don't mind helping with the work?"

He'd asked her the same question at least a hundred times. "I don't mind," she told him.

They both settled more comfortably in the bed and conversation dwindled to an occasional remark and response until he fell asleep.

Jillian stared at the ceiling for a long time as she listened to his steady breathing. The sound reassured her, but their discussion had stirred up haunting memories. She knew if she closed her eyes, she'd see all the disturbing images again. She kept her eyes open as long as possible before succumbing to sleep.

Trey awoke several hours later to the sound of Jillian's whimpers. He reached for her immediately, drawing her close and reassuring her until the effects of her nightmare had lessened. A wave of guilt washed over him. He knew he was responsible for this nightmare.

As he tried to comfort her, he silently vowed to find a way to end the nightmares, even if it meant forcing her to confront her fears. Anything he might do was an emotional gamble. The solutions to her problems could ultimately jeopardize their relationship, yet he didn't want her to live in fear for the rest of her life.

He'd hoped that her being with him would make her feel safe and protected, but it wasn't enough. As long as her conscience refused to let her forget what she'd seen, she would never be free of the bad dreams. She'd convinced herself it was best to hide, but it wasn't in her nature to ignore such gross injustice.

His last thought before falling asleep again was that he had to find a way to help her without alienating her. It wasn't going to be easy. She wouldn't thank him for interfering, but she had given him permission to make the painful decisions.

෨෬

Jillian slept late the next morning and the sun was pouring over the bed before she awoke. She was alone and the house was quiet. She rose from bed and went to the bathroom, then reentered the bedroom at the sound of the telephone.

She never answered the phone. There was an answering machine, so she had no reason to worry about Trey missing an important call. The machine clicked on, and she heard Cade's voice.

"Jillian, it's Cade," he said. "If you're in the house, pick up the phone. I need to talk to you."

She hesitated, then moved to Trey's desk and slowly picked up the receiver. "Cade?"

"Good morning," he responded lightly. "I was hoping to catch you in the house. Is Trey there?"

"Not right now. I just woke up, but I think he's outside already."

"Good," said Cade. "I didn't want him to hear me. Did you know he has a birthday this week?"

"No," she said, feeling a rush of relief. She was wary of any discussions with Cade, but she didn't mind talking about Trey. "I had no idea." How could she not know such a basic detail about her lover?

"He'll be thirty-two on Wednesday. I forgot to tell you while I was out there this weekend, and he'll probably forget it unless somebody reminds him. I won't be able to make it to the ranch, but I have a package for him in my room. Would you mind giving it to him for me?"

"No, of course not," she replied. "I don't have a gift, but I can bake a cake and cook a nice dinner."

There was a smile in Cade's voice when he responded. "I have a feeling he'll like that more than anything else. There's a small wine cellar in the basement. Chill a bottle of champagne, and I guarantee my brother will enjoy his birthday."

"I'll do my best," she promised, her mind already whirling with ideas. She wanted to treat Trey to a really special evening. "Thanks for letting me know."

"You're welcome," he joked. Then his tone grew more serious. "I love my brother, Jillian. He's all the family I have, and his happiness is important to me."

"I understand," she replied, "I want him to be happy, too. You don't have to worry about me hurting him again. I swear that on my life."

Cade's sigh was heavy. "I believe you. I just hope the two of you can make a go of it this time. The last couple years have been hard on him." He didn't mention that his brother had nearly gone crazy without the woman he loved.

"I'm trying," was all she could say to reassure him. "I don't know if he'll ever forgive me for leaving him in the first place, but I'm trying very hard to make him understand and put it behind us."

"So far, I'd say you're batting a thousand," said Cade. "His package is in my bedroom closet. It's wrapped and has a card. I'll call him late Wednesday evening."

They said goodbye, and Jillian hung up the phone. She glanced out the window toward the barns, searching for Trey. A smile lit her eyes when she saw him talking with Wayne. Her mind was already whirling with plans for his birthday. She'd have a romantic, candlelight dinner with all the trimmings.

The thought of a gift made her move to the bedside stand where she kept her wallet. Along with her driver's license and credit cards, she had forty dollars in cash. She had no desire to go shopping, but maybe she could coax Wayne or one of the other men to make a trip to town for her.

Chapter Nine

Jillian spent the first part of the week outdoors helping the men with ranch work. By Wednesday, their dry, sunny weather came to a halt and it rained most of the day, which gave her a good excuse to stay in the house. She fixed lunch for Trey, then really got busy when he went back to work in the afternoon.

She knew he had a weakness for Boston cream pie, so she made one from scratch with the help of Mrs. Cooper's cookbook. She marinated steaks and planned a dinner of all his favorite foods. It took hours to get things just right, but she worked steadily until everything was perfectly timed.

After setting the table and putting a bottle of champagne on ice, she took a shower, washed her hair and put on one of the dresses Sallie had sent. It was sunshine yellow with a bold floral design that looked just right for a birthday celebration.

The dress had a wide, white collar around a square neckline and short, puffy sleeves that looked very feminine. The fit was good, and Jillian was pleased with the overall style. Using some of the bobby pins Sallie had sent, she even managed to secure her hair in a fashionable topknot that seemed appropriate for a party.

By the time Trey entered the house that evening, the kitchen was filled with appetizing aromas. Candles flickered on the table, and champagne was chilling. Jillian greeted him with a wide, welcoming smile.

"Happy birthday," she said.

He tossed his hat on the hook and kicked off his muddy boots, but his gaze never left her, taking in every inch of her beauty from high-heeled sandals to the blush on her cheeks. He sensed more than saw everything she'd done to prepare for dinner. His eyes darkened with pleasure, but he warded her off with strong hands when she would have launched herself against him.

"I'm filthy, and you're perfect," he declared. "Let me go get cleaned up. Then I'll greet you properly."

Jillian rose on tiptoe and gave him a quick kiss. "Dinner will be ready in ten minutes. Hurry," she insisted.

Trey stole one more swift kiss, and then headed for his bedroom. Jillian busied herself with the finishing touches for their meal. She tuned the radio to a station that featured romantic ballads and soft love songs. She wanted everything to be perfect by the time he returned.

Her eyes lit with pleasure at the sight of him. He'd dressed in navy cotton slacks and a pale blue, knit shirt that molded to his broad shoulders and chest. Somehow, the more fashionable attire made him seem more primitively appealing.

His hair was damp from his shower, his dark eyes smoldered with pleasure and he exuded an aura of raw masculinity. The kiss he gave her made her tingle from head to toe. It was a wrench to resist deepening the kiss and turn their attention to dinner.

"Everything smells delicious," Trey told her. He held her chair until she was seated, then sat down himself.

Jillian had already put everything on the table so that she could enjoy the meal with him. She managed to keep their conversation light and cheerful. Trey shared details of his day while music played softly in the background. The lights were low, but the vanilla-scented candles burned brightly. Throughout their dinner, they were cocooned in an intimate, sensually stimulating atmosphere.

When they'd finished their main courses, Jillian poured the champagne and cut two pieces of cake. Then she amazed and delighted Trey by singing "Happy Birthday" to him before feeding him bites of dessert.

They finished their cake with a great deal of teasing and laughter. When they were too full to eat another bite, she insisted that he enjoy his champagne while she cleaned up the table. Trey didn't argue. He leaned back in his chair and kept his gaze glued to her as she moved around the room. After the dishwasher was loaded and the kitchen tidy again, she presented him with Cade's gift.

"So, my brother's the one who squealed about my birthday," he said, then laughed when he read Cade's card. "It's a warning about my advanced age," he explained, handing her the card to read. When he opened the package, he enthused over the new pair of Western boots his brother had chosen for him.

"Cade called earlier in the week. He couldn't come out to celebrate with you, so I told him I'd do my best to see that you had a nice birthday."

"One of the best," he assured her, returning the boots to the box and reaching for her.

She dodged his hand and went to the pantry where she'd put her gift. When she returned to the kitchen, she handed him a long florist's box, feeling slightly nervous about his reaction.

Trey's eyes lit with surprise and curiosity as he pulled the ribbon from the oblong box. Then they darkened with pleasure as he uncovered a dozen ruby-red roses. He lifted them from the tissue paper and inhaled their sweet, heavy scent. His gaze trapped Jillian's.

"Nobody's ever given me flowers," he declared in a voice gone low and husky. It was a sensitive, romantic gesture, reminiscent of the idyllic time they'd spent together when they'd first fallen in love.

"Do you like them?" she asked anxiously.

He smelled the roses again, inhaling deeply, and then laid them in their cradle of tissue. The smile he gave her left no doubt about how much he liked her gift.

"I like 'em a lot," he said, standing to slowly draw her into his embrace. Then he thanked her with a long, deep, wine-flavored kiss.

Their tongues met, warm and wet and seeking. Jillian put her arms around his neck and returned his kiss with a fervor that soon had them both trembling with suppressed desire. It seemed like an eternity since they'd made love, and the timing still wasn't right, but she wasn't going to let her monthly condition dampen his birthday party.

Jillian had a plan. It was bold and daring. She was a little apprehensive, but the feel of his hard body pressing against her stomach gave her courage. She wanted tonight to be a celebration he'd remember for a long time.

She began her seduction by sucking his tongue deeply into her mouth and thrusting her hips as tightly against his as she could manage while standing. Trey moaned and drew her closer. She rubbed against him provocatively.

"Jillian," he rumbled as their mouths parted and his lips scored her face and neck with hot kisses. His chest rose against hers, and his breathing grew rough.

"I want to make this a special birthday." She lifted the hem of his shirt so that she could caress his chest with damp lips. Her tongue tangled in tight curls and then her teeth gently clenched around taut nipples.

Trey's breath poured out in an agonized groan. He heard the blood pounding in his ears, and he let go of her long enough to shrug out of his shirt.

He'd missed her desperately this week, and the longing was much more complicated than abstinence from sex. He missed the sweet, possessive satisfaction of being a part of her, being as close as he could be, making her a part of him. He missed the closeness.

Before he could recapture her in his arms, she'd bent her knees and was sliding wet kisses down his body. Her fingers found the snap and zipper of his pants, and she loosened the fasteners, then exposed more hard flesh to her wandering caresses.

A groan rose from deep in Trey's chest. A hot, aching heaviness filled his loins as blood rushed through him with quicksilver speed. His hands clutched her head when he felt her first hesitant touch on his straining flesh.

"Jillian!" His cry was an agony of need as her caresses grew bolder and his legs grew weaker.

"Jillian!" he moaned, his tone hoarse and heavy with need. He shut his eyes and clenched his jaw. The pleasure was too savagely intense. It made him weak and shaky. His first instinct was to fight the overwhelming eruption of desire.

Jillian wouldn't allow it. She continued to ravage his control with her tender, but ardent loving. He couldn't have held back even if he'd wanted to. He endured the exquisite torture for what seemed an eternity before the unbearable tension snapped, and his control shattered into a million pieces.

His body convulsed, and his knees buckled. He leaned his back against the wall for support, and then slid to the floor, weak and shaky. It was several long minutes before he could speak.

"Where the hell did you learn how to do that?" His voice was a low murmur.

She smiled at his tone. He sounded both awed and jealous at the same time. "I'm not totally ignorant," she whispered. "You're a great teacher, and I learn fast."

His skin nearly sizzled from the intense heat her touch generated. "I'd better be the first and only man you ever love like that," he insisted roughly, resting against the wall and drawing her into the circle of his arms.

She tilted her face toward his. "First and only," she promised softly. "Everything I've learned about loving comes from you. I wanted to show you how special I think you are."

"You're the one who's special." He wouldn't have thought it possible, but he found her more beguiling every time they were together.

"I love you," she managed to whisper past a suddenly tight throat. Her gaze locked with his and the love she professed shone from their emerald depths.

All the breath left Trey's body. A sound rumbled in his throat, but no words escaped. He dragged her closer and hugged her with every ounce of strength he possessed, easing his grip only when the tremors stopped quaking over his body.

Jillian was devastated when he didn't return the words. She couldn't help feeling hurt and rejected. She knew his feelings for her ran deeper than passion and desire, but it would obviously take more time to regain his complete trust. She was willing to wait for as long as it took. In the meantime, she intended to lavish him with attention.

"How about some more champagne?" she asked after he'd regained his composure. She slowly disengaged herself from his arms, rose to her feet and offered him a hand.

Trey let her help him to his feet, and then pulled her close for a swift kiss. "You go to the living room." he said. "I'll be with you in a minute, and I'll bring the wine."

She went without another word. Trey watched her leave the kitchen with his heart pounding heavily in his chest. The feelings she evoked scared the hell out of him. He'd loved her once, and it had almost destroyed him. He couldn't let it happen again. He told himself that all he felt now was obsessive possessiveness, but he wasn't sure he believed himself anymore.

She'd found a music special on television, and was curled up on the sofa when he joined her in the living room. She accepted a glass of champagne and a kiss. He sat close to her and draped his left arm around her shoulders.

He watched her over the rim of his glass. "I have a hard time keeping my hands off you," he stated conversationally.

Her eyes danced with delight. "You won't hear me complaining."

Trey drew her close enough to lick the wine from her lips with the tip of his tongue. When her mouth opened on a shaky breath, he penetrated the tasty barrier and engaged her tongue in a slow, sensuous dance.

"You go to my head," she charged when he finally withdrew from the kiss. "You're more potent than the champagne."

"Good." He wanted her just as intoxicated by him as he was by her. "I want to make you feel the way you make me feel."

"How's that?"

"Unique and important," Trey told her in a careful, measured tone. "Unique, important, strong, sexy, special."

"You are all those things," she insisted, her eyes adoring, "plus beautiful, gentle and passionate."

Trey grinned. He didn't agree with her, but he swelled with pleasure at her praise. "You sound just a little bit prejudiced."

"I'm allowed to be, because I have an intimate knowledge of your finer qualities," she argued, loving the sound of his husky laughter.

She raised her glass for a toast. "To your special day, with many happy returns."

They touched glasses lightly, and then twined their arms to drink from the wine goblets. The smiles they shared were lover's smiles, intimate and adoring.

The ringing of the telephone shattered the mood. Trey reluctantly dragged himself from Jillian's side and answered it.

"Langden."

"Hey, big brother, happy birthday."

"Hey, little brother, thanks for the boots. It's about time I started breaking in a new pair."

"I know that. Since it takes you about two years to break a pair in, I thought you'd better get at it."

The sound of Trey's happy, relaxed laughter pleased Cade. "Jillian said she was going to fix a special dinner for you. It sounds like you've been enjoying the evening."

"Yeah," was Trey's only reply, but he conveyed a wealth of emotion with the one word. His gaze rested on Jillian, and heat raced over his body as he thought of how much he'd been enjoying his birthday.

Cade laughed. "Damn, but I envy you."

"Every man should be so lucky," Trey told him, thinking of Jillian's warmth and generosity. "She bought me roses."

"Roses?" Cade repeated, surprised. "Nobody ever gave me flowers.

"Me, either, until tonight." Trey's deep satisfaction was evident in his tone. She'd given him much more, and he promised himself to give it all back to her with interest. As soon as she was able, he intended to love her like she'd never been loved. He wouldn't be satisfied until she was sobbing with pleasure.

"Trey, are you still with me?" Cade asked when his brother was quiet for so long.

"I'm here," said Trey as he dragged his attention back to their conversation. "I got a little distracted."

"By Jillian and the champagne, I'll bet."

"You'd win."

"How about giving me your full attention for a minute? I have something important I need to talk to you about."

Trey didn't really want to let anything pierce the golden haze of satisfaction he was feeling, but he recognized the seriousness of his brother's tone. "What's up?"

"I've had my men checking on Lieutenant Mitchell for a couple of weeks. He seems genuinely concerned about Jillian, and he's getting desperate for some evidence against Stroyer. Apparently, he knows he's dirty, but he needs proof. I think he can be trusted. What do you think?"

Trey didn't respond immediately. Jillian was approaching him and offering to take his empty glass. As soon as she'd headed for the kitchen, he breathed a heavy sigh of resignation. He knew the time was coming to make decisions, but he didn't like it.

"Have your men get word to Mitchell through the Miami vice detective. Let him know that she's alive and well, but not interested in testifying. Make sure she can't be traced through your people, then watch for a while and see what he does with the information."

Cade knew it was the right thing to do, but he hated the heaviness that had entered Trey's voice. "Have you discussed this with her?"

"Yeah, but she wasn't any more receptive than the first time it was mentioned."

155

"If this is going to cause you a lot of trouble with her, you can lay the blame on me," Cade offered.

"Thanks, but she said she trusts me to make the decisions. She may never speak to me again, but she's a prisoner of her own fear until this case is settled. I have to help her get past it before she can be rid of the nightmares."

"Right, and we're running out of time," Cade added. "Stroyer might be released from the hospital in another week. He could be on crutches and back on the job in three weeks if charges aren't brought against him. He could hire other dirty cops to do his dirty work or he could try to flee the country altogether."

Trey's sigh bordered on a groan.

Cade wished he could ease his brother's concern. "We'll protect her, Trey. I swear it on my life."

"I believe you. She's not going anywhere or talking to anyone without me by her side, either, but that won't keep her from being terrified."

Jillian reentered the room, and Trey managed a smile for her. He didn't want her to realize she'd been the topic of their conversation, so he changed the subject.

"Will you be out this weekend?" he asked.

"I'm not sure yet. How's the new help working out?"

"They're doing fine. Wayne says they're good men, and they've cut my work load."

"Our security men say everything's quiet," Cade told him. "Nobody's supposed to know they're watching the place, but all you have to do is call and they'll come running."

"Thanks."

Cade realized Trey didn't want to say too much in front of Jillian, so he did the talking. "I'll call as soon as I've contacted Mitchell."

"Sounds good," said Trey. "Did you thank Sallie for Jillian?"

Cade snorted. "I thanked the ice maiden, but she was upset because she'd forgotten to include something in Jillian's wardrobe. She's going to send it in the mail."

"In the mail?"

"I asked her, but she wouldn't part with details. You should have whatever it is by tomorrow."

Trey laughed at the disgust in his brother's tone. Sallie really had a knack for getting under his skin.

"I'd better let you get back to your birthday party. I'm sorry to have interrupted the celebration."

"That's okay," Trey insisted. "I'm sorry you didn't get a chance to share the Boston cream pie and champagne."

A groan came across the line. "Jillian made Boston cream pie? Do you think she'd like to come live with me?"

"Get your own woman, little brother, but thanks again for the boots."

Trey hung up the phone and headed for the sofa and Jillian. She looked especially feminine and appealing as she smiled up at him and handed him another glass of wine.

"What's Cade up to?" she asked.

"He wants you to come live with him," he explained before giving her a long, slow, possessive kiss. "I told him to find his own woman," he mumbled against her mouth.

Her lips curved in a smile, and he decided to spend the rest of his birthday memorizing each of her smiling features with his mouth.

ဆာ

The rain continued throughout the night, and it was past noon on Thursday before the sun finally peeked through the clouds. Jillian immediately grabbed her camera and set out to capture the rain-drenched world on film.

She lost all track of time until the sun began to set, and then she felt the need to capture that on film, as well.

It was almost dark by the time she returned to the house. Trey had been warned that their evening meal might be late, but she was greeted at the door by the smell of chili. Her stomach growled.

"Smells good in here," she declared as she shed her jacket. She moved into the kitchen, put down her camera and went to the sink to wash her hands.

"I just warmed the leftover chili you had frozen," he explained, motioning her to take a seat while he served their dinner.

Jillian didn't argue. She was hungry, and he had everything ready to eat. They enjoyed their meal in relative silence, then shared details of their day over cups of steaming coffee and leftover birthday cake.

"I got some really great shots today," Jillian told him, her tone filled with enthusiasm. "There's one of a colt who slipped on the wet grass and looked totally amazed when his feet flew in every direction. I got some shots of the men sloshing around in mud puddles, and some really terrific angles on a shimmering rainbow and a gorgeous sunset."

Jillian had always looked radiant when she discussed her work. Trey loved watching her eyes light with excitement and enthusiasm over the smallest things. She managed to find beauty wherever she looked. Everything fascinated her, from the smallest insect and flower to great expanses of the sun and moon.

"When you're done with your cake, I have a surprise for you," he told her, finishing the last bite of his dessert.

Her eyes grew wide. "A surprise? How come? It's not my birthday."

"You don't have to have a birthday to get a surprise. This is an un-birthday treat."

She forked the last of her cake into her mouth and washed it down with her coffee. "Okay," she declared. "I'm finished."

He just laughed, rose from the table and took her hand in his. He led her through the hallway to a large, walk-in closet. He opened the door, and then stepped aside so that Jillian could investigate.

"It's a darkroom!" she exclaimed in delight. "But how did you do this? I never saw anyone bring supplies."

"I ordered everything from Albuquerque, and the distributor sent a couple of men out to handle the basic construction. They did it all this afternoon."

"It's wonderful!" she enthused, examining every inch of the converted closet. "I have everything I need to start developing. I can't wait! I have so many great shots I'm anxious to see." When she was satisfied that the darkroom was perfect, she came out of the closet and threw her arms around Trey. "Thank you, thank you, thank you," she cried between noisy kisses. "You are an absolute sweetheart!"

He slipped his arms around her waist and drew her closer, then caught her mouth for a long, satisfying kiss.

"There's more," he told her, rubbing his nose gently against hers.

"Another surprise?"

"Uh-huh."

"What is it?"

"It'll cost you a big, fat kiss."

Jillian tightened her arms around his neck and locked her mouth with his until seconds stretched to minutes, and they were both gasping for air.

"Will that do?" she asked breathlessly.

"Yeah," he approved. He picked up a large envelope from a table in the hallway and handed it to her. "Cade said Sallie forgot an important part of your wardrobe, and she was mailing it to you. The package is addressed to me, but I think it's your missing wardrobe item."

Her brows furrowed as she studied the square, padded envelope. It didn't look big enough or fat enough to hold any clothing. "Underwear?" she guessed.

"I don't know, but the curiosity is driving me wild."

Jillian grinned and carefully opened the envelope. She reached inside and pulled out the top of a very skimpy white bikini. A pair of tiny bottoms and a sheer cover-up were also packed in the mailer.

Trey whistled expressively. "The lady certainly has good taste," he declared, studying the little scraps of fabric. He could already envision Jillian wearing them.

"There's a note," she told him as she glanced inside the envelope. "It has your name on it."

He read the brief message. "She said she's sorry she forgot about our pool. Since the weather is improving, she didn't want my guest to be without swimwear."

"I might still be without swimwear," Jillian insisted. "I hate to sound ungrateful, but I don't think this bikini was made for strenuous exercise of any kind."

Laughter rumbled from Trey. His expression lit with mischief. "Whoever designs these things must be men. I'll bet it's completely transparent when it's wet. I can't wait. I might have to clean and fill the pool right away just to see you model it."

Jillian tried to imagine her body in the two scraps of fabric. She'd definitely be more exposed than covered. A sudden image of her naked body brought to mind the ugly scar on her right side. She frowned, but quickly dipped her head to hide it.

Not fast enough to hide her reaction from Trey. He slid a finger under her chin and lifted her face to his. "What brought on the frown?"

She tried to make light of the matter. "Vanity," she teased. "I'm not sure I can do justice to this little outfit. Besides, I'm getting all kinds of strange tan lines. I might look like a clown instead of a bathing beauty."

"Maybe what you need to do is some nude sunbathing," he declared suggestively.

The thought brought another crease to her forehead. "I'd better wait awhile before I attempt anything that bold." She wasn't a vain person, but she

160

wasn't ready to exhibit her far-from-perfect body. Exposing the scar to the light of day would seem like a blatant advertisement of her brush with death.

"You're allowed to be bold with me, remember?" he taunted playfully. "And I'm not about to let anyone else within a mile of you when you're wearing that little number."

His teasing brought a wry smile to her face. "Your possessive tendencies are showing, Mr. Langden."

"I'm working on toning them down," he muttered, pulling her toward him and rocking his hips against the softness of her stomach.

She stopped scolding. "Thank you for the darkroom," she said as she pressed a kiss on the darkening stubble of his chin. "I can't wait to get started."

Trey captured her mouth with his for another kiss, and then set her away from him. "Why don't you go ahead and start some developing. I have to make a call to my tax accountant, so I could be tied up most of the evening. I won't feel guilty if you're busy testing your equipment."

Jillian was hesitant. "You're sure you won't mind? I have a bad habit of getting lost in my work for hours at a time," she warned.

"I don't mind. I'll just come pound on the door if it gets too late or I get too lonely."

Her smile was brilliant. After giving him one last, swift kiss, she dashed to the bedroom to collect the rolls of film she'd already shot. Then she made a more serious study of the darkroom and the wide assortment of supplies. Getting everything in order was a labor of love.

Chapter Ten

Cade didn't make it to the ranch over the weekend, but Trey had enough help that his time wasn't completely taken up with chores. He made time to go riding with Jillian and show her the areas of the ranch that were more accessible by horseback than truck.

Some of the land had an untouched look that made her catch her breath at its wild beauty. Everything on the west side of Langden property was framed by distant mountains, and she used several rolls of film trying to capture the natural grandeur of the area.

Trey had often wondered if Jillian could view his heritage with the same affinity and fierce pride he felt for the land. Seeing it through her eyes was a pleasure more intense than he could have imagined. She loved every aspect of the untamed land and wasn't shy about expressing her delight and enthusiasm.

More and more each day, he felt her opening up to emotion again. As her confidence returned, the nightmares diminished. He knew he was running out of time. Soon he would have to bring up the subject of bringing charges against Stroyer. But he didn't have the heart to destroy her newfound contentment, nor was he ready to risk losing her.

Cade called on Saturday evening while Jillian was taking a shower. He told Trey that Lieutenant Mitchell had been cautiously optimistic about the rumors that she was alive. He was making a media appeal all over Florida in an effort to reach Jillian. He promised her round-the-clock protection by a team of his most-trusted agents.

"I want to contact him personally," Cade said. "I think we can trust him, and the only way we'll know for sure is to make the contact and see if anything goes wrong. I can increase the security at the ranch until we're sure."

Trey knew Cade was right. They would never know who could be trusted until they supplied bait for a trap. He just didn't like Jillian being the bait.

"If Mitchell can't be trusted, then the first place they'll hit is my Dallas apartment," Cade continued. "My security will be tight, and I can let you know the minute Jillian's safety is at risk. You'll have plenty of time to get her off the ranch if we think there's any danger."

Trey ran a hand through his hair in agitation. He didn't like going against Jillian's wishes, yet she didn't show any signs of facing the problem on her own. They couldn't keep on pretending everything was all right, and they couldn't really plan for the future until they'd come to terms with her past.

"Contact Mitchell," he decided. "Let me know his reaction and everything he says. If he sounds the least bit hostile or unsympathetic, tell him to go to hell, and I'll get Jillian out of here."

Cade knew the decision was a hard one for his brother to make. "It's the right thing to do," he assured him.

"I know, but I still don't like it."

"My men tell me everything's been quiet out there except for the guys who came to set up the darkroom."

"They didn't even see her."

"How does she like it?"

Trey laughed. "Wait till you get here and see what she's been doing. Jillian is making an album with photos of every ranch hand and head of livestock on the property."

"Did she get her package from my super-efficient executive assistant?"

"Since when is Sallie an executive assistant? Or is that just a new name for secretary?"

"In some cases, but in her case, it's because she's handling more and more of the executive workload. I offered her a vice-presidency, but she declined. She did accept a new title and a raise. So, you got the latest package?"

"Yeah," he said, smiling at the memory of the tiny bikini Sallie had sent.

"That sounds like a very satisfied 'yeah.' What was it?"

"I'll never tell, and you'll never see it, baby brother," Trey taunted.

"Damn," Cade said in disgust, "nobody ever tells me anything."

"Ask Sallie."

"She begrudges me the time of day."

"Charm her a little," Trey suggested, grinning at the thought. "Buy her some flowers, pay her a few compliments, take her out to dinner."

"And have her breathing fire for a week?" Cade grumbled in disgust. "Every time I try to do anything nice for the woman, she turns into a fire-breathing dragon."

Trey roared with laughter. He couldn't help enjoying Cade's predicament. His little brother had been completely spoiled by women for too many years. Sallie never failed to keep him in line.

"Go ahead, laugh," Cade snapped. "Have a real good laugh. Hell, laugh all damned night at my expense. I'm hanging up the phone. Goodbye."

Trey continued to chuckle after the receiver went dead. He hung up the phone and listened for the shower, but realized that Jillian must be done. He'd showered earlier and was waiting for her to get ready for bed. The thought caused a ripple of excitement.

It had been a week since he'd made love to her, and he ached with need, but he didn't intend to hurry tonight. He wanted to take his time and drive her crazy.

He tapped on the bathroom door, and then pushed it open. Steam enveloped him along with the sweet, womanly scent that was Jillian. Her hair was damp and falling over her bare shoulders. She wasn't wearing anything but a towel. That didn't bother him, because he was wearing less.

"Are you a little impatient?" she teased. A thrill of anticipation quivered along her nerve endings.

"I'm dying," he retorted.

Her laugh was husky and confident. "Because you're totally exhausted and need a good night's sleep?"

"Because I need my woman."

Heat rocked through her at his blatant declaration, and her pupils dilated as he moved closer and released the knot on her towel.

"You won't need this," Trey said, tossing it aside. He scooped her into his arms and carried her to the bedroom.

He'd already turned back the covers. Her eyes darkened more, and her pulse raced with excitement as he lowered her onto a bed blanketed with hundreds of scarlet petals from a dozen red roses. The scent was as intoxicating as that of the man leaning over her.

"I love the roses," he explained. "Now I want to feel and smell them on you."

The petals were satin smooth and some clung to her damp skin. Their sweet fragrance engulfed Jillian, and she knew she'd never smell another rose without visualizing Trey's primitive beauty as he slowly lowered himself to her, suppressed desire evident in every inch of his strong body.

She slid her arms from his neck and stroked his chest. "You'll get no arguments from me, big boy."

ഗര

Trey didn't hear from Cade until the middle of the following week. He was working at his desk while Jillian worked in the darkroom, so he didn't have to worry about her overhearing their telephone conversation.

"I have some bad news," Cade told him.

"Let me have it."

Cade's tone was almost a growl. "The FBI had an eyewitness who saw Stroyer shoot Jillian. After she was shot, she stumbled against his taxi cab, and he got a good look at her."

"Why did you say 'had'? What happened to him?"

"He was killed in a hit-and-run accident. A couple days after he gave his statement to Mitchell."

Trey swore violently. Stroyer had been hospitalized with two broken legs, so he couldn't have been responsible. "You think Mitchell or someone in his agency was involved?"

"I think Mitchell is one frustrated cop. He thinks Stroyer has a partner— maybe a mole in their agency—but he doesn't have a clue."

"Damn it to hell!" snapped Trey. "We have to find out who's working with Stroyer or we can't risk bringing Jillian out of hiding."

"My men are working on it, but nobody has any idea who Stroyer's accomplice might be. He's a bachelor, doesn't have a girlfriend or family and keeps to himself."

"The man has to talk to somebody sometime."

"The only people he associates with are other agents, and none of them feel like they know him very well. All his phone calls are being monitored, but he hasn't contacted anybody outside the agency."

"So his partner has to be another agent."

"That's the way Mitchell sees it," said Cade. "He's watching everyone, but without success. He really needs to talk to Jillian. There's a chance she may know something important without realizing it. He wants a meeting. He's agreed to meet her anywhere we choose."

Trey ran a hand through his hair. "She won't leave the ranch. I tried to talk her into going to Albuquerque, and she won't even go that far."

Cade hesitated for a minute, and then said, "I could bring Mitchell to the ranch."

The suggestion seemed to hang heavily between them while Trey considered all the reasons for not allowing it. On the other hand, Jillian wouldn't willingly go anywhere else. Would she feel completely betrayed if they brought Mitchell here? She considered anyone outside the ranch family to be a threat. Would she accept him more readily if they met on her territory, or would she lose her sense of security and well-being?

"I don't know what to do."

"There's more bad news," Cade offered regretfully. "Stroyer is being released from the hospital next week. There's a preliminary hearing Monday, but the lieutenant doesn't think the written testimony from a dead taxi driver is enough evidence to make an attempted murder charge stick—especially since the victim has disappeared. Until he can flush out the partner, there's no hope of getting conspiracy or murder charges."

"He needs Jillian now." Trey's tone was grim.

"That's about the size of it. If he can't coax her back to Miami, he at least needs her testimony."

Trey swore again. There was no easy answer. Jillian needed to put the whole nightmare behind her. Stroyer and his partner belonged in jail. She had to face the truth and deal with it before more innocent people got killed.

"Bring Mitchell out here," he told Cade. Kregg had assured him that Mitchell could be trusted. "Wait until Friday night, and come out like you normally do."

"I was hoping you'd say that," Cade confessed, relieved. "I know it's not an easy decision, but it has to be done. It will be better for Jillian this way, and we'll both be there to take care of her."

"If she ever speaks to us again," said Trey, the strain evident in his voice.

Cade was silent for a moment. There wasn't anything he could say to make the decision easier for his brother. He was worried, but he knew Trey was both concerned and deeply in love with Jillian.

"I plan to get Mitchell to Dallas first. I won't even tell him our final destination until he meets me, and then I'll be watching him every minute. I'll make sure he doesn't call anybody and that nobody follows him."

"That's the best we can do."

"Are you going to tell Jillian?"

Trey considered the idea, and then rejected it. "No. There's no use upsetting her until it's absolutely necessary."

"It'll be a shock."

"Yeah, I know," Trey conceded. "I just hope she's recovered enough to accept the situation without panicking."

"Me, too," Cade added, not envying his brother's position. "I'd better go. I'll be later than usual Friday, so don't wait dinner on me. I'll call if plans change."

"Right," said Trey. "Goodbye."

"Bye."

After hanging up the phone, Trey stared unseeing at his desk. It was Wednesday evening already, and the fourth week since Jillian had come to the ranch. In less than forty-eight hours their relationship would take a dramatic turn. Would she be hurt beyond his ability to heal? Would she lose all faith in him? Would he lose her forever?

A soul-deep fear kept his muscles knotted with tension throughout the next couple of days. He rarely let Jillian out of his sight and made love to her as if each caress would be the last. He fought to keep the panic at bay each time she favored him with one of her beautiful smiles, or when she eagerly welcomed his body into her own.

There was no way of knowing how she'd react when Mitchell arrived, but his gut feeling wasn't good. He thought about preparing her, about trying to discuss the subject again, but couldn't bring himself to do it. He selfishly wanted more time before he had to face the consequences of his decision. And that time was running short.

Friday evening arrived all too soon. Trey's nerves were frayed as he waited for Cade and Mitchell. He and Jillian had finished their meal and cleared the dishes. He was still in the kitchen, but she was in the darkroom when the men finally pulled in the drive.

Trey went to the door of the porch. As soon as Mitchell stepped from Cade's car, his gaze locked on the agent. The other man had shed his tie, but was still wearing a suit. He was shorter than Cade's six feet, but his stature was straight, and his stride confident.

Cade introduced the two men at the door. Trey was satisfied with the strength of the other man's handshake. Their gazes locked, each scrutinizing and evaluating. After a brief minute, Trey ushered the lieutenant into the kitchen.

The agent appeared to be in his late forties or early fifties. He wasn't a big man, but he was solidly built, with an air of strength and dependability. His lined face and pale blue eyes showed the ravages of years of hard decisions.

"I appreciate this chance to speak to Ms. Brandt," Mitchell said. "I know you're not happy about the circumstances, but Stroyer has to pay."

Trey nodded in agreement. He stood with his back against the countertop while Cade and Mitchell took seats opposite him at the table.

"Anything new?" he asked.

The lieutenant glanced at Cade. "Your brother said he's been keeping you informed. Gardova's murder left us floundering for information on his contacts, but it frees Ms. Brandt from further threat at that level."

"Have you learned anything about Stroyer's partner?"

Mitchell's eyes flared with anger. "The only thing I know for sure is that the traitor has to be a trusted member of my department."

"Nobody knows where you are or why you're here?"

"No one."

"Where's Jillian?" Cade asked.

At nearly the same instant, they heard her calling Trey's name from the front of the house.

"She's been working in the darkroom," he explained.

"You're not going to believe this one," Jillian declared cheerfully, describing one of her photos. She thought they were alone in the house, and her voice grew stronger as she came down the hall. "I got a great shot of Wayne when that angry mama bird dive-bombed his hat."

Her words barely registered as blood pounded in Trey's ears. He hadn't thought it possible to get more tense, but her approach made every muscle in his body coil into knots of pain. He mentally and physically prepared himself for her reaction to Mitchell's presence.

Jillian's grin faded when she caught sight of Trey's solemn expression. As soon as she stepped through the kitchen doorway, she realized they weren't alone. Her gaze shot to Cade, then to the FBI agent.

Her heart stopped, and she went as still as a wild creature trapped by predators. All the blood drained from her face, and a chill invaded her body. Fear and panic briefly flashed in her eyes, but was swiftly replaced by a bone-numbing coldness that sent a chill over every occupant of the room.

After a few seconds of stunned silence, she turned from the table and fastened her gaze on Trey. The smile she gave him was completely devoid of warmth or humor. "And I thought you were beginning to forgive me. If you wanted me to leave, all you had to do was say so."

The accusation sliced through him like a knife, wounding him as nothing else could have done. She thought he'd called Mitchell to get even with her for rejecting him two years ago. *It's not true!* he wanted to shout, but he knew she wouldn't believe a denial.

Cade immediately tried to correct her, but Trey lifted a hand to halt his explanations. His gaze stayed locked with Jillian's.

"Gardova is dead and there's no bounty on your head, but Stroyer's hearing is Monday. We've learned that he's also responsible for the death of a man who witnessed your shooting. You can't let him get away with it."

Jillian remained as stiff as a board. She didn't even blink. "Can't I?"

"No."

They stared at each other for several highly charged seconds. Trey's regard was steady and unflinching. Jillian's was hard, her expression brittle. He watched her withdrawing into the cold, dark place where she hid when she was forced to deal with the difficult and traumatizing emotions.

"If you can't find the courage to return to Miami," Trey taunted quietly, though his heart was being squeezed by an iron fist, "then maybe you can provide information to help Mitchell get an indictment against Stroyer."

His barb went deep, but Jillian didn't show any signs of the pain she was experiencing. She turned to the agent. Her tone was cool and expressionless.

"What do you want to know, Lieutenant?"

The question brought inaudible sighs of relief from Mitchell and the Langdens. Her cooperation was the best they could hope for. Under the circumstances, it wouldn't have been surprising if she'd run screaming from the house or completely refused to cooperate.

"Let me tell you what I know, and then maybe you can fill in some of the blanks," he said. He motioned to a chair, but she shook her head in refusal.

"We have a report from Stroyer that you ran from the safe house, and he chased you. He says two men grabbed you at the intersection and were trying to force you into a car. He fired two shots while he was still in the shadow of some bushes, but we found only one bullet."

Jillian flinched involuntarily, but didn't comment or interrupt. "He says he hit one of the men who were abducting you. However, a cabdriver testified that you were alone and running. He said he slammed on his brakes when you darted into traffic. He saw you get shot and stumble, but he also stated that Stroyer had his gun holstered when he followed you into the street."

"So the cabdriver didn't actually see Stroyer use the weapon?" Trey asked.

"No, but Stroyer admitted firing two shots, and we have other witnesses who heard the shots. What I have to prove is that he was shooting at Ms. Brandt instead of her alleged abductors. Did you actually see Stroyer pointing his gun and firing at you?" he asked Jillian.

"No," she declared flatly. "I was running with my back to him. He threatened to shoot me and fired his gun. The first shot missed. The second one hit me, but I still didn't look back to him until I heard the thud of his body being hit by a car."

Mitchell nodded and pulled a small tape recorder from his pocket. "I'd like to record your description of exactly what happened the night you ran from our safe house," he explained. "Try to remember every small detail."

Jillian crossed her arms over her chest in an effort to ward off the debilitating terror that threatened her sanity every time she remembered her escape from Miami. Her tone was flat but steady as she described hearing Stroyer on the telephone and realizing that she was in danger.

"He was between me and my personal belongings, so I grabbed his hat and coat, knowing I would need some form of protection or disguise."

"Did you put either of them on when you left the house?" Mitchell asked.

"No, I just carried them, but the coat was long and kept flapping against my legs, so I wadded it into a ball around the hat and held it under my right arm." Jillian went on to explain her flight toward the busy intersection.

Mitchell shut off the recorder. "Stroyer says he pleaded with you to return to the safe house."

"He shouted a few warnings about the risk I was taking, but when he realized I wasn't going to fall for it, he started swearing and calling me names. Then he warned me he'd shoot if I didn't stop."

"Explain that again, in detail, with as many of his exact words as you can remember," the agent told her as he switched the recorder back on.

Jillian did as he asked, growing cold and clammy as she relived the nightmare. She explained about the sounds of the braking traffic, the impact of the bullet and then the sound of Stroyer being hit by a car.

Trey automatically shifted closer to her, aching to comfort her but knowing she'd reject his touch.

"You glanced back at that point?" asked Mitchell.

"Just briefly," she explained. "I saw Stroyer hit the concrete."

"You didn't know the extent of his injuries at that point?"

"I didn't care if he was dead or alive," she admitted with chilling candor. "I still had a contract on my head."

"What did you do then?"

"I kept running."

"Where?

"Until I had to stop to catch my breath. I was bleeding, so I took the belt from Stroyer's coat and tied it over the wound. Then I hitched a ride out of the city."

"With whom?"

Jillian's expression grew mutinous. "I have no intention of involving more innocent people in this mess."

Mitchell looked ready to argue, and then changed his mind. "Cade said the bullet grazed your side, but wasn't embedded in the skin. We couldn't find it anywhere in the vicinity of the accident, either. Can you remember hearing it hit something else or ricochet off anything?"

A shiver raced over Jillian as she tried to remember the exact instant the bullet had hit her. She shook her head. "All I remember is feeling the heat of the bullet and being knocked sideways."

"Which side did the bullet graze? Do you mind showing me the wound?"

Jillian was wearing jeans and a T-shirt. All she had to do was lift the hem of her shirt to bare the scar, but she didn't immediately comply with his request. She stared at him for a long time, then uncrossed her arms and stepped closer to the table.

The wound had healed and the bruising was completely gone, but the scar was enough evidence of a bullet wound.

Mitchell didn't touch her, but pointed from front to back as he described the wound for the recorded testimony. "Can you show me exactly how you held yours arms when you had Stroyer's coat tucked against you?"

Jillian let the hem of her shirt drop and tried to place her arms in front of her in the same fashion she'd used while running.

"If the bullet passed through your body, it would have penetrated something else. If Stroyer's coat was bulky and you were holding it close to your body, the bullet might have gotten lodged in the fabric. Did you notice any unusual holes? Do you still have the coat?"

Jillian hadn't given it a thought since she'd shed it four weeks ago. She glanced at Trey.

"At first, I hung it on a hook in the front hall. It didn't smell too good, so I put it on the back porch in case it was needed for evidence," he told them, already heading out of the kitchen.

Mitchell shut the recorder off again. Cade offered him and Jillian something to drink. There was still coffee in the pot, so he poured them cups and made another pot. Trey returned with the overcoat.

Mitchell stood, took the coat and examined it. Jillian heard them suck in harsh breaths when the lieutenant revealed the blood-stained lining. The odor had faded, but she was well aware of the fact that the fabric had soaked up huge amounts of her blood.

"There's a hidden pocket inside the lining of the right lapel," she told the agent. "You'll find a pair of airline tickets for a one-way flight to Puerto Rico."

Mitchell's expression was ominous as he patted the area and found the pocket. Cade and Trey watched intently as he drew the tickets from their hiding place.

"They're a little stained, but the names are legible and they're dated for the night I escaped the safe house," Jillian declared in a level tone.

She'd discovered the tickets soon after fleeing Miami. "One's in the name of John Smith. The other for Gay Smith. I assumed Stroyer had a girlfriend by the name of Gay or that was his friend's alias."

Mitchell stared at her. Then he checked the tickets and verified what she'd told him. "Fake ID's wouldn't be hard for him to obtain," he acknowledged tersely.

"I assume Stroyer and Gay were planning to retire with the million he'd collect by killing me," Jillian continued emotionlessly, having thought it all out on the long ride across the country. "He was probably talking to Gay on the phone at the safe house, finalizing the getaway plans. I imagine she's on your payroll, and probably has access to the evidence room."

Since the first set of prints Jack Carnell had turned over to the FBI had been burned in a suspicious fire, Jillian concluded that Stroyer or his lady friend was directly responsible for the "accidental" loss of the evidence.

Mitchell muttered something that sounded suspiciously like a string of curses. He didn't try to control his fierce reaction to the new information.

"Is there someone named Gay on your trusted list of employees?" Trey asked.

Chapter Eleven

"No." Mitchell's expression became fierce as he racked his memory for a clue to the identity of Stroyer's partner. There was no doubt it was a woman, and probably one of the women on his staff.

"Gay sounds more like someone's middle name," commented Cade. "I know a lady named Tina Gay."

The lieutenant's eyes widened in amazement as the answer struck him. "Thelma Gay," he said. "Thelma Gay Banks. I noticed the middle name on some paperwork recently. I remember thinking she was the least gay person I've ever known. I don't think I've ever seen the woman smiling or happy."

"Thelma sounds like a good candidate for espionage," Trey concluded.

"Thelma Banks," the lieutenant growled. "Who the hell would have thought she and Stroyer were a pair?"

"The idea is obviously a surprise," Cade said. "If she has access to the evidence room, wouldn't she be a logical suspect?"

"She's been with the bureau for twenty years and has a squeaky-clean record. She's a clerk with a high level security clearance—a plain, mousy little woman who never says more than she has to. As far as I know, she's never gotten personally involved with any of our agents or cases."

"I'd say she's pretty involved in this one," Trey snarled.

"Maybe Stroyer charmed her with promises of paradise and a happily ever after," said Cade.

"Was he persuasive enough to get her to run down that taxi driver? That's what I want to know," the lieutenant insisted in a tight voice. He placed the tickets on the table and continued to search the coat. After checking the inside, he turned it and began to examine the exterior.

"Here!" he exclaimed, twisting the coat so that the other three occupants of the room could see the collar. The fabric had a puncture hole. Mitchell ran his fingers over the seams until he felt a small, hard shape between the coat's lining and outer shell.

"Damn! That has to be the bullet," he declared. "Do you have a pair of tweezers? I'll need an envelope or plastic bag, too."

Cade went in search of the tweezers. Trey looked through the kitchen cupboards until he found a plastic sandwich bag. Mitchell slowly tried to maneuver the metal object toward the hole in the fabric.

Jillian drank her coffee in silence while the men concentrated on retrieving the bullet. When Mitchell managed to get hold of it with the tweezers, he lifted it to the light and studied the size and shape.

"I can't be sure, but we'll find out if it came from Stroyer's pistol."

He dropped the fragment of metal into the plastic bag and tucked the bag into his pocket. "If we're lucky, this one will still have some blood and tissue samples to prove it's the one that struck Ms. Brandt," he told them. "We'll need to run a few tests."

Jillian shuddered at the idea. He discussed her flesh and blood as though it were an exchange commodity. She didn't want to be a specimen for the FBI's investigation. She didn't want to testify. She didn't even want to think about it anymore.

Trey noted her infinitesimal reaction to Mitchell's careless words. He stepped close to her and reached out a hand, but she deftly avoided his touch.

"You can't imagine how strongly this new evidence will affect our case," the lieutenant said. "I don't want to give you any false hopes, but with hard evidence and the name of Stroyer's accomplice, we might be able to get a confession and avoid a trial."

"What about the Banks woman?" Cade asked.

"I'll have her picked up for questioning the first thing in the morning. She may not tell us anything, but she and Stroyer will know we're on to them. If the ballistic and DNA tests are positive on this bullet, I'll have Stroyer jailed as soon as he leaves the hospital."

"If the evidence is all you need, then Jillian won't have to testify?" Trey was brutally aware that she hadn't spared him so much as a glance since she'd accused him of betraying her, but she was his main concern. He didn't want her to endure any more stress than absolutely necessary.

"I'd like Ms. Brandt to come to Miami tomorrow for some tests. The DNA tests are crucial. Then I need her to testify at the preliminary hearing on Monday." Mitchell chose his next words carefully. "If the case goes to trial, it may take several weeks or even months. Considering the circumstances, I can press the court for expediency."

Trey didn't like the sound of it. "And in the meantime?"

"We'll see that's she's well guarded in a government safe house."

Cade's and Trey's expression mirrored their disgust. They glanced at Jillian, but she didn't show any reaction at all. She knew the process.

"I want to head back to Florida tonight," Mitchell surprised them by announcing. "I want to question Thelma myself and get this bullet to our lab."

He looked directly at Jillian. "I can escort you back tonight, or you can come tomorrow."

Trey answered for her. "Cade and I will see that she gets to Miami tomorrow."

"I'll make arrangements for hotel accommodations. There won't be any need for her to come to the bureau's lab. I'll personally bring a technician to her hotel room, and she'll have round-the-clock protection," he assured them.

Neither Trey nor Cade responded. Mitchell could make all the arrangements he wanted, but Jillian would stay with them, in a location of their choice, and with their men guarding her.

The lieutenant looked at the tight expressions on each of the room's other occupants and knew he wasn't going to have the control he wanted over this operation. At this point, he was willing to settle for the new evidence and any further cooperation he could get.

"I can have one of my men drive you back to Albuquerque," Cade offered. "Would you like something to eat before you go?"

"No, thanks," Mitchell said. "I'll get something at the airport. I would like a bag of some kind to carry this coat back with me."

Cade found him a plastic trash bag, and they crammed the coat into it.

Jillian turned to the sink and rinsed out her coffee cup. She was trembling violently, but was determined not to let it show. Staring blindly at the sink, she felt rather than saw Trey step beside her with more cups. The heat of his gaze increased her trembling. Knowing she would shatter into a million pieces if she stayed close to him, she mumbled an excuse and left the room.

The men watched her leave with varied expressions of concern. Mitchell hoped she wouldn't run again. Cade hoped she wouldn't be troubled with nightmares all night. Trey hoped she'd give him a chance to comfort her and explain that he wanted to help her, not hurt her.

When he went to his bedroom a few hours later, he found Jillian in bed. His relief was so intense, it hurt. He'd been afraid that she wouldn't even share his room tonight.

After a quick shower, he climbed into bed beside her. As always, he slid close to her warmth. Her back was turned to him, but he didn't hesitate to envelop her in his arms and cradle her against his body. She remained rigid and silent, but she didn't struggle or withdraw from him.

Trey buried his face against the silky softness of her hair. He would have given anything he owned to be able to absorb her pain and help her fight her emotional battles, but he knew she wasn't going to give him a chance to help. He'd betrayed her trust, and she believed he'd done it for revenge. He didn't know what to say or how to prove she was wrong. He searched for words, but they didn't come. All he could do was hold her.

The only thing he knew to do was protect her and stay with her every step of the way until she was free of the burden she'd carried too long. By then, maybe he'd have found a way to reach her again.

‽‽

When Jillian awoke on Saturday morning, the sun was just beginning to lighten the bedroom. She was more exhausted than she'd been when she went to bed. It had taken hours to get to sleep. She'd tossed and turned and awakened several times from nightmares.

She heard the shower running and knew that Trey had already been outside doing early-morning chores. Now he was getting cleaned up for the trip to Miami. She allowed herself a small moan of pain.

Instead of dwelling on her problems, she rose from the bed and began to function like a robot—without serious thought. She stripped the bed and threw the dirty linens in the clothes hamper, ignoring the sting of pain as she discarded bedding that still held Trey's scent. She remade the bed and tidied the room so that no evidence of her stay was apparent. Then she dressed in the underwear, jeans and the neon truckin' shirt she'd worn when she arrived.

By the time the shower shut off, she'd run a brush through her hair and was heading to the kitchen. Cade was starting breakfast. They exchanged brief greetings and then worked together in silence.

Trey joined them shortly. Jillian was aware of him the instant he stepped into the room. She felt his gaze lingering on her, but she suppressed all reactions to him. For her, it was a simple matter of survival. She didn't have the emotional stamina to deal with his betrayal and a trip back into her worst nightmare.

The men were wearing boots, jeans and long-sleeved cotton dress shirts, Trey's dark green, and Cade's light blue. Their look was casual, yet suited for almost any occasion. They discussed ranch business while they ate.

Jillian forced herself to eat, but all her actions became mechanical. She wouldn't allow herself to feel again until she could put the past to rest forever. Until then, she would just have to get through one hour at a time.

Despite the light tan she'd acquired, she looked pale and had dark shadows under her eyes. Trey wasn't surprised. The night had seemed unending. She had eventually eased herself out of his arms and endured hours of unrelenting nightmares. She hadn't been comforted when he tried to soothe her; he'd become an extension of her troubled dreams. Neither of them had gotten much sleep.

"How soon do you want to leave?" Cade asked him.

Trey's gaze settled on Jillian. She hadn't said a word except for succinct responses to specific questions. She stared into her coffee without looking at either of them.

"We can leave as soon as you want. Wayne'll take care of everything. Delia will be back tomorrow evening, so there's nothing to worry about here in the house."

"Are you packed, Jillian?" Cade asked.

"I didn't pack anything," she replied. "Now that I don't have to worry about being traced, I can buy whatever I need in Miami."

"You'll want some personal items," Cade argued.

She gave him a blank stare. "I don't need anything."

The brothers exchanged frustrated glances. Jillian was making it clear that she didn't want anything they'd supplied for her. She considered them both traitors. Cade wanted to argue, but Trey had already warned him not to pressure her. She had to deal with the situation in her own way.

Within an hour, they were ready to leave the house. Trey and Cade loaded their suitcases in the car along with a case Trey had packed for Jillian. She might be too obstinate to use anything he'd packed, but he wanted to make sure she had some personal items if she needed them.

Cade's security men followed them to Albuquerque, and they all flew to Miami on a private plane. A bulletproof limousine was pulled up to the steps of the plane when they were ready to get off, and Jillian was whisked from the airport with amazing speed.

"Where are we headed?" Trey asked his brother as the limo wove through traffic.

"I have reservations at the Sheraton downtown. We'll go by there first, but we'll be staying in a beach house that belongs to a friend of mine."

Trey nodded his approval. If Mitchell had a hotel room or safe house reserved for Jillian, and Cade had separate reservations, then it would take a while for anyone to realize they weren't using either.

"The beach house is completely secure?" he asked.

"My men spent days getting it ready," Cade told him. "They knew we'd be needing it sooner or later. Security is tight."

"We can use the hotel room until Mitchell has his lab samples," Trey said. "Let him think we're settled, and then we'll head to the beach house."

"Good idea. I don't plan on telling the lieutenant exactly where we'll be staying. I trust him, but there are too many leaks in his bureau."

Trey's jaw clenched in anger. There were definitely too damned many leaks in Mitchell's organization. He wasn't trusting anyone with Jillian's safety.

She was gazing out the window, sitting as still as she'd been during the whole journey. He watched her with worried eyes. She'd done everything they asked without comment. She hadn't complained or questioned their instructions.

Apparently, she trusted them to some extent, but he wished she would give him a clue as to what she was feeling and thinking. If she continued to hold her emotions in such tight check, her control was bound to shatter and she could have a serious breakdown.

It would have been easier to defend his actions if she'd thrown a temper tantrum or raged at him for making decisions which he knew she wouldn't approve. He wanted her to scream at him, to rant and rave—anything that would relieve some of the tension.

Her quiet, withdrawn attitude was slowly driving him crazy. She hadn't asked for reassurances. She hadn't refused to do as Mitchell had asked or denied the necessity of making Stroyer pay for his crimes. She seemed resigned, and he didn't know how to cope with her calm indifference.

Cade telephoned Mitchell from the car. He agreed to meet them at the Sheraton. Once at the hotel, Jillian was taken through a private entrance and they rode the elevator to the penthouse. It was big and luxurious, but nobody really cared.

The lieutenant arrived shortly after them with a lab technician who took samples of Jillian's blood and skin tissue. The process was brief and painless.

"The bullet is definitely from Stroyer's gun, and the lab found particles of blood and tissue," Mitchell told them as they all gathered in the living room of the suite. "If Ms. Brandt's samples match, we'll have substantial evidence for the preliminary hearing."

"What about Thelma Banks?" Trey asked.

Mitchell frowned and glanced at Jillian. Trey assumed the lieutenant had learned something he didn't think she'd want to know.

"What is it?"

"When I told her she was the prime suspect for the cab-driver's murder, she broke down and confessed. She set the fire in the evidence room, and she was planning to run away with Stroyer. She knows she's guilty of conspiracy, but she swears she didn't kill the cabdriver. I believe her."

"Then who did? Stroyer couldn't have done it from his hospital bed," Cade argued.

Trey supposed the lieutenant wanted to keep them in the dark about new information, and it made him furious. Without their assistance, he wouldn't have a case. "Mitchell?" he growled, his expression tight as he stepped closer to the agent. "Level with us, or we're out of here."

The lieutenant clenched his jaw in anger. He didn't like being threatened, and he didn't want to discuss what he'd learned from Banks, but he wasn't stupid.

"Stroyer hasn't contacted anybody since he was hospitalized, but Banks said he slipped her an envelope one day when she visited him with some other bureau staff members. There was a letter for an ex-cop named Trudeau, Tommy Trudeau. She had the letter delivered, and the next day the cabdriver turned up dead."

"So there's another player?" Cade said with a frown.

Trey wasn't pleased with the information, either. "What do you know about Trudeau?"

"He was thrown off the police force for a variety of offenses, ranging from brutality to misuse of his badge. He's unstable, at best, and thinks he's a one-man commando squad. He's apparently willing to do whatever Stroyer asks just for the thrill of it."

Cade groaned. Trey's expression grew more grim. Jillian walked across the room and sat down in an easy chair.

"How good is he?" Trey wanted to know.

"He's well trained—a sharpshooter and a martial-arts expert with experience in a variety of guerilla warfare tactics."

"Do you have a folder on him I can give to my security chief?" asked Cade. "We'll need a recent photo."

Mitchell hesitated again, and then nodded. "Send someone to my office, and I'll have a copy made for you," he said as he turned to leave. The technician followed him to the door.

"I didn't figure you'd want agency protection, so I found a female agent who resembles Ms. Brandt, and we'll be using her as a decoy at the safe house. I can have a couple of my best men back up your men, or we can concentrate on the decoy and leave you alone."

The lieutenant would probably try to keep men on their tail regardless of what they said, but Trey told him not to. "Your decoy won't be very effective if your men are guarding two different locations."

"Have it your way," Mitchell said as he walked out the door. "Call me if you run into trouble. The hearing is in the federal courthouse at ten Monday morning."

"We'll be there," Cade assured him.

Mitchell nodded, told them to be careful and closed the door behind him.

Cade and Trey exchanged glances. They would wait a while before moving on to their next destination.

"We might as well make ourselves comfortable," said Cade, heading to the suite's fully stocked refrigerator. "Anybody want anything to drink?"

"Beer," said Trey. "Jillian?"

"Anything cold, please," she replied. "Juice or cola."

The men took their drinks and joined her in the sitting area. They were all lost in thought for a few minutes, and the room was quiet. When Cade had drained the last of his beer, he gave Jillian his attention.

"Is there anyone you'd like to get in touch with while we're in town? It would be safer to do it from here than from the beach house."

Jillian shook her head.

"Anything special you'd like to do?" asked Trey.

She wondered if they'd really let her do what she wanted. "I'd like to go shopping."

The two men stared at her as if she'd lost her mind. "Shopping?" they chorused in unison.

"I don't have anything to wear to court," she explained calmly. "I haven't been able to buy anything for myself for months, so I'd like to go shopping."

The Langdens displayed matching frowns. Since it was the first request she'd made, they hated to refuse her, yet the idea boggled their minds.

Cade touched a button on the small radio at his waist. "I'll check with Steven."

A few minutes later, Langden's chief of security joined them. Steven Tanner, like most of his men, didn't fit Jillian's image of a bodyguard. Instead of being big and burly, he was tall and lean. Instead of sounding rough and tough, he was unusually soft-spoken.

His hair was pale blond, and his eyes piercing blue. Her impression of him from their brief acquaintance was that he could be dangerous. He'd never blend into the scenery, but she doubted if anyone would dare to cross the man.

"Jillian wants to go shopping," Cade told Steven.

The security chief's expression showed no reaction. "Is there anywhere in particular you want to go?" he asked, turning to her.

"There's a shop I used to visit regularly. It's not far from the downtown area. It's small and fairly exclusive."

"Just one shop?"

"I should be able to get everything I want there."

Cade was relieved she didn't want to go to a mall. One store might not be too bad. They hadn't been in town long enough for anyone to plan an attack. "What do you think?"

"Give me the address and an hour to check the place out," Steven said. "I'll take the limo, and then come back here to pick you up. All the activity will at least confuse anyone who's watching us."

Trey agreed. "A detour for shopping will give us a chance to lose any tails before we head to the beach."

Jillian gave Steven the name and address of the shop she wanted to visit. "The store manager's name is Kathleen Simons. She helped me replace some of my clothes when my apartment was destroyed. She's a friend, she's aware of my situation, and I'm sure she'll help you any way she can."

The security chief didn't bother to write down the information, but Jillian didn't doubt that he had it securely fixed in his mind. "Would you like me to call and make sure Kathleen's working today?" she asked.

"That might be a good idea," Steven said. "But don't give your name to anyone except her. Let Ms. Simons know that I'll be stopping by shortly, but don't mention that you'll be coming later."

Jillian put through the call and one of the store clerks connected her directly with Kathleen.

"Jillian!" Kathleen's normally calm and collected tone rose with affection and genuine concern. "Are you all right? I haven't heard anything for weeks, and I've been so worried."

"I'm fine, thanks, but I can't say much. I just wanted to let you know that a friend of mine will be stopping by the shop this afternoon. His name is Steven Tanner. Would you please help him for me?"

"Of course I will. Are you in town? Will you be staying long? Is there anything special you need?"

"I'm under tight security," she explained.

"Of course," said Kathleen. "I shouldn't be asking so many questions. Please just take care of yourself and have your friend ask for me. I'll be waiting."

"Thanks. Steven will be there in a few minutes."

Jillian replaced the receiver and turned to Tanner. "Kathleen is a petite redhead with hazel eyes. You won't have any trouble identifying her."

"Thanks," Steven said. He turned toward the door. "I'll take Matthews with me. Pearson will stay outside the building, and Davis is in the lobby. Just be extra-careful until I get back."

Trey assured him they would. When he'd gone, Cade moved to the telephone. "I'm starving. I'm going to order something to eat while we wait. You guys want anything?"

The three of them ordered a meal and ate the late lunch while they waited for the security chief to return. When Steven came for them, they left the hotel and climbed into the limousine again, then headed for the boutique.

Jillian felt like a round peg in the center of a square of broad-shouldered men each time she was escorted from a building to the limo or vice versa. The men were all at least a head taller than her. Trey and Cade kept her securely clasped between their big bodies. Steven always took the lead and another man stayed close behind. If she'd been in a better frame of mind, she'd have found some humor in the situation.

Kathleen Simons was not a demonstrative person, but her eyes lit with joy when she saw Jillian enter her shop. The two women hugged each other, and then Kathleen took a step backward to better study Jillian.

"Your hair has gotten really long. It suits you. So does the tan. You look good. Despite that awful T-shirt."

Her words drew a rare smile from Jillian. "I've gotten rather fond of this T-shirt, but I do need help."

"What all do you need?"

"Everything."

"Again?" Kathleen's tone was filled with compassion.

Jillian nodded, but didn't elaborate. "I go to court Monday. The main thing I need today is a presentable suit with accessories."

"Of course," said Kathleen, her tone becoming brisk and efficient. "How much time do we have?"

Jillian glanced at the security chief. He already had men posted in strategic places.

"How long do you think you'll need?" Steven's desire to be quick was obvious.

"I'll have one of my clerks collect some basic necessities," Kathleen told him. "Jillian and I can have the more important items picked out within an hour."

"Fine," said the chief as he left their side.

Jillian introduced Kathleen to the Langden brothers, and then Cade excused himself to help Steven. Trey's gaze locked with Jillian's. The current of electricity sizzled between them. "I go where you go."

Protesting would be a waste of time, so Jillian didn't bother. She didn't feel threatened in Kathleen's shop, but this was the first time in weeks that she'd been in public, and she felt exposed.

It didn't take long for the women to choose a few outfits in styles, colors and sizes that suited her. Trey took a seat in one of the elegant chairs outside the dressing room when she was ready to try on her selections.

Kathleen entered the room to assist her, but gasped in surprise when Jillian pulled off the T-shirt and revealed the scar on her side. "My God! I heard you'd been shot at, but nobody confirmed whether or not you'd been hit."

"Believe it or not," Jillian said, "I was lucky."

Kathleen snorted indelicately. "I don't think I'd want your luck of late," she insisted, then qualified the statement. "However, you are lucky to be traveling with some gorgeous companions. Are they all new acquisitions?"

"I just met Steven today, but I've known the Langdens for a long time."

"Are they working for the government?"

"No."

"Is there something special between you and your tall shadow who never takes his eyes off you?"

"Trey?" Jillian hedged. "He's just making sure I don't do anything stupid."

"I've been watching him watch you," Kathleen admitted. "It's fascinating. His expression is so carefully controlled; you'd think he was made of stone. But his eyes!" she exclaimed softly. "If eyes are the window to the soul, then he must have a hot, passionate soul."

Jillian felt herself blushing. "You really did miss your calling," she told her friend. "With your imagination, you should be writing fiction." Her tone made it clear she didn't want to discuss her relationship with Trey, and the subject was dropped.

Both women agreed that the emerald-green suit looked and fit better than their other choices. The suit, and all other necessary accessories, were purchased and bagged within the allotted hour. Kathleen gave Jillian a hug and wished her well. Jillian promised to call her as soon as she regained some measure of freedom.

Cade, Trey and Jillian climbed back into the limousine with Steven and a man named Matthews in the front of the car. The rest of the security team followed in separate vehicles. The whole entourage wove in and out of traffic until they were certain they weren't being followed. Then they headed for the beach house.

Under different circumstances, Jillian would have been thrilled to spend time in the borrowed house. It was open and airy, yet isolated enough that no nearby neighbors intruded on their privacy. More of Langden's security team were in evidence at the house, and Jillian felt like a goldfish in a bowl. She couldn't do anything without several pairs of eyes trained on her every move. After a light evening meal, she decided to settle in one spot with a book and try to ignore them.

At bedtime, Trey accompanied her to her room, and she realized that he intended to spend the night with her. The idea didn't please her, but she didn't argue. She showered and donned a nightgown she'd gotten at Kathleen's, then climbed into bed and closed her eyes.

Trey showered and redressed in his jeans. He wasn't going to try sleeping with Jillian tonight. He ached to hold her, but he knew she didn't want him touching her. Neither of them had slept much last night, so he decided to stretch out in a recliner near the bed.

When Jillian realized he wasn't coming to bed with her, she relaxed and fell asleep. A nightmare woke her later in the night, but she was able to get the fear under control without bothering her bodyguard. Her gaze focused on Trey. His presence made her feel safe, and she gradually fell back asleep.

Sunday was a quiet day. Jillian would have liked to soak up some sun, but she was an easy target outdoors, so she was encouraged to stay inside the house. Another book was her solution to the problem. She enjoyed reading, and it was a good way to escape thoughts of what tomorrow might bring.

The men played cards. The only blight on an otherwise pleasant day was when Cade called Mitchell, using the phone in the limousine to avoid a trace. He learned that an attempt had been made on the life of the FBI's decoy. She'd been shot at, but hadn't suffered any injury.

Cade relayed the information to Trey and the others.

"Did they get Trudeau?" Trey asked.

"No," Cade said. "They think he's aware of his mistake, but they're only guessing at what he'll try next."

"What's happening with Stroyer?"

"He's officially under arrest. Mitchell told him to call off Trudeau, but Stroyer's lawyer advised him not to admit any association with a madman. The lawyer doesn't want him to say anything."

"Until he's sure Trudeau won't be successful in eliminating the only eyewitness?" Steven summed up the information without realizing how the comment might affect their charge.

Jillian stared at the security chief, refusing to react to the latest atrocity in a long list of atrocities. She turned her attention back to the novel she was reading without commenting.

Trey watched her with brooding eyes. He'd insisted that nobody keep secrets from her now, but he hated having her hear one grim fact after another. Even worse was watching the totally detached way she handled every new development.

She'd completely withdrawn from them, especially him. She avoided looking directly at him. She talked, ate and moved around the house, but she never really communicated her feelings. He didn't know if she was hot, cold, tired, hungry, angry, afraid or even sad. He didn't want to push her, but each passing hour increased his concern.

In another twenty-four hours it might be finished, he reminded himself. They would ensure that Jillian safely testified against Stroyer. If the evidence was incriminating enough, which it undoubtedly was, Stroyer's lawyer would ask for a plea bargain.

At that point, it would be to Stroyer's benefit to see that no harm came to Jillian. Providing he had some control over Trudeau, the hit man would be offered as a sacrifice.

෨෬

The sun shone brightly on Monday morning. The limousine cut a wide path through traffic as it approached the federal courthouse. Once there, the occupants waited inside the vehicle until they were given an all clear sign from both Lieutenant Mitchell and Steven Tanner.

Armed men, dressed in bulletproof vests with FBI emblazoned across their chests, were positioned on either side of the path Jillian would traverse to the doors of the courthouse. Plainclothes security men were positioned up and down the street, all of them alert and watchful.

The Langdens were dressed in lightweight suits that made them look more formidable than civilized. They stepped from the limo, and each reached a hand to Jillian.

Everyone knew that the hundred or so yards from the curb to the courthouse door were Trudeau's last chance at her. She was most vulnerable here, out in the open, because of the crowds and clusters of buildings where a sharpshooter could hide. Metal detectors could keep firearms out of the courthouse, but first she had to get there.

Her hand was ice-cold as Trey grasped it in his. He lifted it and placed a brief kiss on her fingers as he drew her close to the protection of his body. Cade helped him sandwich Jillian between them.

Her blond hair was a beacon, so she'd secured it in a chignon at the nape of her neck and Mitchell had given her protective headgear. They'd also given her a bulletproof vest to don over her clothes. She had to fight for breath as she was crushed between Trey and Cade. They didn't waste any time once she was out of the limo. Their pace was swift, and they all but dragged her through the columns of armed men.

Despite all the precautions, she wasn't out of danger. They were only a few feet from the courthouse door when they heard Steven shout a warning, and Jillian found herself facedown on cold concrete. A succession of shots from a high-powered rifle shattered the silence and slammed into the pavement near them with frightening accuracy. More men fell around them. The weight of Trey's body completely blanketed Jillian, nearly smothering her. She fought for breath, too stunned to even scream.

Orders were being shouted and men were running in all directions. The agents couldn't return the fire, because they couldn't pinpoint Trudeau's exact location, and the area was too heavily populated to start random shooting.

Steven had seen a flash of metal, and he ordered his men to block all the exits of the building where he believed Trudeau was hidden.

"Get her inside!" Mitchell shouted when the hail of bullets ceased.

Jillian felt herself being hauled into strong arms and crushed against a hard chest. She didn't even have time to wrap her arms around Trey's neck before he had her through the doors of the courthouse.

Once inside, he gently lowered her feet to the floor. She was trembling, so he waited until he was sure she could stand before releasing her. Her expression was blank as she brushed dust from her clothing and made an effort to tidy her clothes. Trey didn't take his eyes off her.

Cade and Mitchell were beside them in an instant, and the four of them were swiftly ushered to the courtroom where Jillian would testify.

When she could catch her breath again, she speared Mitchell with emerald eyes. "Do you do this often, lieutenant?"

"Too damned often," he replied succinctly. "Are you all right?"

"I'm alive," she retorted, knowing her dignity was a small price to pay for survival. "Thank you all," she added with an encompassing glance at her three concerned protectors.

"A couple of my men got hit, but their vests protected them. It's almost time for you to testify," Mitchell said, his tone dropping to a whisper as they entered the courtroom and made their way up the center aisle. "I'll ask for a short recess if you need a little more time to catch your breath."

"No." Jillian's response was firm. She wanted this thing over and done.

Mitchell nodded in agreement. "We'll be notified as soon as they have Trudeau in custody. Just have a seat. You know the procedure."

Jillian took her place between the Langden brothers. She tensed when Stroyer was brought into the room. He was on crutches, but his ankles were chained. She gave him one cursory glance, and then dismissed him, hoping to never lay eyes on him again.

Trey hadn't thought it possible for her to crawl more deeply into herself, but she'd managed just that. Wherever she'd hidden her deepest emotions, they were truly buried. Cold fear clutched at his heart. He was more afraid for her now than he had been during the skirmish with a gunman. She was alive, but would she survive emotionally?

The hearing started on time, and the government's attorney stated their case before the court. Significant facts and evidence were presented, and then Jillian was asked to give her testimony. Her legs trembled when she rose, but she stiffened her muscles and crossed the floor to the witness stand. She swore to tell the truth, and then did so with little emotion.

She knew what to expect from the cross-examination. Even though this was a preliminary hearing, and she was a victim instead of the criminal, Stroyer's lawyer would badger her and try to discredit her. When she'd first testified against Gardova, she'd been shocked by the aggressiveness of the defense attorney, but Mitchell had explained back then that charges would be dropped if her testimony didn't stand the test.

Stroyer's lawyer was a short, elderly man with a thin face and shiny bald head. He looked very grandfatherly. His tone was soft and coaxing as he approached Jillian.

"Ms. Brandt, you've obviously suffered a great deal of trauma in the past few weeks. Witnessing a murder and having a contract on your life would unnerve most people."

Jillian immediately knew what angle he was going to use to try to discredit her. He was going to insist that she wasn't in her right mind, that she'd overreacted and had behaved like an irrational female. She didn't know if he expected a response, but when she didn't give one, he continued.

"You've stated that you heard my client speaking on the telephone, but you admit that you didn't hear his exact words. You only imagined you were in danger."

Jillian stared at him, but still made no comment.

"You've told the court that Special Agent Stroyer chased you from the safe house, warning you to stop. Wouldn't any man responsible for your life do exactly the same thing?"

"Probably."

"But you've charged that my client acted with malice, that he was a threat to you even though you had no proof."

"He proved it to me when he told me to stop or he'd shoot. I wouldn't expect an agent to shoot me, even for my own protection."

Her comment roused a lot of muttering in the courtroom and the judge called for order. Jillian remained still, her eyes never leaving the defense attorney as he paced in front of the witness stand.

"You've testified today, under oath," the attorney reminded as though in warning, "that you were shot from behind while dodging through congested traffic. Is it accurate to say that you were distraught at that point? That you were exhausted from running, confused about which direction to go and trying to put distance between yourself and my client?"

"I wasn't confused about anything," she responded with certainty. "I knew my life was in danger, and that Agent Stroyer was chasing me with the intent of doing me physical harm. You're correct in that I was putting as much distance between us as possible."

Another round of whispering was generated by her comments, and Stroyer's lawyer frowned in annoyance, but his tone remained patient. He basically ignored her contradiction of his earlier statements.

"So you thought you were running for your life?" he suggested with emphasis on the word thought. "You were alone, frightened and unwilling to trust anyone."

He was determined to make her sound too weak and confused to be completely sure of what had transpired that evening. Jillian's cool, controlled demeanor didn't lend much credibility to his case. After a few more suggestive comments that she handled just as smoothly, he told the court he didn't have any further questions.

Becky Barker

The hearing concluded before noon. Mitchell excused himself to check on his team of agents. Before leaving, he pointed to a side exit door for them to use. Trey, Cade and Jillian rose from their seats and stretched a little. At the main exit of the courtroom, a throng of reporters was being held at bay by FBI agents.

Cade headed for the side door. He and Trey would have to get Jillian out of the side exit while the guards watched the front. "Let me check this route first," he told his brother. "Give me a couple minutes, then come on out."

Trey watched Jillian fidget restlessly. The knot at her nape was loose. She pulled the pins out and shook her hair free, but didn't put the hat back on her head.

She still didn't want to look at him. He wanted to grab her, drag her close and demand that she admit he'd done what was best for everybody concerned, especially her. It took monumental control to restrain himself from pressuring her.

"I think we can leave now. Cade will have found the shortest, safest route out of here." Trey slipped a hand beneath her elbow and guided her toward the side exit.

He stepped through the door first, then ushered Jillian into a long, narrow anteroom off the court. Cade was at the end of the room with two women. One was short, gray-haired and elderly. The other was younger, a tall, thin brunette holding a baby in her arms.

Trey and Jillian paused until Cade brought the older of the two women to meet them. "This is Eva Carnell," he said in introduction. "She's Jack Carnell's mother and was hoping for a chance to meet Jillian."

Jillian stepped ahead of Trey and offered her hand to Mrs. Carnell. "I'm pleased to meet you," she said in greeting. "Your son was a very brave, honorable man. I can't tell you how sorry I am about his death."

"Thank you, dear. He thought you were special, too. I'm just sorry we had to meet this way."

"Me, too."

196

"I wanted to thank you for testifying today," Eva told her. "I tried to reach you after you replaced him as a witness against Gardova, but it wasn't possible."

"Things were pretty hectic then. I didn't even make it to the funeral."

Eva Carnell shook her head. "That's not what was important. We believe that Bill Stroyer was responsible for the breach of security that got Jack killed. We wanted him tried and sent to jail."

At Jillian's nod, Eva continued. "Did you know Jack's wife was seven months pregnant when he died?"

The shock that registered on Jillian's features was answer enough. Her eyes flashed to the woman cradling the baby. She was pale, gaunt and looked fragile. She must have been devastated by her husband's murder.

"I almost lost my daughter-in-law and my unborn grandchild, too," Eva explained. "Samantha didn't want to live or bring a baby into a world that could cold-bloodedly kill the man she loved. She stopped eating and refused to take care of herself."

Jillian made a small sound of distress.

Eva continued. "The only thing that saved them was your courage. When you put your life at risk to uphold the justice Jack so valiantly defended, you gave Samantha the courage to keep living and bring her child into the world. You saved both his wife and child."

Jillian was shaking her head back and forth in furious rejection of the suggestion that she deserved praise. "I am not courageous," she insisted fervently. "I was scared out of my mind. I gave up on the justice system."

"It doesn't matter," Eva declared just as fiercely. "Justice will be done because of you. Samantha and I came here today in hopes of thanking you personally."

Eva motioned for the younger woman to join them. She brought the baby closer. "This is my daughter-in-law, Samantha, and my granddaughter," she added, unwrapping the folds of a receiving blanket to expose the sleeping infant. "She's two weeks old now."

The proud grandma fussed over her grandchild. The baby was dressed in a pink outfit with plenty of ruffles and lace. She had a head full of dark, fluffy curls, and long lashes rested on her cheeks as she slept peacefully.

Jillian's face softened into an awed smile as she studied the baby. "She's beautiful. So little and so perfect," she whispered, reaching out a hand to touch the tiny, delicate fingers that were curled into a fist.

"We think so," said Eva.

"May I hold her?"

Samantha smiled and shifted her bundle into Jillian's arms. As soon as the warm little body was cuddled close to her breast, she felt a slow warming in a heart that had been chilled too long. Jack's daughter was so tiny and delicate. She represented all that was good and innocent.

Jillian's gaze swung from the baby to Trey. She hadn't realized there were tears in her eyes until she had to blink to bring him into focus. "Isn't she precious?"

Trey nodded and smiled. The sight of Jillian cradling a baby in her arms made his throat constrict. He couldn't find any words.

Jillian's attention went back to the baby, then to her mother. "What's her name?"

Samantha spoke for the first time. Her voice was low and it quivered with emotion. "We named her Jillian."

The unexpected honor stunned Jillian. Something shattered deep inside of her, some brittle emotion at the very core of her grief and bitterness. A tumult of conflicting emotions erupted within her, and pain radiated throughout her body. She began to shake convulsively.

Her voice was barely audible. "Thank you."

Trey knew the instant Jillian's defenses started to crumble. He was close enough to feel the tremors that shook her. He slid his arms along hers and supported the baby until she could carefully hand her back to Samantha.

"We'd better not keep you any longer," Eva put in, "but we hope you'll come visit us sometime."

Jillian could only nod. Her throat was completely blocked by tears.

Eva and Samantha turned to Cade. He escorted them from the room, and Trey turned Jillian in his arms.

The trembling was uncontrollable now. Tears poured down her cheeks. She felt as if she were coming apart, piece by shattering piece. She slid her arms under Trey's jacket and clung to his waist, burying her face against his chest.

His arms tightened around her as violent shudders racked her slender form. The crying began slowly, but soon escalated to ragged, gasping sobs torn from the depths of her heart where an agony of pain had been locked for too long. He ached to absorb some of the pain, but all he could do was hold her tight. He sunk his fingers in her hair and held her head close to his chest.

"Let it all out, baby," he crooned gently. "It's okay. Just get it all out of your system."

Jillian grieved for the death of her friend, for a baby who would never know her father, for love lost, for broken hearts and broken dreams. She sobbed for the loss of good, decent people, for the destruction of innocence and optimism. She wept over the senselessness of violence and greed that demeaned the value of human life.

Once she started weeping, she couldn't stop. Scalding tears gushed from her eyes, and sobs ripped through her until she was alternately sobbing and gasping for her next breath. She was aware of being totally out of control, but she couldn't do anything about it.

"Everything's going to be all right," Trey whispered against her ear as he tried to console her. He buried his face in her hair and continued to reassure her. "You did the right thing, sweetheart, and the worst is over now."

Cade had seen the Carnells out of the room and returned for Jillian and Trey. The two brothers exchanged glances over her head. Their expressions were etched with concern. Cade offered a handkerchief, and Trey coaxed Jillian to ease her death grip on him long enough to accept it. She blew her nose and hiccupped. Then she collapsed against him again, crying more softly, but no less painfully.

Trey held her closer. He'd never had to endure anything as devastating as her pain and heartache. "It's all over, baby. You're safe, and they're not going to hurt you or scare you again."

After another few minutes, Jillian's grip on him began to relax, and her body slowly lost its stiffness. Her crying gradually subsided, and he thought she was regaining her composure. Instead, her legs buckled, and she slumped against him.

"She fainted!" he cried in astonishment. He tightened his hold on Jillian and lifted her against his chest. Her eyes were closed, and she didn't respond to him.

"She just went limp and passed out. It can't be good," he insisted gruffly. "Let's get her to a hospital!"

They didn't waste time getting out of the building. Mitchell and his men ran interference for them until Jillian was in the limo and headed for the nearest hospital.

Once there, a doctor examined her while the Langden brothers paced in the waiting room. A psychiatrist was consulted, and Trey explained Jillian's situation. The doctor concluded that she was suffering from post-trauma exhaustion. He assured them that it wasn't abnormal or life threatening.

The doctors advised Trey to have her admitted for a few days of observation, but the matter of her security negated the option. Trey assured them she would get the best of care and as much rest as she needed. They also prescribed a mild sedative, told him not to worry if she slept around the clock and warned that it might take a few days for her mind and body to completely recover from the recent trauma. Her bout of crying had allowed a release of tension that was more therapeutic than anything he could do for her.

It was late evening by the time everyone returned to the beach house.

Trey carried Jillian to the room she'd been using, stripped her to her underwear and put her to bed. After he covered her with the blankets, he sat beside her and tenderly brushed the hair off her cheeks. His fingers strayed to the softness of her cheek, and he slowly stroked the silky flesh. He needed the physical contact, however slight. She hadn't done more than mumble a few disjointed sentences since leaving the courthouse, and he couldn't help but worry.

Cade knocked at the door, then opened it and looked into the room. "How is she?" he asked quietly.

"The same," said Trey, rising from the bed and turning toward his brother. "She's not feverish, and she seems to be sleeping peacefully."

"That's what the doctors said she needs most," Cade reminded him after a glance at his sleeping friend. Then he added, "Steven's back. Do you want to come talk to him?"

Trey didn't want to leave Jillian for long, but he needed an update on Trudeau. He followed his brother into the living room.

"What happened?" he asked the security chief.

"We trapped Trudeau on the roof of a building. He tried to shoot it out, but one of the FBI marksmen got him."

"He's dead?"

"Yeah."

Trey raked his hand through his hair. "I can't say I'm sorry," he growled. "That's one less threat to Jillian."

"I think it was the last threat," Steven told them. "Mitchell said Stroyer's lawyer is already trying to strike a bargain. Stroyer will confess to conspiring to commit murder and armed assault against Jillian. He's claiming to have valuable information about the drug trade in town. In exchange for the information, he wants a promise that he won't be held responsible for the murder Trudeau committed."

"He's hoping to get a death penalty sentence reduced to life in prison with a chance of parole," Cade surmised.

Steven nodded. "Mitchell says he has a chance if the information he can provide is valuable enough. Stroyer has over twenty years of service with the bureau, so that will count for something when they consider his plea."

Trey snarled. "He should be put away for life."

201

"In most cases of a cop turning bad," Steven told them, "the judgments are harsh. He probably won't get a chance at parole for thirty years."

"If he's trying to improve his image, then he sure won't want anything happening to Jillian," Cade injected.

"I think she's out of danger," Steven agreed.

Trey hoped they were right. He kept telling himself she was going to be fine, but he wouldn't be convinced until he knew she wouldn't have to suffer through a long legal battle. He returned to the bedroom, pulled a chair close to her bed, and kept himself busy for the next hour reading several days' worth of newspapers. He ate the dinner Cade brought him on a tray, but declined his brother's offer to spell him.

It was late when the brothers finally called it a night. Trey stripped to his shorts and climbed in bed with Jillian. Sliding next to her, he slipped one arm over her waist and rested his head on the soft cushion of her breasts. He needed to be close to her—to smell her, feel her warmth and hear the steady beat of her heart. A shudder ripped over him as he remembered how close Trudeau's bullets had come.

He'd never been so scared in his life, and he hadn't liked the feeling. That brief instant in time had proven to him, as nothing else had done, that he couldn't live without her. Being parted from her for two years had been hell, but it dulled in significance compared to a world without her in it. The thought of losing Jillian made him break out in a sweat. He shivered, and pressed closer to her warmth.

When he finally fell asleep, he slept deeply and awoke before dawn. For a few minutes after opening his eyes, he watched Jillian sleep. Her breathing was slow and deep and steady. Trey was relieved that she'd slept without nightmares. He brushed a kiss over her lips, pulled the covers up to her neck and climbed from bed.

After pulling on a pair of jeans, he headed for the smell of coffee, wondering what the future held once Jillian awakened and life could get back to normal.

Chapter Twelve

"Morning," Trey greeted his brother as he entered the kitchen.

"Any change with Jillian?" Cade asked.

"She seems okay," he said as he accepted a cup of coffee. They moved into the living room. "She's still asleep, but she seems to be fine."

Cade took a seat, and Trey carried his cup to the window facing the beach. He sipped the coffee while watching the sun rising over the water.

"I talked to Wayne last night," Cade said.

On Sunday, the foreman had told them it had been raining heavily since they'd left the ranch. "Still raining out there?" Trey asked.

"Yeah. He said the weather bureau is starting to issue flood warnings."

"Any storm or wind damage?"

"Nothing too serious yet. He said they had to rescue some newborn calves, and they're trying to move the cattle to higher ground."

Trey stared at the horizon as he considered the work that needed to be done on the ranch. He didn't like burdening Wayne with all the responsibility.

"If Mitchell tells us Stroyer's case will be settled out of court, do you plan to go home soon?" Cade asked.

"It depends on how long he wants Jillian to stay in town."

"You're planning on taking her back with you?"

Trey shot a glance at his brother. "Why wouldn't I?"

Cade hesitated. "She doesn't need to hide anymore."

"What if she decides to stay here and get on with her career?"

The thought had been nagging at Trey, too. "She'll go home with me if I ask her to." His tone held more certainty than he felt.

"Are you going to ask her to?"

"What the hell kind of question is that?" he snapped irritably. "You know I want her with me."

The two brothers stared at each other in silence for a few minutes. Then Cade said, "I always thought Jillian had the heart of an eagle. She's a free spirit."

"And you don't think she'll be happy to soar on a ranch in New Mexico?" Trey asked between clenched teeth.

"I don't know," Cade admitted honestly. "The ranch might be the perfect home for her, but only if it's her decision."

"You think I'm going to pressure her?"

"I don't think either of you will ever be happy unless you give her a little shove out of the nest and force her to try her wings again. Then she can decide what she wants most."

"I let her go once." He didn't want to think about letting Jillian leave him again.

"She came flying to you when she needed someone she could trust," Cade pointed out. "You know she loves you."

"But what if she doesn't need me anymore? What if the love isn't strong enough to carry her back to me?" Trey wondered aloud. He turned his back to the room and stared out the window.

Cade could feel his brother's pain, and he understood his reluctance to let Jillian fend for herself. But he also understood that they each needed to have their love proven beyond a shadow of a doubt.

"I think she'll come to you this time."

Trey's spine was straight and stiff, his whole body rigid with tension. He splayed one hand on the cool glass of the window as he stared into the distance. "You don't understand," he told his brother quietly. How could anyone understand the desolation and fear? He continued, his voice just a whisper of raw emotion. "If I lose her again, I won't survive."

¹∞²

It was almost noon when Jillian finally awoke. She yawned and stretched, opening her eyes to unfamiliar surroundings. She propped herself on her elbows and glanced around the room. Trey was sitting in a chair at the end of the bed. Their gazes met, and she gave him a tentative smile. "Hi," she said.

His heart quickened at her smile. He hadn't seen it for days, and it made his pulse race. "Hi, yourself."

The covers had fallen to her waist, and Jillian realized she was wearing a slip. She frowned. Then it all came rushing back to her. She was at the beach house in Miami. She had to go to court, she thought in alarm. No. She didn't have to go. All the memories began to surface—the attack on the courthouse steps, her testimony, Jack's tiny daughter and Trey comforting her when she'd broken down and bawled like a baby. She couldn't remember ever crying so hard or so long. It embarrassed her.

"I'm sorry," she told him.

Trey had grown tense while he watched the emotions passing over her features. "For what?" he asked softly.

"For crying all over you."

He relaxed again. "The doctors said it was your mind's way of cleansing itself."

"Doctors?"

"You collapsed, and we took you to the hospital. The doctors said you just needed to rest, and you'd be fine."

Jillian glanced toward the window. "What time is it? How long was I asleep?"

"It's Tuesday morning. You've been out of it about twenty-two hours."

"Twenty-two hours!" she exclaimed. No wonder she felt so rested and relaxed. She'd lost a whole day. "Did I miss anything important?"

"Trudeau's dead, and Stroyer is locked in jail. He's ready to cooperate with the authorities. If the case goes to trial, you'll have to testify, but there won't be any more threats on your life and no more safe houses."

Her eyes widened. It was almost too good to be true. In a low, hesitant voice, she asked, "It's really all over?"

"The worst of it."

Jillian gave some thought to the new developments. It was hard to believe that the threats against her life were finally at an end, yet she felt a deep sense of well-being she hadn't experienced in months. It was probably due to a combination of reasons—her emotional release of tension, putting the testimony behind her and the hours of sleep.

Whatever the reasons, she felt good, really good. She felt whole again—stronger, healthier, happier. The only thing she was really worried about was Trey. She'd treated him badly. He'd been trying to do what was best for her, and she'd accused him of betraying her for revenge. Would he ever forgive her?

She crossed her arms over her knees and rested her chin on her arms. Her gaze didn't waver as she studied him intently. He was so devastating to her senses that it almost hurt to look, yet she couldn't drag her eyes from him. He was so gorgeous, so strong, so dependable. He'd known that she couldn't hide forever, and he'd forced her to face reality. She'd been hurt and furious, but she'd been in the wrong. She'd shut him out, yet he'd stood by her every inch of the way.

Now she couldn't even find the words to express what was in her heart. Did he want her to apologize and beg his forgiveness? She wasn't too proud. She'd do anything for the man, but she didn't want to embarrass him by throwing herself at him if all he wanted to do was be free of her. She didn't want him to feel responsible for her anymore.

"Did you get some sleep last night?" she asked, her gaze locking with his. At his nod, she continued. "I'm sorry for causing so much trouble. I don't remember anything after that crying fit. I must have been pretty poor company."

"You haven't been too bad," he declared lightly. "Cade snores, drinks my beer and wants to argue all the time. You're a lot better company than he is."

Jillian smiled. Then her smile widened, her eyes danced and she began to chuckle. The sound slowly grew from a low, husky chuckle to enchanting, exuberant, infectious laughter.

Trey hadn't heard the carefree, irresistible melody for two years. He'd missed it more than he realized. It made his heart swell and his pulse accelerate. Jillian's eyes were clear and bright. They'd lost their haunted look. The burden of pain and fear had been lifted from her slender shoulders. She was going to be all right.

He wanted her mouth. He wanted to taste the laughter, and hold her in his arms. He wanted to lose himself in her, to love her until the rest of the world disappeared, and the two of them were all that mattered. There was nothing he wanted more than to carry her home, and keep her with him forever.

But he'd had plenty of time to think about what Cade had said. He didn't want Jillian to stay with him out of a sense of duty or gratitude. He had to give her some freedom and pray she would come back to him, this time because she loved him and wanted a future with him. He forced himself to stay in the chair.

Jillian's laughter gradually subsided. Despite Trey's answering grin, he didn't look particularly happy. He was tense, his eyes guarded. She wondered if he was anxious to get back to the ranch. She also wondered if he and Cade resented having to baby-sit for her. They were both busy men whose time was valuable. Would this mess destroy her relationship with both of them?

"Is Cade still here?"

"He's going back to Dallas tonight. He didn't want to leave until you were awake and he had a chance to say goodbye."

"What about Cade's security team? Will they go back to Dallas with him?"

"Steven and a couple of the men will stay here with you for as long as you like."

His words immediately dampened Jillian's spirits. Trey was planning to leave, too—without her. She realized it, but didn't want to believe it. He was going to dismiss her from his care. The Langdens had protected her and stood by her in a time of need, but they were undoubtedly anxious to get back to their own lives.

She felt free of fear for the first time in months. She wanted to share her joy with Trey, but he wanted to put distance between them. It was entirely her fault, yet the knowledge didn't ease the hurt. She couldn't let him leave without making an effort to apologize for her mistakes.

Her fingers plucked at the bed covers as she searched for the right words. "I'll never be able to thank you enough," she began.

Trey grunted in disgust. The last thing he wanted from her was gratitude.

Jillian didn't like the way he was glowering at her, but she had to apologize. "I'm really sorry for the way I acted after Cade brought Lieutenant Mitchell to the ranch. You were right, and I was wrong. I know I've been a real witch, but I'm truly sorry I've treated you so badly."

Trey quickly dismissed the apology. "It was my fault for not telling you in the first place, but I didn't want to face it any more than you did," he admitted. Then his tone grew cold and grim. "I'm sorry you couldn't trust me enough to know I wasn't exacting some kind of revenge."

Jillian flinched, realizing how much anger he was suppressing to avoid an argument and keep his real emotions under control. His expression hadn't changed much since she'd wakened, and it wasn't very warm or encouraging. She'd hurt and angered him. She'd rejected him again, and he wasn't the sort of man to tolerate that from any woman.

She considered trying to rationalize her actions or blame her behavior on temporary insanity, but her excuses sounded weak, even in her own mind.

She couldn't think of any way to prove that she loved him, trusted him and wanted to spend the rest of her life with him. He wasn't likely to believe anything she said at this point.

"When are you going back to the ranch?" she asked, dropping her gaze.

Trey noticed she didn't say "we." Did she think he wouldn't want her, or was she relieved that she wouldn't have to hide anymore? Had the idea of living with him on the ranch lost all appeal now that she was free to return to her previous life-style?

"I can't stay much longer," he said. "What do you plan to do?"

Jillian looked him directly in the eyes. What did he want her to do? she wondered. "I haven't given it any thought," she confessed. All she'd been thinking about was surviving.

"There must be a lot of things you want to do now that you don't have to worry about death threats."

She lowered her lashes to conceal the pain his words caused. He sounded as if he wanted her to stay in Miami. "I would like to get in touch with Jack Carnell's editor, and maybe visit his family. I need to do some banking and buy some more clothes."

"Will you be looking for an apartment?" he forced himself to ask.

Her gaze flew to him again. She searched the dark depths, but didn't find a clue to what he wanted from her. "Are you trying to tell me I'm not welcome at your ranch anymore?" she mustered the courage to ask.

Trey's heart lurched. Every muscle and nerve in his body felt stretched to the snapping point. He might be doing the right thing again, but he didn't like it any more than he had the last time he'd watched Jillian spread her wings and fly from him.

"You're always welcome," he answered in a clipped manner, his tone taut with repressed emotion. Going back without her was going to tear him apart.

Jillian searched his face. "Do you still want me?" she asked in a soft, unsteady voice.

He nearly went wild at the question. His hands clenched into fists, and he forced himself to stay in the chair. He couldn't stand her insecurity and vulnerability. Still, he had to know she wanted him as much as he wanted her. He couldn't survive a one-sided love affair.

"I haven't stopped wanting you," he growled, his eyes glittering with intensity, "but the decision has to be yours. You've been at the mercy of too many other people for too long. It's time to think about the future and what you really want now that you're independent again."

Jillian noticed that he was still talking about wanting, not loving. What would he expect if she returned to the ranch? Would she just be a live-in lover for as long as it suited him? Would he ever trust her enough to commit himself to a long-term relationship? Was he ever likely to risk offering her marriage again?

୫୦୯

Twelve hours later, Jillian stood gazing out the living room window of the beach house. Moonlight sparkled on the water, and the sky was laden with stars. It was a beautiful, romantic night, but she was alone except for her bodyguards, and so very lonely.

Lieutenant Mitchell had stopped by to explain that the district attorney had made a bargain with Bill Stroyer. The agent would plead guilty on conspiracy charges, but not murder, and the FBI would gain some valuable information to help fight the ongoing drug war. Jillian was finally free of the whole horrible mess.

Trey and Cade had left shortly after dinner. They'd seemed determined to keep the goodbyes brief and unemotional. Cade had business to attend to, and Trey was needed at the ranch. Jillian understood. She knew they both had heavy responsibilities. She was deeply appreciative of everything they'd done for her, yet she still felt abandoned.

Everyone seemed in agreement that she needed time to sort out her personal life and prioritize her objectives. She knew better, but she hadn't bothered to argue with them. All she really needed was Trey's love, yet she'd decided to take the time he thought was necessary to evaluate her emotional needs, and then she would go to him.

The next day, she stayed close to the beach house, swimming and soaking up sun. Shedding the burden of fear wasn't as easy as she'd thought, so she took her time readjusting to a normal existence. She was aware of the presence of Cade's security men, but they were unobtrusive.

On Thursday, she met with Jack Carnell's editor. He offered her a position on his staff and the opportunity to cover an upcoming conference of world leaders. She declined his generous offer, but agreed to write a full account of her experience with the drug cartels.

She visited Jack's family and left them with a promise to keep in touch. Next, she went to her bank and collected some things from her safe-deposit box, and then she took care of her personal finances before making one last stop at Kathleen's shop for more clothes.

By Friday morning, she was on a plane to Dallas with Steven. Once there, she stopped by Cade's office and met his assistant, Sallie. Jillian personally thanked the other woman for helping her when she'd been unable to help herself.

Cade wasn't going to the ranch for the weekend, so Steven continued to escort her until their plane landed in Albuquerque. Once there, Jillian insisted that he return to Dallas while she drove herself to the ranch.

During the two-hour drive, her emotions fluctuated from an extreme high at the thought of seeing Trey to an extreme low that he might not want her. It took all the courage she could muster to drive onto his property in a rental car loaded with everything she owned.

The ranch was an oasis of green shimmering under the late-afternoon sunshine. The heavy rains had ended, the land was drying and spring was in full bloom all around her. The temperature was hotter than when she'd left, and everything was alive with the brilliance of renewal.

Jillian felt the same sense of renewal. She felt as though she'd experienced an emotional rebirth, a complete metamorphosis. The beauty of nature appealed to her more than any of the world's wonders she'd seen in the past. She intended to spend the rest of her life photographing and highlighting what was beautiful, innocent and precious, and she planned to do that from Trey's corner of the world.

Providing he wanted her, Jillian thought with renewed anxiety. She parked in front of the ranch and took a minute to catch her breath. Once she'd bolstered her courage, she stepped from the car. Instead of going to the front door, she rounded the house and headed for the barns.

Wayne greeted her before she'd gotten far. "Miss Jillian! You're back."

"It's good to see you, Wayne," she said with a smile. "This time I'm here to stay." I hope, she added silently.

He returned her smile with a grunt of approval. "Glad to hear it. The boss hasn't been too cheerful this week. A regular bear. I don't think he's been sleepin' or eatin' much. Delia got so disgusted, she went to spend the weekend with her daughter and new grandbaby."

Hope flared within Jillian. Maybe Trey was missing her just as much as she'd been missing him. "I didn't know if Mrs. Cooper was here or not. I didn't go in the house yet. I've never met her, and I wanted to see Trey first."

"He's out by the pool. Spent a couple days gettin' it cleaned and filled," Wayne supplied. "He probably decided to take a dip once he'd finished."

Jillian glanced back at the house and changed her mind about how she would greet Trey. "I'll find him."

With a parting thanks to the foreman, she headed for the back door and entered the house through the kitchen. It was cool and quiet inside, welcoming her with a rush of homecoming pleasure unlike anything she'd ever experienced.

This was the home of the man she loved and generations of his family. She'd been traveling like a nomad for months, not calling anyplace home, but now she basked in the feelings of belonging, of permanency. Trey might not be sure he wanted her or that he could trust her, but she intended to make him a believer.

Jillian felt rumpled from her journey, so she headed for the bedroom she'd shared with Trey. Upon entering, she stood still and inhaled the now-familiar masculine scents while absorbing the exquisite feel of being near him again.

Everything was just as she'd left it. Most of the clothes that had been bought for her were still neatly arranged in the closets and dresser. Jillian rummaged through the drawers until she found the tiny white bikini Sallie had mailed to her. After only a second of hesitation, she shed her traveling clothes and donned the skimpy suit.

A glance in the mirror verified her suspicion that the triangles of satin barely covered her feminine curves. The lacy cover didn't conceal much, either. The outfit made her feel exposed yet incredibly sexy and increasingly bold. Her body was far from perfect, but nothing to be ashamed of. A bullet scar would always mar the taut skin of her right side. Trey had already seen it many times, and had never acted as though it repulsed him.

Once freed from the constraint of clothing, Jillian felt cooler and more comfortable. The sexy outfit bolstered her confidence. She'd never doubted that Trey found her desirable, only that he didn't love her enough or trust her to make a commitment.

If that desirability was all she had going for her right now, at least it was a strong start. She was willing to work for his trust and prove herself worthy of his love. After another short pep talk, she headed to the opposite side of the house and outside again.

Chapter Thirteen

Trey was alone in the pool. His dark hair and bronze skin glistened with pagan beauty in the sunlight. His powerful body cut through the water with sure strength, and the sight of him made Jillian's heart go wild with joy. Her lungs constricted, her stomach tightened and her nerves sizzled with sensual pleasure.

She was able to cross the patio, move to the edge of the pool and drink in the sight of him for a few joyful minutes before he noticed her presence. When he realized she was near, his head snapped up, and for several long minutes, they devoured each other with their eyes. Neither uttered a word of greeting as sizzling tension vibrated between them. Then Trey broke the visual contact, dove beneath the water and swam toward her.

The sight of him made her legs go weak, and she sank to the edge of the pool near the shallow end. She'd just dipped her toes in as he surfaced a few feet from her. When he rose from the water, he shoved his hair from his face with both hands, causing a ripple of corded muscle in his arms and chest. The water was only thigh-deep, and he was totally naked—gloriously, primitively nude, and one hundred percent male.

He stole her breath. For an instant, Jillian's pulse pounded so loudly in her ears that she was deafened. Despite the intimate nature of their relationship, she felt herself blushing, but the heat suffusing her body was due more to excitement than shyness. She couldn't take her eyes off him.

A soft breeze blew a strand of hair across her face, and she lifted a hand to brush it back. The diamond solitaire on her ring finger flashed in the fading sunlight, instantly capturing Trey's attention. His eyes narrowed, and his body grew even more tense. He hoped Jillian's presence, her brief attire and the ring were clues of her intention to stay with him, but he was beyond the point of leaving anything to chance.

He stepped closer and grasped her left hand to study the ring on her finger. The first touch of skin on skin sent a shaft of pure pleasure through him. Blood surged hotly through his body.

"You kept it," he said, gently stroking the finger bearing the engagement ring he'd given her two years ago. He wanted to believe she was ready to make a commitment now, but he'd been hurt too much in the past to trust his first instincts.

"I was afraid to wear it when I was traveling, so I put it in a lock box," she explained, her voice low with emotion. She was thankful she hadn't kept it at her apartment where it might have been destroyed with the rest of her belongings.

Trey didn't say anything—he just kept holding her hand and staring at the ring. His emotions were in such a tumult, he didn't know where to start. The hunger in him was violent, nearly debilitating, yet he needed more proof that Jillian was here to stay.

When he made no comment about the ring, Jillian found the courage to ask, "You're not sorry I kept it, are you?"

Trey's chest tightened, and his eyes flashed to hers. "It depends on what it means to you."

Jillian realized he wasn't going to give her a hint about how he felt until she'd completely clarified her own feelings. She'd spent hours wondering what she would say once she saw him again, how she could explain her feelings. It was hard to express what was in her heart.

"It still means the same thing it always did to me," she told him quietly. "It means we share a special love, and we were meant to be together. I might have delayed the normal course of events when we argued and I left, but my feelings for you never changed."

Trey's jaw clenched as anger washed over him. If she had really loved him, how could she have walked out on him and left him in so much pain? How could she have sentenced him to two years of hell without her? He dropped her hand and took a step backward. His gaze turned hot and scorching.

"Then talk to me," he growled in angry demand. "Make me understand. Convince me you really loved me. Explain how you could walk out on what we had."

Finally. After continuous efforts to avoid the real issue, the most important questions were being asked. He was addressing the matter that presented the greatest threat to their relationship. Jillian wanted to explain her feelings.

"I was pretty naive and determined not to let you dictate to me. I wanted you to respect me and my right to have a career." She repeated all the old arguments. They sounded just as shallow now as they had two years ago, and she knew they wouldn't convince Trey.

"I never stopped loving you," she insisted. "You were always my anchor, my port in a storm. I always knew you were here. There were so many times when I ached to be with you, but I guess pride kept me from coming sooner."

Her words stoked his anger. She wasn't telling him anything he hadn't already heard, and he was tired of the same old excuses. "You knew I wanted a wife and family. What if I'd decided to marry someone else?" he snapped.

She'd lived in fear that he would find someone to replace her in his heart. Cade had kept her informed of his brother's life-style. She would have known if another woman became important to him.

"I'd have known," she told him.

Maybe she would have known, but would she have cared? Trey asked himself. He asked her. "Would you have come running to stake a claim?"

"In a heartbeat," Jillian declared roughly.

The intensity of her response made him shudder. He wanted to believe she'd cared that much. "Then why in the hell didn't you tell me that? Was asserting your right for independence so important?" he demanded furiously. Hadn't she realized that he'd been proud and vulnerable, too?

"What I really wanted was your unconditional trust," she confessed, dropping her lashes. Then she lifted them to gaze searchingly into his.

"I thought that if you really loved me, you would trust me, regardless of the circumstances," she explained. "But what I hadn't learned then is that trust has to be nurtured. We hadn't been together long enough to have that much faith in our love. It was too new and so fragile," she admitted on a husky whisper.

Trey knew she was right. They'd both been at fault in the past, and past mistakes were better forgotten. It was the future that concerned him. He needed assurances.

"And now? What about now, Jillian?" His tone was rough with emotion. "Do you trust me? Do you trust what we have? Is it enough?"

Her head tipped slightly backward as Trey stepped closer, never taking his eyes from hers. Her breathing faltered when he was close enough to touch.

"Are you here out of a sense of obligation?"

"No." Her tone rang with certainty.

"Are you here to say goodbye before you accept a new assignment?"

"No."

Trey put a hand beneath her chin. "What about your career?"

She wanted to be totally honest. "You taught me that I can't deny my creative tendencies, but I have a new perspective now. I don't want to travel much, and never without you. Jack Carnell's editor gave me the name of some contacts in this area. I can work if I want."

"That's why you're here?"

"That's the very least of it," she murmured. "I mostly came because I love you and want to be with you."

"For how long?"

217

Jillian had to lower her lashes again. The intensity of his gaze was scorching. "For as long as you want me."

A shudder racked Trey's body. "Be sure, Jillian," he commanded hoarsely. "Be damned sure, because if you marry me, I'll never let you go again. I can't help being possessive where you're concerned, and I won't settle for anything less than a lifetime commitment."

Her gaze flew to his, and his eyes glittered with excitement. Her heart began to race. Was he willing to forget the past and plan a future with her?

"You still want to marry me?"

"I never stopped," he admitted roughly, "but I couldn't force you to want it, too."

Relief and exhilaration washed over Jillian, but she still yearned to hear him say he loved her. He might want her, but that didn't mean he'd forgiven her or would trust her again.

"I love you," she whispered softly.

"Do you?" Trey asked, stepping back into deeper water. His gaze remained locked with hers. "How much?"

"More than words can say," she swore vehemently, baring her heart to him. "I've loved you since the first time we met, but now I love you more than I knew it was possible to love someone. I ache with loving you. I want to marry you and spend the rest of my life proving how much I love you."

Trey's eyes flared with emotion, and then his gaze narrowed. He stepped deeper into the pool until his lower body was hidden beneath water.

"Then come here," he insisted gruffly. "Come to me as naked and vulnerable as you make me."

Jillian blinked. Did he mean emotionally naked or physically naked? Just like him, she pondered, knowing he wanted both. She glanced around them.

"We're completely alone," he assured her. "It's just you and me. Either you trust me or you don't."

His expression compelled her—eyes that reached deep into her soul and touched the very fiber of her being. Jillian didn't hesitate any longer. She stepped into the pool and slipped off the lacy jacket, then tossed it onto the deck. She reached behind her, unfastened the clasp of the bikini bra and threw it toward the jacket.

Savage desire exploded through Trey. His pulse roared in his head while all his blood boiled and pooled in his loins. The sight of Jillian's beautiful, bare breasts made him quake with need. He clenched his fists beneath the water and forced himself to remain still until she came to him.

Jillian returned his steamy gaze while reaching for the bikini bottom. In another agonizingly slow movement, she was tossing the last barrier after the others. Then she was as exposed and vulnerable as she'd ever felt in her life.

Trey's voice dropped an octave and his eyes were dark with turbulent emotion. "Come to me," he coaxed huskily.

She was ensnared by his tone and the gleam in his eyes. A tremor quaked over her. Her nipples puckered from exposure to the cooling air, but she resisted the urge to cover herself with her arms. Instead, she moved steadily toward the man she loved beyond all reason.

He contained his impatience until he felt her soft body rubbing against his hard one. When her plump breasts were crushed against his chest, and her arms slid around his neck, his control shattered. Desire seared him to the depths of his being.

He crushed her against him with arms that were bands of steel. He lifted her up and pulled her completely against him, holding her tightly while rubbing the hard evidence of his arousal against the cradle of her thighs. Then he slowly moved back to more shallow water. They exchanged moans of pleasure as their mouths locked and shared a long, hungry kiss that only began to satisfy a need to touch and taste. Tongues entwined, stroked, danced.

Jillian grasped Trey's face between her hands, and implored, "Do you really want to get married?"

"Yes."

"And have lots of babies?" Did he trust her enough to risk giving her his child?

She felt him tremble. His eyes gave her the answer she wanted. She hoped her next questions would get the same response. "Can you ever trust me again? Have you forgiven me for not trusting you?"

His growl was low and rough. "You're here," he said. She'd renewed his faith by coming to him on her own.

"You want me as much as I want you?" she queried as she nipped at his lips with her teeth.

Trey opened his mouth and coaxed her tongue inside, then sucked it before responding. "I want you more."

"Do you love me?" she made herself ask. It was the only thing he'd neglected to mention. His affirmation was murmured against the tender curve of her ear, but she needed more. "I need the words," she insisted huskily.

He grasped her thighs and pulled them around his own. His eyes were locked with hers as he locked their bodies in the most intimate of fashions.

Jillian sucked in her breath, and then he stole it with a kiss that clutched at her heart and soul. She had his trust again. He'd regained his faith in their future. He was proving it in the most elemental of ways. She arched against him, loving the feel of his possession.

When their mouths parted minutes later, his lips roamed down her throat. "Welcome home," he whispered before his mouth fastened on her throat. He felt Jillian's muscles clenching around him and his body bucked in reaction.

"I love you," he declared with raw emotion.

Jillian melted against him. They swallowed each other's moans of pleasure as their bodies danced in an ancient, primal rhythm.

She was everything he'd ever wanted: his woman, his lover, his only love. She'd flown back to him on wings of love. He'd cherish her with his life, and give her all the babies she wanted. The future looked very bright for the next generation of Langdens.

About the Author

Becky Barker is a multi-published author whose work has been translated into many different languages and has been made available in several formats, including, electronic, mass market paperback, hardcover and large print library editions. She's an avid reader who writes very sensual contemporary romances that incorporate humor and/or suspense. She invites readers to visit her website at: http://www.beckybarker.com

Burke Black wanted something he could live with,
but ended up finding someone he could live for.

Discovering Dani
© *2006 NJ Walters*

Book 1 of Jamesville

Dani O'Rourke has had the responsibility of raising her two brothers, Patrick and Shamus, since the death of their parents. As sole owner and operator of O'Rourke Cleaning Services, she is no stranger too hard work, but she is a beginner when it comes to men.

Burke is a very rich and successful businessman whose brush with death has made him question his priorities. He's traveled to Jamesville for peace and quiet while he plans the rest of his life.

Their lives collide when Burke accuses her of breaking into his cabin to steal from him. Their attraction to each other is immediate, and after a series of misunderstandings he finds himself caught up in the lives of Dani and her brothers.

But can this gentle, giving woman get a man as hard and cynical as Burke to believe in the power of love? Or will Burke leave town without ever discovering the wonders of life with Dani?

Available now in ebook from Samhain Publishing.

Just because it's convenient doesn't mean it's easy.

The Way Home
© 2006 NJ Walters

Book 2 of Jamesville.

"So, will you marry me?" Although not a particularly romantic proposal, Rebecca Gentry seriously considers accepting because it comes from Jake Tanner, the man who she's secretly loved for years.

Rebecca has been alone for most of her life, but she's made a life she's content with. She has her own sewing business, a lovely apartment, and a few good friends. But it's her yspecial friendship with Jake that has always been most important to her. Now, he is proposing a marriage of convenience as he finds himself in need of a wife to help him raise his orphaned niece.

Convinced that she can teach him to share a real marriage rather than one of convenience, she agrees to his offer. But, becoming a family is not an easy journey for any of them. Both she and Jake have their own insecurities and challenges to overcome if their marriage is to have a chance to survive. But unforeseen problems test their new relationship and threaten to destroy what they've just begun to build.

Available now in ebook from Samhain Publishing.

Samhain Publishing, Ltd.

It's all about the story…

Action/Adventure
Fantasy
Historical
Horror
Mainstream
Mystery/Suspense
Non-Fiction
Paranormal
Red Hots!
Romance
Science Fiction
Western
Young Adult

http://www.samhainpublishing.com

Printed in the United States
68070LVS00003B/133-243